REDEEMED FROM THE ASHES

REDEEMED FROM THE ASHES

Leah Lindeman

Lindeman Publishing House

The mass of men lead lives of quiet desperation.
Henry David Thoreau
Walden Economy

Chapter 1

The creaking oak floorboards betrayed the footfalls of an intruder. Evelyn Richardson was aroused from her reverie. She swivelled her head to peer around the back of her crimson cushioned chair, a shaky breath escaped her chapped lips. Casby, the dear old butler who had been in her family's service for the last three and a half years, was standing beneath the dark-veneered door frame. His greying eyebrows were drawn up tightly, his eyes protruded from their wrinkled sockets, and his mouth was slightly parted.

"Madam, are you all right? Please forgive me. I had no intention of frightening you." He recovered well, she had to admit. His air of quiescence, momentarily disturbed by her skittish behaviour, had returned.

"Uh, yes—yes, I am quite well, thank you. Is it time?"

"Yes, it is. Shall I accompany you?"

"You're very kind, Casby, but no, thank you. I'll return shortly. Would you see to supper being ready for when we return?"

"Very well, Madam." Casby, with white-gloved hands at his bony sides, strode back into the darkened hallway, which consisted of a maple hall tree situated to the right of the gold-gilded mirror which her mother had given to her as a wedding present and a single entrance table upon which stood a glass vase of fresh-cut lilies.

Casby was the sole asset of her household that impressed her mother. The first time she had had her mother over for a visit after moving to Richmond was a serious matter. She had ordered Casby to clean the house until each surface was brightened by a sunny, dust-free luster. And he had done just so. Her mother had admired the house, of course, since she had had a hand in choosing it. She had not taken so well to Casby whose emaciated features gave him—Evelyn had to admit—a gloomy appearance, but his excellent deportment in service and manners redeemed him from further harsh criticism and anchored him within her mother's good graces.

Evelyn managed to rise from her chair, shaken from the interruption. Her reverie was still fresh in her mind. Her only intention had been to sit in her favourite chair which was situated in front of the sash window overlooking Grafton Street to bask in what little sunlight tore through the dense blanket of clouds and to watch the young lads play in the street. She had also welcomed the smell of fresh bread drifting from the kitchen into the living room, no doubt a loaf which Casby had made that morning. He was not only their butler but their cook, as well. The snowflakes falling from heaven had impelled her to close her eyes and imagine the sensation she would feel were they to land upon her face and open mouth. She had heard the clomping of horses' hooves and the buzz of conversation in the street. But as she had been admiring the grim beauty of the predictability of her neighbourhood and soaking in all the bedlam, the smell of fresh bread had suddenly become the stench of smoke and fire. The snowflakes had become ashes; the clomping of horses' hooves had turned into shouting and screaming, the buzz of conversation had ceased. And instead of seeing healthy young lads, she had seen them all lying on the ground, filthy and motionless, dead.

She exhaled a deep breath. Everything was all right. She plodded toward the hall tree to collect her long fur coat and departed from the house. Eyeing her surroundings, she was relieved to see life had not stopped, had not died even though it was the tiring, same old play.

"Oh, sorry, miss! Watch out! Oh...!"

"What in…!" As she bent down to grab her throbbing ankle, she saw a young boy attempting to push himself from the ground and right his fallen bike. "Are you all right? Are you hurt anywhere?"

"Only a little scrape, miss. See here." He exposed his reddened palms. "I'll be all right, miss. I'm so sorry I caused you hurt. Would you like me to retrieve some ice from my icebox?"

"Do you live nearby?"

"Uh, no, miss, but if you'll wait a little while, I wouldn't mind getting some."

"That is very kind of you, but I think the cold air will do just as well. Try to be more careful next time...I'm sorry. I don't know your name."

"Oh, Clyde. My name's Clyde."

"Clyde, it was a pleasure to meet you even under these painful circumstances." She extended her hand.

"Oh no, the pleasure is all mine, miss." He clasped her hand and shook it with vigour, unaware that his slightly incorrect use of words under the circumstances amused Evelyn greatly.

"Is that your friend waving to you down there?" She pointed above Clyde's head to a young brown-haired boy who was waving both of his arms in wide arcs above his head.

Clyde swirled around and waved in return, grinning mischievously. "Yes, it is. That's Tommy. I should go; he's not a very patient fellow. Thank you, miss. Goodbye!"

Evelyn hailed a horse and buggy and asked to be taken to the harbour. She paid the driver his fee and bid him a good day. Gliding off the buggy, she was met with a familiar sight, a boat such as the one in front of her had come to collect her husband and his comrades in 1914 to fight the present war in Europe.

What a blessed place the harbour had been, and what a dismal place it had become. The people of Halifax had used to welcome distant friends, or bid a temporary goodbye to a loved one. Now it had become a shrine of despair where wives came to procure their mutilated husbands; where sons and brothers were met with weeping from broken-hearted families; and where marred soldiers came to kiss the beloved ground of their home country, many unaware that the haunts of war would soon dispel those feelings of safety. Would things ever be the same again?

At last, the ship's ramp was set in place. Evelyn was eager to welcome her husband home. It had been so long since she had seen his effulgent face. Of course, she had looked at her one wedding picture almost every day. But to see him and to touch him would be transcendently real. A great flux of men began to disembark. She was scanning every woebegone face, trying to find the one dearest to her heart. She became distressed after the final person's step withdrew from the plank. She pushed her way through the throng. "Excuse me, thank you. Carl! Carl!"

"Evelyn!"

That voice she had been aching to hear rang through the chill air. All she would have to do was follow it to the source.

"Carl?"

Where is he?

She looked to her right. "Oh, there you are!"

She moved past two men, each having had one arm amputated, and straight into Carl. She buried her face beside his stiff uniform collar and nudged her nose closer to his neck to smell his chaffed skin. "How was your journey?" She fervently kissed his gelid hands.

"It could have been much worse."

Evelyn gazed into his eyes. How she had missed those luminous blue diamonds! They had always sparkled for her, yet something wasn't quite right anymore. The spark, the light had vanished, and now those depths were hollow. "Come. Let us get you home to a warm supper and a hot bath."

During the ride home, Carl remained silent, looking out into the passing streets. Evelyn couldn't help but take in the sight of his missing leg. His leg had been cut off right below the knee. The left pant leg fully covered his limb while the right one was rolled up to the stump. He had been discharged from the army because of his impairment. She had seen many of the home boys return with a missing leg, but this was different.

"Here we are. It is so good to have you back home again. I've missed you."

"Home."

"That's right. Shall I help you out? Do you need...?"

"No." He edged over to the black door and leaned over to swing it open. He grabbed his crutches in one hand and held onto the handle with the other. He stepped out with some difficulty and motioned for Evelyn to take his proffered hand.

"Thank you." She felt guilty taking advantage of his help even though it was perfectly adequate for him to offer it.

He anchored himself in front of the steps leading to home. Evelyn stood by his side, listening to the steady rhythm of his breathing. She pivoted her head to regard the mild expression appearing upon his handsome face. His eyes did not stray from the sight of their home. He squeezed her hand gently.

"Carl, tell me, what are you thinking?"

"It is just...I've not been home for a long while, and I was thinking I almost don't know what to do."

"Shall we go inside?" She held his arm as she helped him hobble up the stairs, his crutches *clacking* against the slabs of stone.

As they entered their abode, Casby appeared from within the dining room adjoining the entrance hall to the left. "Welcome home, sir."

"Good old Casby. It is a pleasure to see you after so many years. Have you been taking care of Mrs. Richardson?"

"Yes, sir, I have. And I do quite agree. It's been too long. Do you have any bags for me to take up to your room, sir?

"Yes, Casby. Here you go. Thank you." He handed Casby his "ditty" bag.

Casby took Carl's bag and began to walk up the stairs. "Madam, did your airing replenish you?"

"Yes, thank you."

A furtive glance darted from Casby's eyes. The muscles in his neck stood out as intensely stressed chords. A little unnerved, she led Carl into the living room, situated directly across the dining room separated by the main hall. They both sat upon a light blue sofa, embellished with an oriental floral design. It had been a gift from Evelyn's mother before the war years. A couple of feet to the left of the crimson chair which was across from them was a small wooden table, graced by a figurine of a man and a woman dancing in evening attire.

"Do you remember the night we met?" Carl whispered.

So he had glanced at the figurine, as well.

"Yes, I was just thinking about it."

"I saw you not very far from where I was standing. You were the prettiest girl in the room. Your curls bobbed as you danced with the other men; I was quite jealous. Oh, God, you were a sight. And I will never forget."

"You finally had the courage to ask me to dance when one of the last songs was playing. What you didn't know was that I was waiting a very long time for you to whisk me away. Was not the band splendid? I can still hear it...in a past where..." She fumbled with his faded collar then slowly inched her fingertips closer to his Adam's apple. "Where our lives were untouched by what has consumed them now."

"But that was all I needed to know...it would forever be you."

"Sir, supper is served," Casby brusquely announced as he entered the living room.

"We'll be there in a minute."

They both looked at each other, thinking of happier days that had once been. But such thoughts could never settle in Carl's fragile mind; for they were always quickly overtaken by torturous images which played continuously as if a film reel had been implanted inside his brain.

Little did Evelyn know of her husband's true state of mind; and yet her own thoughts could not dwell in happy places for long periods of time either. Many times, grim embitterment and hopelessness of present circumstances would upstage her parade. Both sincerely hoped that the other was truly content, not wanting the other to know the truth about themselves.

***

Carl and Evelyn dined in silence, their mouths watering with every bite they took. No roast lamb was left, and each of their stomachs paid dearly for it. Both husband and wife were fatigued and looking forward to sleep. Carl settled into a bathtub filled with soothing hot water. Evelyn perched upon a nearby stool and read Charles Dickens' *Little Dorrit* to him. Before the war had occurred, she had customarily read to him while he bathed. After reading a chapter, she gently closed the book.

"Carl?"

"Yes, dearest."

"When you wrote to me you would be coming back because of what had happened to your leg, you never wrote how it had happened."

"Would you like to know?" Evelyn nodded her head.

"Ah, where to begin?" He rubbed his calloused fingers over his eyes. "We were fighting at Vimy Ridge. I was in the trenches—awful places they are—with my comrades. We were ordered to retreat from the trench; as we were retreating, shrapnel hit my leg. I was one of the last of the men to abandon our position; as a result, nobody was aware of what had happened to me. It burned badly, I could barely breathe. Pain invaded my leg, I was defenceless. For one night and one day, I wallowed in the mud while an abundant number of rats scampered around. I tell you, those little devils…we could never keep them away.

"Time had never moved so slowly for me then during that day and a half. I thought I was going to die. I thought…I would never see you again." He raised his hand from beneath the water and stroked Evelyn's porcelain cheek.

"Thank God, our troops didn't let the enemy snatch the trench; for if my comrades had failed, I wouldn't be alive, or maybe I would. From what I've heard, the Huns' prison camps have been relegated to a miserable breeding place of all kinds of illnesses. The Allied armies retrieved the trench early in the morning and found me.

"They sent me to the hospital immediately. The stationed doctor said it would be hopeless to try to save my leg because the gas gangrene infection was too widespread. The only thing they could do to save my life was to amputate my leg.

"I wouldn't wish any man to experience this plague. War is a terrible thing. The depravity of men...Young and old fantasize about the honour and glory that come from serving their country; yet they don't understand the terrors that are sure to invade one's every thought. Yes, honour and glory come; but so does pain and horrors darker than the blackest night."

He closed his eyes and rested his head against the rim of the tub. "In spite of it all, I am proud to have served my country. I love my country. I love you. Protecting my country means I protect you and our livelihood. If we don't have love for our country, then do we truly love those closest to us?"

She closed her eyes and rested her forehead upon her fist. "You are...very honourable in the things you say. But you should not have suffered such as you did. You didn't deserve it."

"Evelyn, there will be many times when horrible acts fall upon the most undeserving of people. What can we do? I cannot control the acts of others."

The flooring near the door groaned. Evelyn jumped. The door was slightly ajar. A shadow slithered out of sight.

"Carl, did you see that?"

"See what?"

"There was someone at the door listening to our conversation."

"I didn't hear anything. Come, you are probably very tired. Why don't we retire to our bed now?"

"Yes, I...I am tired."

Was her imagination playing tricks? Whom could it have been?

***

Evelyn slept fitfully. The dark reverie she had seen earlier returned as a nightmare. The snow turning into ash, the crying, the flames, and the shouting were all the same; however, this time Casby, wearing an ashen mask and having a devilish glint in his eyes, promenaded through the chaos unharmed.

A chill glided over the hairs of her uncovered arms. In the darkness, she grappled for the sheets. Warmth immediately settled over her cold form.

Wait, that was too easy. He always...

Emptiness and some untold dread covered her in a cocoon. She rolled over to watch Carl sleep, but to her surprise, he was missing. "Carl? Carl?"

Where could he be at such an early hour? She threw her cream sheer robe over her clingy nightgown and ran down the stairs. She surveyed every room until she found him dressed in a casual suit in the dining room eating some bread, cheese, and grapes while reading the previous day's edition of the *Halifax Herald*.

"Carl?"

"Yes?"

"What are you doing?" She combed her fingers through her unkempt hair.

"Excuse me?"

"When I woke up, you weren't beside me. So I thought perhaps something had happened and..."

While she rambled on, Carl just looked at her, unaffected by her anxiousness. "Evelyn."

She took a deep breath. "Yes?"

"Just because I lost my leg doesn't mean I cannot function on my own. I appreciate your concern, my dear, but it isn't necessary. By the way, that is a lovely robe."

Having been disarmed by his suave voice, she was tranquil enough to notice his sensual gaze upon her normally over-clothed body. So ignited was the passion burning within his eyes that she crossed her arms over her chest. "Th...thank you," she stammered. "but have you not seen this robe a hundred times before?"

"I have. What of it?"

"Well, I thought perhaps the novelty of its...design would have worn off by now."

"Remember, I haven't been here for the last two and a half years...so, no, I still find it extremely attractive draped like so upon your figure."

"Really?"

"Evelyn, let's not play games." He pushed back his chair, walked toward her, and clutched her to himself, planting tender kisses along her exposed collarbone and feeling his way down her curves, his breath warming her to her toes.

Her body tensed, and her breath was released in irregular spurts. "Carl...I...just, what were you doing up so early?"

"Why?" He continued his increasingly feverish kissing.

"Carl. I just...want to know."

He paused, his touch gone cold. "All right, I'll desist."

"Carl, please." She frantically tried to grab his hands, but it was too late. He had already retreated to his former seat.

Instead of blushing from her husband's physical assertions, she coloured in shame.

Why did I stop him? Did I not want this to happen? Have I not been pining for his caresses, his touch? I did expect this to happen. Of course, I did. Stupid girl! How am I to mend this?

"Frankly, the reason I am up so early is when I awoke I felt the best I have ever felt in a long time. The bed was like heaven, and there was no damn noise keeping me awake at all hours of the night. I felt so rejuvenated; I wanted to start my day right away." He offered her a curt smile and flapped the wings of his newspaper as if he were trying to fool himself into thinking he was all right.

And I have just ruined his perfectly good morning.

"Carl, that is...wonderful." She approached cautiously, knowing he could not have easily forgotten or forgiven her rebuttal, and gave him a kiss upon his broad forehead. "I will return with some food for myself."

After filling her plate with the same delicacies Carl had taken, she rejoined him at the dining table. "What are you reading in the paper?"

"News about the war."

"Oh."

Carl devoured the remnants of his food, gulped down his coffee, and hastily left her presence. Not a word could leave her lips; so stunned was she by his disquieting behaviour.

I am definitely in a kettle of hot water now.

***

As the day dragged on, Carl's missing presence produced a state of tension within Evelyn's mind and limbs. At one point she was writing a letter to her mother and was very tempted to disclose the very frustrating feelings she had toward herself and Carl. But no. No good would come of it. Mrs. Moore didn't need any more ammunition against Carl.

Evelyn was seated alone at the table for lunch and supper. Carl had asked his plates of food to be brought to the study. Before she retired to bed, Evelyn knocked upon his study door without receiving a reply. The only sounds she could perceive were the flipping pages of a book. Only at midnight did Carl venture to the bedroom and slide into bed, careful not to touch her. She was lying next to a stranger.

The next morning she again found him in the dining room, his head hiding behind the newspaper.

"Good morning."

"Good morning," he replied.

At least, he's not ignoring me.

"I'm looking at the job advertisement section. Evelyn, I've been thinking. I need a job to support the both of us, without your mother's continual financial contributions."

"Do you not have a pension? And what is wrong with her contributions?"

"Yes, I do have a pension. Concerning the contributions, there is nothing inherently wrong with them. What I mean to say is we are our own family, and I would like to be the sole provider for this family."

"You have never slighted them before."

"Well, things are different now."

"How so?"

"You ask too many questions; I care not to answer at the moment."

This is not about a job. This is about me.

After a few moments, Carl slapped his hand upon the table. "I've got it! Look here! The *Halifax Herald* is looking to employ another editor. It's just in my line of work."

"You already found something?"

"Why? You don't approve?

"I do—it is just that—well, you have recently returned from war. And now you want to leave me again?"

"Come now, Evelyn, I'm not fighting this war anymore. You will have me for probably most evenings, Saturdays, and Sundays. I won't be in some far-off country. The office is down the street, hardly a jog away."

"It is a few blocks of a jog away."

He rolled his eyes. "You know what I mean. The point is I would like to inquire at the office today."

Her heart was aching for him to stay put. When she had known he was to return, she had dreamed of having him all to herself, stroking back the hair from his face as he would tell her how much he had missed her. And she would tell him how much she loved him. But present circumstances would not bend to her fanciful wishes. She also wanted to mend the damage she had done.

"Would it be all right if I came along? I mean, of course, I wouldn't be in the way. I'll stay put in the lobby."

"You'll be bored." He jutted his chin.

"Please, I'd like to."

He slammed his fist upon the table. "Dammit, woman, can't you take no for an answer?!"

She shrunk into her seat, tremors traveling down her spine.

He sighed, interlacing his fingers across his forehead. "I'm so…I…Fine. Let's."

They walked down the crowd-infested blocks always a few paces separating them and arrived at the office. Evelyn sat in the waiting area while Carl was being interviewed for the position of editor.

The waiting area was large enough to accommodate two simple wooden chairs facing the main oak desk. The bottom half of the walls had been painted a hunter green that was now blemished with scratches and grooves. The upper half was ivory. The walls were adorned with black and white photographs of the official ceremony commemorating the opening of the office, the editor-in-chief with the office manager, and a few landscapes of the Nova Scotia shore. She peered behind the front desk to see a large room separated into small, even cubicles. The air was abuzz with conversations. Tips were being whispered between writers and orders were shouted.

Evelyn thought more of the grief she had caused during yesterday's breakfast and the monstrous manifestation of Carl's grudge.

What if he is only trying to get the job to stay away from me? Will he hold a grudge against me forever? He needs to rest more.

Carl returned to the waiting room with a smug grin on his face. "I got the job!"

"So fast?"

"Yes, my reputation as an editor with *The Gazette* in Montreal precedes me. My previous editor-in-chief and my now present editor-in-chief are acquaintances. It seems my past editor-in-chief spoke very highly of my work."

"Ah, this was before we ever met."

"Precisely."

Carl and Evelyn walked out of the office and were greeted by a cold wind compelling them to draw their coat collars higher up their necks.

"Carl."

"Yes?

"Please forgive me for not being so enthusiastic at first when you mentioned the possibility of acquiring the job. I was being very selfish. I just wanted to spend more quality time with you. I now realize you enjoy spending time with other people and want to be employed in some kind of work. And I need to let you be free to do that, without having to cater to my whims or without having to suffer my frustration against you."

"I...There's nothing to forgive."

"Carl... this is ridic—"

"Shall we go have some lunch?"

He was too stubborn. Could he not see she was trying to right her wrong?

Perhaps, I'm not saying the right thing.

When they returned to the house, no one was home. Casby was always ready to greet them from any excursion they came from.

"How strange!" Evelyn untied the scarf from around her neck.

"What?"

"Casby is nowhere to be found."

"Well, perhaps, the old chap went out for a stroll."

"But he's always here."

"Oh, what does it matter? I'll prepare a light lunch for the both of us."

After they ate lunch, Carl rose from his seat. "I'm going to rest in the study for an hour or so."

"All right."

Evelyn sat upstairs in her sewing room embroidering a cushion she had started the week before. All was quiet in the house. It reminded her of the days when she had to deal with the frustrating silence that ensued after Carl had left home for the war in Europe, those days when she had cried till she had no more tears to give because of the loneliness that had sunk within her soul. She thought she could faintly hear her cries in the distance of her memories. But then she realized it was not her past cries she was hearing. It was someone else's moaning. She lay down the cushion immediately and followed the sound into the study downstairs.

"Carl?" Worry overtook her. She had never seen him so distressed. "Are you all right?"

"Go away!" His sobs sounded as violent waves crashing upon the seashore. He moaned, hiding his head beneath his wracking hands.

"I'm not going away whatever you say." Evelyn put her arms around him and laid her cheek upon his bent back until he fell asleep peacefully.

Evelyn watched him sleep. She was disturbed by her husband's change of disposition ever since he arrived home. His refusal to forgive her (although he always had to put a great effort in forgiving the wrongs of others), his violent outbreak, and mad swing of moods—this was absurd.

The sun had set. Carl started to shift from side to side until he was finally aroused.

"Carl?"

"Mmm."

She slowly helped him to a sitting position. "Carl, what happened?"

"Uh—oh, I'm sorry. It was nothing."

"Please, Carl, tell me what happened?"

Carl swallowed slowly, bowed his head, and whispered, "I saw them."

"Saw whom?"

"My comrades all around me were dying, screaming. Blood was seeping from their open wounds. Their cold dead eyes stared back at me. In the chaos, I could not close their eyelids. Cannons were setting off. Then I saw heaven break open. You were picking flowers from the back garden and smelling them, and you looked at me with longing. I tried to reach out for you with my hand but I couldn't touch you, feel the warmth of your body. Then you vanished, and I was on the battlefield again." He touched her face with both of his hands, feeling every plane. "Evelyn, I need you. Don't leave me."

"I won't. Neither you nor I are leaving each other, ever." Evelyn put her arms around him. "We will always be together. I promise."

Chapter 2

During the next few days, Carl and Evelyn were newlyweds, trying to adjust to the other's schedule and to each other's sleeping arrangements. They woke up together at seven in the morning. When they arrived at the round dining table, breakfast was being served. Carl would stand behind Evelyn's chair and pull it out of its place for her to seat herself upon it. He would then fetch the newspaper from the front steps of his home, where it had been discarded in a hurried fashion, and bring it into the dining room. He read about the war in Europe as he leisurely ate his breakfast. He related any prominent news to Evelyn, and she would view him with concern, hoping he would heal from his battle scars and cast off his obsession of needing to know any more of the dreadful war that had altered the lives of so many, including theirs. Every day, he left home at eight o'clock to walk to work. And some days, when he returned from work, he would hide in his study. She could never tell what he was doing in there. Sometimes she would walk up to the door with a glass in her hand. She would put the glass against the grain of the wood and press her ear against it to hear whatever secrets he hid. But she never heard anything. It was almost as if he knew she stood on the other side and would wait until he heard her retreating footsteps to let go of the pain seeming to build inside him. The only evidence of tears she could see after his hour in hiding was the subtle red streaks that had been painted across his eyes. She felt hopeless, knowing she could not do a single thing to help him. Her fortitude was gradually being crushed by the myriad of concerns she carried day after day.

***

"Carl?" Hearing the front door groan, her eyes peeped out from behind the top of her novel.

"Yes?" He unravelled a black and white checkered scarf from around his neck and hung it upon one of the lower branches of the hall tree. He came into the living room and settled down upon their blue sofa.

"How did you fare at work today?"

"Well, some of the writers are very hesitant to...converse with me. I sometimes feel their stares piercing me through my office walls. They are civil enough. I just need to work hard and show them I am a man they can trust. I must demonstrate my approachability."

"That must be somewhat unnerving."

"It's not so bad, really. How was your day?"

"Same as the day before."

After a small conversation, he would again retire to his study, and she would sit upon her chair brooding over her misfortune of having a husband with whom she could no longer commune.

***

The next morning, husband and wife languidly sat at the dining table as they heard the *pit-pattering* of the rain beating upon the window. "This damn weather…I shall have to walk in this rain."

"Why do you not take the cab this once?"

"There is no point of my hailing a cab to drive me a few blocks down. It is a waste of money and time of entering and exiting the carriage. No, I shall walk. Wait! Don't we have a parasol?"

"We…did. I had to dispose of it because one of the ribs cracked."

"Well, I shall have to bear it. Mmm…" he shook his newspaper.

"What is it?"

"The *Imo*, a relief ship from Brussels, Belgium, arrived at the harbour yesterday. It's supposed to set sail later on this week for New York to then return to the war front and bring more supplies to the troops. Splendid, how there are many people who want to see this war ended."

"What sort of supplies would they be collecting from New York?"

"Clothing, bandages, food, and war supplies. A lot of these necessities are supplied by women who have entered the workforce to continue outputting goods. They are some of those who are filling in for the men overseas." He quickly sipped the last of his coffee, folded the newspaper, and reached for his crutches. "Well, I should be getting along now."

"Will I see you later?"

"Yes, except I won't arrive home at my usual time. I have an extremely important piece for the newspaper I need to work on along with the usual others. Do not expect me earlier than ten."

"Ten?!"

"Yes, ten. Goodbye! I'll see you then." Carl gave her a quick kiss. "My dear, you'll eventually catch a fly with such an open trap."

"Right…ten. I understand."

"Good. Goodbye."

Guilt washed over her. A bitterness had settled within the pit of her stomach ever since she realized Carl was not the same man anymore. Only hints of his previous amiable personality would protrude during those times when he left his walls unguarded. But those moments were so few.

Perhaps, I'm not the same anymore.

So many neighbours, friends bore the same despondency she did, yet they were doing so much more to help the war effort, giving their loved ones a greater reason to come back home. Many bought victory bonds, knitted clothing; served overseas as nurses, truck drivers and so on. She had hardly done anything to help.

At the start of the war, she had been involved with many volunteer services. The joy of giving had infected her to the point she had spent most of her days out and about helping in any way she could. She and many other women who sat quilting in a circle on Saturday afternoons would comfort each other with the hope that the war would be over by Christmas, that their men would come home. But Christmas passed, and there was no sign of any immediate withdrawal from Europe. Little by little she lost any incentive to spend her time giving herself to a seemingly hopeless cause.

***

The day dragged on. Evelyn became fidgety and anxious. Every little creak from the old flooring or scratch from a scampering mouse inside the walls made her jump. She tried to finish embroidering one of her pillows, and she tried to read. But nothing would do. She could only hear the clock go *tick, tock, tick, tock.*

"Casby?" She called out, hoping he was nearby to answer.

"Yes, Madam?"

"I...I need to go out for a stroll. When will supper be ready?"

"Six o'clock. Would you like me to postpone it?"

She glanced at the grandfather clock which stood at the northeastern corner of the room. However, despite her intense gaze upon the clock hands, she could not read the time. Her eyes blurred as they became sheathed in translucent wetness.

"You have an hour before supper, Madam."

"Yes, yes, of course." She darted from her chair, jerked her coat from the hall tree, and almost ran outside. How did it come to this that she could not find proper peace in her own home but would have to venture into the miserable world around her to find some note of healing?

Where do I go?

All around her people bustled about, some accidentally shoving her from one side to the next. Without any conscious thought, she let her feet propel her toward the harbour away from the stench of apathetic souls. She couldn't remember the last time she came across a familiar face during a rare airing. She let her tears fall freely, knowing no one would care to or dare ask what the matter was.

Reaching the harbour, she wiped the drying tears from her cheeks. She milled through the small crowd of soldiers that must have been dropped off not more than half an hour ago. Many seemed to have no family or friends to greet them. They were alone just as she was. Some sat upon benches staring off toward the sea, and others walked off in haphazard directions. One or two actually looked her way and smiled, raising their hands in friendly greeting. She didn't know why. Their kind gestures warmed her heart in a way she couldn't understand.

This is all I was looking for, some human warmth although a few feet distance away.

She wanted to stay, to talk, to sense or fathom she was not the only person in the world who felt the way she did, day in and day out. But she left, knowing dinner would be ready soon.

Such a convenient excuse.

***

Evelyn retired to her bedroom after dinner. She tried to do some more reading, but her eyes roved over the words so quickly they became a blur. Letting out a deep sigh, she snapped the book shut.

"This is ridiculous! I can hardly do anything!"

She began to pace up and down her room. Her steps strode in unison with the flickering flame. Only her steps were lit—a small candle she held—the rest of the room engulfed in darkness. She thought of changing into her nightgown and snuggling into bed. Perhaps the preparation and actual act of sleeping would calm her nerves. But she was so agitated she could not even undo the buttons down the front of her dress. Her fingers fumbled and slipped. Pausing from her taxing chore, she blew out the candle and sat down in her chair facing her mirroir.

Breathe, she willed herself. *Breathe*.

The air was cold enough that puffs like smoke escaped her open lips. The moon's macabre light washed over the room. Her rosy cheeks had acquired a ghostly complexion, and even paler still as she saw its reflection. Winter's chilly breath blew down her partly exposed spine, the hairs on her back tingling.

"Oh dear! I've left the window open."

She crossed the room to close it. In the darkness below, she noticed a shadowy figure approach the front door and slip from her sight under the porch roof. She glanced back at the clock to faintly see it was not yet ten. Perhaps Carl had finished his work sooner than he had expected. And if it was not Carl, who else could it be? She knew there were to be no visitors tonight. Besides, it was much too late to entertain any guests. In the silence, she heard the front door swing open.

For ten minutes she waited for Casby to come up and inform her of the visitor's arrival, or for Carl to fumble into their room and allay her incoherent fears. But neither one knocked upon her door. What kind of game was this? Her knees quaked, her hands quivered. She slumped to the floor and could hardly breathe, nulling any previous effort of calming herself. This stranger was up to no good. What should she do?

"Oh, God, wherever you are, please help me."

Inhaling deeply, she shut her eyes to shut out the fear overtaking her body with its vise-like grip.

All right. I'm going downstairs. I will not be afraid.

She proceeded into the darkness with extreme caution, relying only upon her instinct and weak night-vision. Every step she took she held her breath and was aware of every muscle she moved in her feet. With sweaty, trembling hands she managed to turn the doorknob and steal her way into the corridor. After five minutes of groping around, her foot finally encountered the edge of the staircase. She took great pains descending the old stairway so that the steps would not creak. However, as she was about to sidle from the last step onto the main floor, the step's moan betrayed her vulnerable position. Her heartbeat ceased for a moment. The next second it accelerated to the sky. She pressed herself against the wall, putting her hand to her heart to stop its insanity. It was all at an end. She had been discovered. She could only wait for her fate.

But five minutes passed, and no one had come. Had they not heard her stumble? She could hardly believe her good luck. She resolved to continue her mission. As she slid along the wall opposite the staircase, she accidentally smacked into the entrance table. The bottom of the glass vase teetered precariously until she deftly amended its balance.

Of all things!

She stayed still for a minute, determining whether she could continue. Not a sound approached her. She neared the kitchen toward the back of the house, stopping at the halfway open door. Casby's hoarse voice streamed through the opening of the door. Had he been drinking? She strained to listen to what the other's voice sounded like. She deemed the stranger to be a man from the tones of a lower register. Unfortunately, he spoke so softly she could hardly hear him.

"Good wine, isn't it?" drawled Casby.

The other man's murmurs were inaudible to her prying ears.

"Compliments of the good master and mistress, Mr. and Mrs. Richardson. Ha! Oh, if they only knew."

What is he doing? And whom is he with?

Casby continued. "Oh, well, if you must know the master is hard at work this evening. I've known for a few days—had the foresight to ask him of what his schedule might be like. And his wife..." He chuckled. "She's a bag of nerves, probably sleeping like a baby. Now you have five more deliveries to make. Make use of the friendships you have with the officers. You'll know where to find me. And always watch your back. Only then will you be released from your side of the bargain."

The unknown man muttered something.

"Yes, well, I know it's going to take time; but you must be hasty. Our country is counting on you. I'm counting on you."

Which country did he mean? What was he talking about? And five more clandestine meetings in her house? Evelyn would not stand for it.

The men's conversation turned to war politics. She left her sleuthing position, grabbed her shawl from the hall tree, and exited the house. She wished she had taken a little more time to find her coat. Although the office was only a few blocks away, she was sure she would nearly freeze to death; the temperature had dropped to an even lower degree than it had been during that day. Already, the wind cut through her shawl and was biting her skin. The little snow which painted the streets was shimmering in the glow of the moon. The street lamps had been extinguished due to the curfew imposed upon the city since the war. She ran as quickly as she could to the office of the *Halifax Herald*.

By the time she reached the office, her legs were tingling. She bent over to breathe in the snappish cold. Her hand flit to her heart to rest its pounding. She beheld a single lit room on the second floor. Carl! She stumbled to the door and rested against it for a moment. After catching her breath, she tried to open the door, fully knowing it would be locked. But to her surprise, it wasn't. She threw open the door and trampled up the stairs to Carl's office.

"Carl!"

"Evelyn?!" A worry took hold in Carl's surprised gaze. He shot out of his seat and fastened his arms around her. "What's the matter?"

"Casby... home... he...."

"Come, come, now, take a seat, rest a little. Did you run all the way here in the freezing cold wind with only a shawl upon your shoulders??"

All she could do was nod her head, and close her eyes knowing the notion was preposterous. "We need...to...to go home."

"All right. We'll go. But you must put on my coat. I will not have you gallivanting about in such a miserable condition. You can tell me everything once we are on our way." He touched her frozen cheek.

"Thank you. Wait. What will you wear?"

"We're just going to be outside for a few minutes. I can endure. I'll tell you what, I'll wear your shawl. See. How do I look?"

"Carl... you're not serious, are you?"

"Of course, I am."

"But that's a women's shawl!"

"Yes, I know." He flung it across his shoulders in a dramatic fashion. His mischievous grin forbade her from infringing upon his circus any further.

"Where have *you* been this whole time?" she whispered searching his visage for more of *him*.

"I'm not sure." He stashed a pile of papers into his desk, blew out the lamp, and guided Evelyn out of the building.

"What about your work?"

"I was able to finish most of it. I'll come in early Monday morning to conclude it. Now, Evelyn, what is the matter?"

She told him, the story pouring out of her as they hurried through the deserted streets. "Can you remember anything else?" Carl asked.

"No."

They approached the house in silence.

"Evelyn," Carl whispered. "I want you to stay at the bottom of the steps. Wait for me to let you know if it is safe to come in. Do you understand?"

"Yes."

Carl clumped up the stairs and entered the house. The darkness swallowed him. Evelyn waited and waited. Five minutes seemed like an hour. Finally, Carl's head poked outside the entrance door. He waved her forward, holding in his right hand a gun.

"I never knew we had a gun!"

"I bought it in case of an emergency."

"Well? Was anyone there?"

Carl shook his head. "No, Casby's gone."

Chapter 3

Carl and Evelyn stumbled into their bed and slumbered deeply after conducting a thorough search of the house. They had examined every room, even the tiny attic that could be accessed through the ceiling of their master bedroom. Surely just as Evelyn had recounted, the wine had been touched, having been discarded on its side and a small amount of wine left to dribble on the crude kitchen worktable. The whole bottle was empty. Carl had scrutinized every corner of Casby's spacious bedroom, situated on the second floor above Carl's study. No vestige of his previous presence was left.

Carl and Evelyn arose at nine o'clock the next morning, much later than their usual time. Carl managed to scoot himself to the edge of the bed to put on his Sunday trousers. "I'm so glad I don't have to work today," he yawned. "I don't think I would be able to function properly having had hardly any sleep. I'm thinking, perhaps I should check the whole house again. Maybe I missed something; it was very late."

Evelyn propped her drooping head upon her outstretched arm. "True. Shall we look again?"

"Yes."

Even after the second search, they saw nothing with their fresh eyes. When they entered the dining room, they were cognizant they had no butler and, therefore, no prepared food.

"Do not fear. Your stomach shall be satisfied," Evelyn announced.

Carl cocked his head to the side displaying a rather facetious-looking face of surprise.

"I don't think I've told you this before…" she put on an apron. "When I was a young girl, my mother forbade me from approaching the kitchen. She would continually bellow in my ear, 'The kitchen is the servants' quarters. You are not to associate with them in this way. Do I make myself clear?' Trust me, she did; just the effect she had hoped for never came to fruition and…"

"That's no surprise."

"Ssh, as I was saying, I was curious as to how they made such delectable meals. Eliza, the cook, taught me the art of cooking when I was able to steal away from my mother's company at certain outings. I was very clever at hiding my secret. She never knew nor was suspicious of my…illegal activities."

"My dear, I didn't think of you as a rebellious child."

"You didn't know the trap you fell into by marrying me."

"I must conjecture you are perfectly right." A chuckle escaped his lips. He smiled.

Evelyn searched Carl's eyes for a sign…his laying down of arms in the unbroken silence. She cleared her throat. "So now you know my terrible secret; I'll prepare some lunch." She spun on her heel and strode into the kitchen.

Is this the dawn of something new? Will the walls we've built finally break down?

She tried to read between the lines of their moment of openness as she prepared lunch. She returned with two bowls of potato soup, two slices of bread and butter, and two glasses of water on a tray. She placed the food in front of him.

He reached for her fingers and placed them in between his hands, his thumb caressing each ridge. "Thank you, my dear."

"You're welcome," she breathed out. A dusty rose shade bloomed upon her cheeks as she sat down.

He tentatively took his first sip all the while gauging her reaction to his false performance of hesitancy.

"Well?"

"I must say...it may need a bit of salt."

"Wipe away that Mephistophelian grin!"

"Ah, Faust. I don't know what you're talking about."

"That book has been sitting on its shelf for far too long. You never finished it."

"Yes, thank you for reminding me."

They resumed their meal, both exhibiting pleasing expressions of delight.

"Carl?"

"Yes?"

"What will we do now? I mean, we have no butler. Should we advertise for another?"

"I think not. We could save quite a bit of money if you were the one who prepared all our meals from now on."

"But I'm sure mother wouldn't mind hiring another one for us."

"Evelyn, don't you remember what I said concerning the matter? I believe it's best if we not be living off of your mother's money anymore. Because she helps supports us, she has great influence over the important choices we make; and she believes she has the right to force her ideas down our throats. Don't you remember what problems we had in purchasing our own house with your mother breathing down our necks? There was that lovely cottage you wanted on...oh, I can't remember which street it was on. I believe it was on the other side of town. But no! She insisted upon this one. And we accepted it because, well, it was generous of her. The thing is is that we are our own family; she has no right to dictate what we do with our lives. I cannot accept any more money from her. I appreciate that when I was off to war, your mother gave much for you to live on. Now I have returned and am able to support you myself without her monthly financial donations." The tension in his face slowly drained.

"I'm so sorry. I didn't mean to...make you frustrated." She tenderly placed her right hand upon his outstretched forearm which had been moving around quite vigorously during his previous overwrought speech. "I do know what you mean. Sometimes her overbearing presence is overwhelming. Do you really think if we cut off from her financially she will be less inclined to put her nose where it doesn't belong?"

"I don't know. But it's worth a try. And look, aren't you grateful you learned to cook and clean behind your mother's back?"

"Yes, quite." She picked at her food. "Last night was quite the adventure. I...I remember something else from last night."

"What?"

"Casby said, 'Our country is counting on you. I'm counting on you.' What does 'our country' have to do with what they were doing?"

"You are sure that's what was said."

"Yes, I'm sure."

"Perhaps he was talking about national espionage for...the Allied Nations?"

"Then why all the secrecy?"

"These men are bound to secrecy. I'm sure there is a very good reason why he left without telling us."

***

Evelyn was not reassured by Carl's words. The nightmares that continued to haunt her while she slept made it impossible for her to dispel the distrust she had for Casby. When she closed her eyes that night to succumb to the sweet kiss of sleep, poison penetrated her realm of dreams. Fire engulfed her, snow froze her, a horrendous noise shook her, smoke choked her, and darkness attacked her. Her husband suddenly disappeared in a wisp of cloud, and she was all alone in her torture.

"Carl!" She lunged upright in her bed.

He stirred softly.

Realizing it had just been a dream, her rapid breathing started to slow. She lay back down, thankful her husband was still there, right beside her. Exhausted, she closed her eyes and surrendered once more.

Soft lips pressed upon her, a hand cupping her cheek. She groggily opened her eyes. An angel of light was bending over her. The planes of his face touched and moulded against hers, reflecting the sun's dancing rays. Slowly, he pulled away from her, letting his kiss linger in the space between them.

"Good morning, my love."

"Good morning." What an awakening this was. This touch of romance had been gone for many years. Now that the spark had been ignited, she wanted more.

"Shall we get an early start?"

She nodded, unable to utter a single word; for his advances had stolen away her ability to breathe, unlike the first time when they had caused her to blench. After getting dressed, Evelyn prepared a simple breakfast of oatmeal. Although not many words were spoken, the newborn lovers passed the fondest looks between each other.

"You're different today, Carl."

"Yes, I am."

He seemed to be in the best of spirits. And the way he had kissed her. She could only think of that kiss.

"Carl, that kiss...what made you think I was ready? How did you know *you* were ready?"

"The possibility of your being in danger in our own home made me realize I've been holding onto things that were much less precious than you. I've been observing you the past few days to see whether you would welcome my…touch."

"Oh."

Now is a good time.

"I want to say I am truly sorry for the way I reacted the first time you touched me. My apology is long overdue. You were in need of physicality and..."

"Please, don't say anymore, Evelyn. I realize I gave you no warning. It had been a long time since...the last time. I shouldn't have expected...I also want to ask for forgiveness for holding it against you for too long."

"I know you and I in our stubbornness could bicker back and forth over how the blame should be upon ourselves and not the other for the next hour. So let us each forgive one another for the offenses we have laid out. Truce?"

"Truce." He downed the last drop of his coffee. "Well, I'm off."

"Already?"

"Yes, already."

"Hmm, all right. I'll be waiting for you when you come back."

"Good. And tonight...I have something special planned for you." At that moment, Carl leaned out of his chair and planted a passionate kiss upon her lips, locking her in his embrace.
The table and arms of the chairs could not stand in the way of his hands caressing the frame of her body.

She could only melt at his attentions. As she pulled back slightly to catch her breath, their heads knocked together.

"Ow!"

Evelyn touched her lip and winced while Carl rubbed his nose. They burst out laughing.

"I'm sorry, Evelyn."

Another kiss took place, one that glided over their lips as silk over skin.

"There now, perhaps that shall take away the pain." He rubbed his smooth thumb over her bottom lip.

"It already has."

"All right, then. Goodbye, my love."

"Wait! I'll see you out the door." She followed him out, chuckling. The air was crisp, and the clouds did not hinder the sun from making an adequate appearance.

"Carl, look." Evelyn whispered, pointing toward a young boy leaning over his bicycle, a flustered expression crossing his face.

Carl stepped toward him with Evelyn following behind. He placed a hand upon the young boy's shoulder, making the boy jump.

"Oi, what...!? Oh, pardon me, sir."

"Tommy?" Evelyn remembered him as Clyde's impatient friend.

"Yes, how'd you know...? Wait! Now I remember. You're the pretty lady Clyde was fool enough to bump into." He darted his gaze toward the Narrows. "What, in tarnation, are they doin'?" He swiped a chunk of hair falling into his eyes.

"Whom are you talking about?" Evelyn wondered aloud.

"Those two ships there." He pointed his finger at a point in the Narrows where two ships were about to pass each other.

"What's wrong?" Carl scratched his head. All seemed calm in the waters.

"Them both are on the wrong sides of the channel."

"Oh." Carl and Evelyn both felt a little foolish for not being able to see such a simple explanation; although the reader cannot blame them for not knowing such things, seeing they had never received nautical knowledge or experience.

Carl cleared his throat. "And how do you know all this, Tommy?"

Tommy's brows were knitted even deeper. "My father works in the shippin' business. He tells me things.There's them regulations that ships need to obey. A collision can happen if the ships don't meet proto...protocol? And if it happens to a ship carryin' guns, gunpowder, bombs...? Now that one isn't, I don't think—I can't tell! There're lots of dangerous ships comin' through here now 'cause of the war."

"Do you think any parties will suffer damage?" Evelyn asked.

"Well, if these two ships do run each other astern, the mess can be a fixed, I think."

"I never knew they had such regulations. Then again it's only logical that they should. Thank you, Tommy, for the nautical lesson. I really must go. Goodbye, Evelyn."

"Yes...I—I need to get a goin' myself." Tommy shuffled his clumsy feet toward the harbour, hopped onto his bicycle, and grazed past swinging skirts and striped trousers.

Carl invaded her thoughts continuously throughout the next forty-five minutes. Memories of their past secret meetings in her childhood garden while her mother was out visiting, of the inconspicuous loving looks they had cast each other's ways at public dinner tables, and of the day they had been united in matrimony rushed forth from their prison cell. She was skipping across the wooden floors and singing, not caring who might hear her through her home's walls. She took a respite from her housework to drink a glass of water. As she sipped her water, she moved toward the dining room to look out the sash window overlooking the harbour. A few buildings blocked parts of her view, but she could mostly see what was happening in the harbour below. Instead of beholding a clear blue sky, she gazed upon a gigantic mushroom cloud of smoke coming from a point in the Narrows.

"Oh, goodness!"

She backed up into a chair, turned it around, and slowly sat upon it. From what she could tell, two of the ships had collided. One of the ships sported a large gash at its fore-hold. Many people, including children, had started to gather in the streets and near the docks to watch the spectacle. Flames burst from the ship's hold and licked the sides of steel. All she could do was stare at the roiling smoke. She had seen smoke like this...her dream. Her nerves began to tingle; her fingertips shook. She swallowed her growing terror, rose from her chair, and stared into the middle of the swirling pillar of smoke. The smoke, furling in continuous circles, hypnotized her.

She could not fathom what had caused this strange beauty manifesting its fearsome strength. Was it a munitions ship? Tommy had said something like this might happen. Suddenly the smoke vanished, and a brighter light than the sun flooded her entire vision. Awestruck, Evelyn covered her squinting eyes with her hands and could not breathe.

Oh, dear God, what is this?

She knew not what to think. As quickly as she could, she crawled underneath the oak table. She was hidden on all sides by the draping tablecloth. She hugged her knees to her chest. Soon the ground began to shake beneath her. Would the earth swallow her deep into its pit? And Carl…. She hoped he would be all right. An ear-shuddering strum grew louder and louder until…. She squeezed her eyes closed; Death was near.

*****

Dark grey light, spattered with black blotches, pervaded her sight. Different sounds meshed into one jumbled flow. She licked her lips to taste a bitter metal substance. She tried to spit it out immediately but failed in doing so. She felt a soothing touch sweep over her brow. A sweet low voice spoke to her. Evelyn raised her hand to see what was covering her mouth. "Ah!" Excruciating pain shot into her right arm.

"Sh! Sh! It's all right, dear. Everything will be okay."

The bright light Evelyn had seen was gone. The world was now black with death. The sun had been defeated. Everywhere ash rained down from heaven upon ruins and rubble. Her house and others had either warped, broken in pieces, or fallen to the ground. Trees and telegraph posts had snapped in two.

"Where am I? What happened? Where—where's my husband?"

"Here let me tend to your arm."

"Who are you?"

"I am Nurse…"

"Nurse Randall. Come here immediately. I need your help," a man's voice called from within the bleak wilderness.

"I'm coming, doctor." The nurse turned to Evelyn and said, "I'll be right back, dear. Stay here. Don't move around and keep this blanket on your arm." Then she left, as a ghost slips through the shadows.

What had happened? Had the Germans attacked?

I need answers. I need to find Carl.

She tried to summon her strength. Attempting to rise, she fell to the ground on her back. Again she tried and then succeeded. Slowly she removed the blanket on her arm to see the damage. Her arm was burnt close to the bone, charred and white in some areas. The edges of her burn were welting her tender flesh. She covered her arm with the blanket again because of the extreme pain searing her. Her head twisted from left to right. As far as her eye could see, houses had turned into ash-covered ruins, people were dead, people cried in pain, fire licked its victims. Her dreams, her reveries were manifesting themselves. What on earth had happened? Carl. He was supposed to be at work. But the whole of Halifax had not escaped the wrath of Fate. Had he survived? Had he...? There was only one thing to do. She would find him, no matter what the cost.

Chapter 4

Determination had settled within every fibre of Evelyn's will although her frail mettle insistently persuaded her to lie down and drift into a state of unconscious debilitation. She took a few small steps forward and wandered into the rolling smoke about her. Her eyes burned from the fumes intoxicating the area. She looked down to see her skirt ripped to shreds and her top outerwear missing from her person. She placed her unscathed arm over her thinly covered chest for modesty's sake.

Soldiers, servicemen, and medical personnel entered the area in a trickle aiding those who were trapped within the rubble of unrecognizable homes. They helped drive the greatly injured to the nearest hospitals in whatever civilian or army automobiles they could find. All the streets looked the same.

Evelyn tried to find her bearings but could not distinguish anything.

"Dear me, what are you doing up and about?" Nurse Randall's face came into view.

"I...I need to find my husband."

"I'm sorry, dear. You can't in this condition. How are you going to help him when you need help yourself?"

Evelyn's head drooped; she felt a deep pressure throbbing in her forehead. She lifted her grimy hand to the side of her temple, feeling splotches of dry and wet blood.

"You've been cut in some areas by shards of glass. Come now. I'm sending you to the hospital. Don't you go running off right now. We're going to get you some help." She bustled off.

Evelyn, weak and hurting, could not stand any longer. She lowered herself to the ground. Nurse Randall came back in several minutes, with two men and a stretcher.

"There's space for you on an automobile. They'll take you to Camp Hill Hospital." The men lowered the stretcher onto the ground and offered her their hands. Weakly, she settled her body into the tarp, a bloodied canvas, worn from being painted upon. The two men grunted as they picked her up and started walking...God knew where. The rhythm of their shuffling feet and the strokes of their encumbered breathing guided her mind into oblivion. And even in her rest, peace was not to be found.

She woke up a minute later not being able to sleep properly because of the automobile's stop-go rhythm. She lifted her head an inch to see the destruction had uniformly blanketed the entire area. She wondered how widespread the damage really was. People were everywhere, walking around in confusion. Some were sifting through the corpses that had been laid on the side of the road to see if they could find their deceased loved ones. She could not tell one person from the next, for all their faces were covered in oily soot.

My face looks the same, as well.

Suddenly she felt a crinkling of paper beneath her aching fingers.

Ah, I still have it.

She pried open the petite slit in her dress which was the opening to a secret pocket, within which she always kept a photograph of Carl on their wedding day. Gingerly, she placed it upon her bosom.

The whole grimy scene faded once again into nothing

***

Groans, hushed voices, a child's whimper—Evelyn's eyes wearily opened to view a dark mesh of movements. Throbbing pain grasped her right arm. The images started to clear. She was surrounded by other victims wearing masks of misery and stalwartness. The doctors and nurses crammed as many beds as they could into one room to fit the astounding number of people who had come for medical attention, yet even so many lay in between the beds on the floor. Halifax's hospitals were not ready for such an influx of damaged people. One nurse was administering painkillers. Another was soothing a hurting child.

Evelyn's head lolled to the left. A gentleman of approximately seventy years of age stared at her with drooping eyes. A smile curved at the corner of her lips. Her small amount of emanating compassion was enough to bring some light back into his eyes. He then turned his eyes upward and shut them, his breathing calm and light.

Time was of no consequence when all one could do was lie in bed and share the sad fate of so many others. Eventually, the little air coming through the boarded windows became considerably cooler. Night had fallen. Evelyn hoped the relief workers had rescued all the survivors. She could hardly imagine still being alive to suffer yet another bad element, Winter's freeze.

She was starting to fall asleep when Nurse Randall came into the room to ascertain all the patients' conditions and administer any necessary medicine. After passing four beds, Nurse Randall sat on the side of Evelyn's bed and held her hand. "How are you feeling, dear?"

"I'm very tired. And I'm still in pain though it is much more bearable then before. Tell me, what happened?"

"Well, Doctor MacCrae spent hours performing a very risky operation on you. You had a third-degree burn on your right forearm. The subcutaneous layer suffered some damage. He had to graft in its place skin from your thigh onto your arm. You were monitored for a day to see if any complications would arise. But you're a fighter. You seem to be recovering very well. And the pain you're feeling, it's normal. I don't know if you remember this or not, but you also suffered from some cuts on your face and other arm. However, those were much less critical than the burns you had."

"Well, I'm glad the worst is over. Please thank Doctor MacCrae for his care."

"I'll be sure to do so."

"What really happened...out in the harbour?" Evelyn gazed upon the sea of bodies filling the room. "Was it the Germans?"

"No, goodness, the *Imo* collided with the *Mont-Blanc*, a munitions ship, in the Narrows. The whole harbour face has been demolished. Homes are now ashes. A lot of people died in horrible ways from the force of the explosion. The factories have been laid flat. So much devastation...one mistake...so many victims. They were still searching for the living the night of the explosion. But there was a ghastly snowstorm; I don't believe they found many more survivors...after that." She put on a thin smile. "A few towns in New Brunswick and Boston, that city in Massachusetts, were the first few to send relief and..."

"The *Imo*...the ship my husband read about in the *Halifax Herald*...Nurse Randall, I need to find him. Do you know what happened to the newspaper office?"

"Is that where your husband was working?"

"Yes, he's an editor."

"Where was this building located?"

"A few blocks down from our home on Grafton Street."

"I believe most of the buildings near the harbour have been laid flat. I'm sure you'll find each other if...I'm sorry."

"There isn't much hope he has survived?" Evelyn's lips trembled.

"No."

Evelyn folded her hands in her lap, breathing deeply. "Thank you for telling me the truth."

"It's what you deserve. By the way, call me Betsie."

"Betsie."

"I'm sure you're eager to determine if your husband is all right. If your recovery goes well, you may leave in approximately four weeks."

"Four weeks?"

"Now, now, if you do not rest properly, you will be staying longer; but if you do exactly what I tell you, then you may leave sooner. It all depends upon you."

"Of course."

"Oh, before I leave...I believe this belongs to you." She produced from her pocket a folded photograph.

"Oh, thank you. I don't think I can go on without it."

"When the soldiers carried you in from the car, one of them noticed you had dropped it. I'll see you later."

Betsie rose from the rumpled bed and left.

Evelyn quickly glanced at the older gentleman who was fast asleep, hoping nightmares would not invade his seemingly sweet sleep that night.

***

The next morning, Evelyn awoke, aching all over her back and limbs. The little cold air continuing to seep through the cracks of the boarded window saved her from being stifled amongst all the patients. Two nurses were on duty bringing in trays of food to everyone. She received hers. Her heart drooped as she saw what little food there really was for her to ingest. This food would not fill her stomach compared to the portions she usually gave herself at home. But that was all gone now. No turning back. And that last breakfast together—it had been the setting where the healing of her relationship with Carl had taken place. But that had been ripped from her as well. He was lost.

The old gentleman laying beside her turned toward her when he heard her sniffling. He studied her face, painted by several tears. "May I have the pleasure of knowing your name?"

Evelyn's head snapped to her left, surprised the gentleman had uttered a sound. She thought she had been alone in her misery

41

and no one would care to pay any attention to her weeping. "My name is Mrs. Richardson, sir."

"And your Christian name?"

"Evelyn."

"Evelyn, that is a beautiful name. May I call you by your first name?"

"Yes, you may." She wiped away her tears with the back of her hand.

"Evelyn, why the shedding of tears?"

She let out a heavy sigh. "Oh, sir, forgive me. I...I was thinking of how little my portion is, how I would like a lot more on my plate. But I chide myself, knowing I am not the only one whose stomach will be suffering from this small meal."

"Don't continue to bruise yourself unnecessarily. You are human; and because of this very fact, you are bound to do wrong. What is important is that you find this error and correct it. Endeavor to expel it. Think of others." He reached out his hand, beckoning hers to join.

Grateful for his friendship, she returned the gesture. "And what is your name, sir?"

"My name is Matthew Cox."

She noticed a scarlet leather-bound book in his hand.

Mr. Cox followed her questioning gaze. "It is the one book that offers me true hope; it is my constant guide throughout life's trials and happy times. It is my family's Bible. And did you know, this was the only object I had on my person when these good people found me? Not even my clothes could be found."

How could God have let this...devastation happen to me, to Carl, to Mr. Cox? So many good people have lost loved ones, their livelihoods. And yet he still turns to Him for comfort.

When she was younger, she had attended church with her mother. Yes, she had believed in God, in His miracles. But the older she had grown, the more insightful she had become. Through the *good morning*'s and *I hope you feel better*'s she saw the undeniable hypocrisy stemmed in many of the hearts occupying the pews. It had especially poisoned her mother. Her mother—so many people looked up to her tasteful decor, her overwrought courteous manners, and righteous living; but they had never seen the transition from brief godly living to stuffy hypocrisy once the door shut out the world's prying eyes. They never saw the mask she drew upon her face when she went out into the public eye. No, there was not a single shred of truth to her faith. And Evelyn didn't want any part of it. She wouldn't be naive and let her mind be comforted in...in what? A lie? A crutch? A truth? No, she didn't care to think of it.

"Mr. Cox, I believe I'll finish my breakfast if you don't mind."

"Of course."

***

Evelyn regained her complete bodily strength as well as some of the strength in her recovering arm through some effective exercises Betsie had shown her throughout the following weeks. Every night of the week, she looked upon Mr. Cox with confusion as he ritually read his Bible and prayed. She couldn't understand his devotion to Someone who was unfair in his dealings with men. Despite his obvious faith, she and Mr. Cox became fast friends; she even volunteered to help him with his leg and foot exercises.

"Mr. Cox, what happened to you during the explosion?"

"Some older woman found me completely naked two streets up from where I was watching the cloud of smoke. The force of the explosion must have carried me over. She quickly threw the coat she wore on her back over my lower body. She asked if I was able to walk. I tried, but I just couldn't. She went to find some help for me, later returning with two soldiers driving an automobile. Ah!"

"Oh, I'm sorry!"

"No, no, don't be. That particular movement was painful."

"I will try to be more careful."

"Thank you. As I was saying, the men picked me up and drove me to this hospital. When I arrived, a nurse took a look at my legs. She said my right ankle was broken and my left thigh had sustained some lacerations."

So much did her heart form an attachment to him and his predicament that she stayed more than her mandatory weeks of recovery until he was able to take a few steps on his own. When she wasn't occupied with him, she would help Betsie nurse the other patients still filling many of the hospital's rooms. Because there was an overload of people receiving treatments at the hospital, Evelyn had to give up her cot for another patient. For the next little while, she settled with sleeping upon the floor in the corner of Mr. Cox's room, where no one would think of her being in the way of traffic. She had no other place to go. And Carl…he was most likely dead. She could hardly give herself any hope of his existence when it might be dashed to pieces when she would find out he truly was dead.

***

One day, she and Betsie were changing a patient's bandages when Betsie exclaimed, "Oh, dear me. I forgot to get some new ones to replace these. Evelyn, would you mind putting these old ones out and bringing me some new ones?"

"Of course. I won't be more than five minutes." She left the room and glided into the corridor, trying to remember in which room they could be found. Once she found the correct room, she drifted toward the closet where some of the clean bandages were stored. She picked up five and walked out.

"Doctor MacCrae, your services are needed immediately," a voice called out nearby.

Evelyn swivelled her head to the left to see Doctor MacCrae and a nurse standing side by side.

"Yes, I'll be there directly," he answered. "Thank you."

With a nod of his head, the nurse left.

As he was walking her way, he espied Evelyn a few feet from his side.

So this is Doctor MacCrae.

His face sported lines of fatigue across his brow and mouth. He centred his gaze upon her recovered arm and hardly peeked a glance at her. A step in the hallway curtly drew his attention away, and he ambled into a room.

She stayed still for a moment trying to draw a conclusion from their strange encounter. It was of no use. This conundrum was to stay within her mind, not to be unraveled.

The rich man in his castle,
The poor man at his gate.
God made them, high or lowly,
And order'd their estate.
Mrs. Alexander

Chapter 5

"I shall miss you, Evelyn. What will I do without you? You always fetch those darn clean bandages for me." Betsie tried to compose herself in public view by sniffling away the rebellious tears continuing to threaten to spill over her weak lids. She bit her lip hard and laid her right palm over her heart.

"And I you."

"Where will you go? Are you going to see family?"

"Yes, I'll first try to find my mother in Dartmouth to see if she is well. I've heard some of Dartmouth suffered from the blast. Which parts, I don't know. Then after I find my mother I shall look for my husband, even though…he may be dead."

"I hope he isn't."

"Thank you. I hold to the same hope." Evelyn gave Betsie a large embrace.

All her life did she only have a handful of good friends. She never was part of a posse or a close group of gossips. She preferred to keep to her own company than indulge in public outings. But

Betsie…she was the closest friend she had ever had even though Betsie was twenty years her senior.

"Now, I'll go see Mr. Cox and bid him farewell before I take my leave."

"All right."

Evelyn waved goodbye and then a minute later entered Mr. Cox's room. "Mr. Cox, how are you today?"

"Oh, I'm getting better day after day. Although sometimes, I wish I could jump out of this cot and run back home to the comfort I love. But then I don't even know if my home is still standing. It probably isn't. I don't know what I'll do once I'm released. And you…you are doing just that today, aren't you? You're leaving me today?"

"I'll come back. I promise. I need to see if my mother is all right, and I must try to find my husband. I hope it won't be difficult to find a new home. There must be some committee in charge of aiding those who have no place to sleep."

"Yes, I'm sure there is. Well, now I'll have to fend for myself with you gone and Betsie having no one to restrain her…feisty personality. You know how stubborn the woman is."

"Ha, I know. How will you be able to stand it for more than a few days? I'm sure she'll drive you mad." Evelyn's chuckles were intermingled with choking runaway tears.

"I'm praying for you, dear girl."

"During our time of getting to know one another…I know I haven't voiced any of my own personal beliefs or lack thereof—truly I cannot see what good your prayers will do but thank you." Evelyn displaced her hand from his and kissed his brow. "Goodbye."

***

Exiting the hospital, every step she took seemed as lead, the earth not able to bear the tremendous weight of her uncertainties. A strangeness invaded her body as she noted the way people milled about; their faces couldn't hide the hurt they had suffered. Would she be able to hail any familiar-looking neighbours, no matter how little she had known them? Or was this populace a new class of breed, one that had been raised overnight to shun the past and push toward a brighter future?

What is there left to live for?

That was all she needed, to find him. But first she had to see her mother, to see to her present state. She owed the woman who had raised her that much.

The coaches and tram services had returned to the streets. Presently, she cared not to be transported by anything nor to share the means of it with any stranger; instead, she decided to walk down to the harbour, which had been rebuilt and was again receiving incoming ships. She wanted to see whether a ferrying service had been established so that she could cross the channel to the other side. As she neared the docks, men were hauling goods off the ships. They shouted commands to each other, and she could faintly hear the merry seamen's tunes along the breeze. A ship whistled its leave as it was expertly maneuvered away from the docks and out into the channel. The ferry, two hundred feet away from her, was just about to leave.

I must make it. There's no time to lose.

With no decorum, she dashed to the ferry's dock and planted her toes upon the edge. "Sir, sir, please let me board."

"All right. Come on in." He waved his hand briskly, beckoning her to hurry. After he examined all his equipment was set and all his passengers were safely on board, they sprung from the dock's hold and out into the open sea. Multitudes of fish scattered from the ferry's bottom as it chopped through the waves. Evelyn sidled along the edge of the ferry to lean over the railing to drink in the sea air, embracing its crisp savour from the salt, flavouring the deep.

What will Mother think when she sees me? Does she think I'm dead? Will she even let me into her home? I haven't visited her since I wrote her saying Carl and I wouldn't take any more money from her.

Discouraged by her tumultuous thoughts, she turned around and observed the other people on deck. A mother with a small child of about four years huddled together to ward off the wind's chill. They fondly gazed at another child's knitted sweater to which the present child clung. Perhaps it had belonged to an older brother or sister. An older man had his arm around a young woman who sobbed her tears onto his chest. And an old woman grimly stared out into the abyss, shaking her head back and forth. The captain of the boat was moving through the small mass of still hurting souls, seeming to want to assure himself all his passengers were at least physically well.

"And how are you, Missy?" he asked.

"As well as can be, sir."

"The slight rocking motion doesn't disturb you?"

"No, I happen to enjoy it."

"Good, I enjoy hearing of another hearty spirit who enjoys the sea's waters as much as I do. Yes, well, I better be moving on." With a quick nod of his head, he cast a glance back to his position and returned post haste.

Evelyn continued to watch him for several minutes. He seemed to have brought his own company aboard the ferry. The man (she assumed) was covered from head to toe in a deep ocean blue cloak shielding the calm grey light from his eyes. His back was bent, the crinkled planes a harsh contrast to the gossamer clouds lazily drifting in the background. The old seafarer exchanged a few words with his esoteric company, patted his back, and returned to his duties.

After some time, the ferry approached the Dartmouth shore. As it did, excitement ruffled its way throughout the throng.

"Did you hear that one of the *Mont Blanc*'s gun barrels flew all the way to this side of the Narrows? It landed near Albro Lake. Have you been there before? I could show you the sight today if you like." A young man wearing a large brown tweed coat accosted a pretty girl and her chaperone.

"Oh, yes, that would be very pleasant. Do you not think so Aunt Hilda?"

"A lake? We aren't prepared for such an outing. Would you not rather book into our inn straight away?"

"Oh, no, please say yes. I wasn't here when the explosion occurred. To see a piece of history, a part of the wreckage…And this young man seems quite amiable!"

You were lucky not to have been here. You might think differently if you had been.

Evelyn lumbered through the crowd trying her best not to push through linked arms and bent together heads as it would be very rude and unladylike. After freeing herself, she instantly hailed a coach.

"Please take me to the Nova Scotia Hospital on Pleasant Street."

"Yes, miss."

Once she arrived, she swung open the door, paid the man his fare, and walked briskly into the hospital only to stop shortly at the receptionist's desk.

"Good day, what can I do for you?" A young woman with glasses perched atop her nose sat behind a desk with several papers neatly stacked in a corner and three pens loosely scattered about.

"Good day, I'm looking for a Mrs. Moore, a Jane Moore."

Evelyn had decided to go to the local hospital first (it was on the way) to see if her mother was or had been a recent patient. If she was, Evelyn wouldn't be wasting time going to the house only to discover her mother wasn't there.

"One moment, please." Her head disappeared behind a stack of files. She took one out and scanned its contents. "No, I'm sorry. We don't have a Jane Moore nor has she been admitted here for some time."

"Oh, thank you. Thank you for your time…" Evelyn peered to the right of the desk to look at the receptionist's name card, "Lucy."

"Have a good day."

"Thank you."

With a burden lifted off her already cracked heart, a lighter step pervaded her walk. She decided to go to her mother's house on foot since it was only but a twenty-five minute walk from the hospital.

On this side of the Narrows, devastation had also come. However, it wasn't as widespread as it was to be found in Halifax. The closer she approached her mother's house on Hastings Drive, the sparser the damage.

The smell of fresh bread wafted along the street through a slightly open bakery window, reminding Evelyn of her restricting childhood. As a secret helper to the cook in her mother's kitchen, she would slip out before her mother's arousal from sleep to fetch the fresh bread for the day. The cook could have easily made her own homemade bread; but Evelyn's mother had said, "Instead of wasting your time making bread, you can be doing other things. We can easily afford it from the bakery. "

Evelyn cocked her head to the right to gaze longingly at the delectably displayed bread in the large shop window. She would quickly veer from her mission to step in, fill her tickled senses, and say hello to Mr. Longsworth, the shop owner.

Ding! Ding! The bell jostled back and forth signalling her entry into one of her favourite abodes. Entering, she found the store to be empty of shoppers and an owner. It was overflowing with all different kinds of breads, baguettes, croissants, and more. A shadow in the back room knocked over a large box. Somewhat fearful to identify another as the present owner and not dear Mr. Longsworth, she turned to leave. But as she did, she saw him entering with a load of tarts on a tray.

"Mr. Longsworth!" She clasped her hand over her mouth, horrified at her lack of propriety. "I'm sorry. I shouldn't have shouted, but I was…so overjoyed to see you again alive and well."

He came around the counter and put his lean hands upon her shoulders. "There's no need to apologize Evelyn. I'm glad to see you, dear girl."

"Your family…?"

"My wife Florence is no more. The good Lord took her away after the explosion happened. She was on her way to the grocer when…" He rubbed his wrinkling hands over his eyes. "I still have little Matthew. He misses her an awful lot, but he has hope he'll see her one day. And so do I."

"I'm so sorry, Mr. Longsworth."

"Thank you. I know I might sound somewhat insensitive, but I say this with confidence. Good will come out of this; I know, somehow. Tell me, what brings you out here?"

"I'm here to see to my mother's health. I haven't seen her for quite some time."

"Ho, I would love to hear her comment if you said that within her hearing's reach."

"Yes, well, heaven and earth couldn't escape her brutal honesty."

"Would you like a-pound loaf of fresh bread, free of charge?"

"Bless you! Your generosity means a lot to me."

He wrapped the loaf in parchment paper and tied it closed with a string. "And your husband?

"My husband…I don't know where he is. I've been at Camp Hill Hospital for the last five weeks recovering from a severe burn. I saw him last the morning of the explosion. He must have been at work when it happened. He hasn't come by…?"

"No, I'm sorry."

The bell jingled several times announcing the arrival of more customers.

"Well, I must be going." A little awkwardly, Evelyn stepped close and wrapped her arms around the lanky man.

"Thank you, Evelyn, for stopping by. God bless you!"

"Thank you." As she was leaving, she brought the fresh bread up to her nose inhaling the glorious smell when she suddenly ran into the same heavily cloaked gentleman she saw on the ferry. Over his shoulder, she saw the captain of the ferry.

"Begging your pardon, miss," the old sailor said.

"Pardon granted, good day." She exited the bakery. "Now I can finally see to my mother."

So they were married—to be the more together—
And found they were never again so much together.
Louis Macniece
Novelettes, II. Les Sylphides

Chapter 6

Evelyn strode onward, her skirts swishing in the violent wind. She neared the stately Georgian house and its dressed grounds, almost as delicious as an ornately arranged garden salad. The whole property was enclosed by a pearly white gated fence. Instead of being framed by superfluous elegant crimson curtains, all of the windows were boarded up, locking the darkness within. The rest of the house was intact. Her childhood home had once effused such a majesty, but now it was shrouded in mediocrity.

Dare she hope her mother still lived? She swung open the creaking gate, ran up the steps, and furiously knocked upon the door. The door was gently opened a few moments later by an elderly woman whose brow was creased with impatience.

"Mother!" Evelyn enclosed the stricken hostess in a fierce embrace.

"Calm yourself, now, Evelyn." Her mother tried to right her perfectly pleated dress and return balance to the silver comb holding up most of her thinning grey hair. "What is the meaning of this brashness?"

"Why, Mother, I've come to see if you're well."

"Well, of course, I'm well. How could you think I wasn't?"

"I heard Dartmouth had received some damage from the ship's explosion that happened..."

"Yes, I know, five weeks ago it was. Thompson relayed all the details to me when I returned."

"Returned?"

"I was out of town when it occurred. I was visiting with your Aunt Gladys and her scoundrel of a husband in Montreal. I stayed with them for a week and a half to help settle some of their money troubles. And I also travelled there to look at some property."

Property?! And she didn't think to tell me she was all right?! Is she so blind to the fact that I care?

Evelyn coolly inquired, "Is it in your keep?"

"No. I took one look at it and happily relinquished it to your uncle and aunt."

"Why Montreal? You've never expressed interest in the city."

"Just because I have never talked to you about it doesn't mean I haven't considered the notion. Your aunt and uncle live there, and I would like to stay there during the summertime to see the hubbub of industrialization."

"It must be quite fascinating." Evelyn muttered.

"It is."

"And you didn't read about the explosion from there?"

"No, why on earth would I do so?"

"Well, the newspaper, of course."

"All there is in the newspapers these days is ghastly reports of the war. No lady of breeding would interest herself with the politics of the world. When I returned I was horrified to see my lovely windows boarded up. I went to Thompson immediately to demand an explanation. He told me what had happened. As you can see I'm all in one piece."

An uncomfortable silence ensued.

"Will you not come in? Would you like some tea?"

"Yes, thank you."

She never even bothered to see if I was all right this whole time.

"Come this way." She waved toward the parlour. She gave a nod to the newest employed servant girl and then sat down with a regal air upon an ice blue chair.

Evelyn followed suit choosing the buttercup yellow divan, shuddering at how her mother could be so cold to a daughter she hadn't seen in so long.

"The weather has been quite ghastly recently," Mrs. Moore murmured.

"I wouldn't know. I've been at Camp Hill Hospital these past five weeks."

"The hospital—such a filthy place. What for?"

"My right arm was burned in the fire that consumed my home after the explosion. All the burning debris of the ship and the blast must have knocked over many wood stoves in the homes of the city. When I regained consciousness, I could see the flames rising all around me. I don't know who, but someone retrieved me from the fire. It might have been a soldier. There were so many crawling about trying to find and save survivors.

"I stayed in the hospital for five weeks; four of them were for my own recovery. I stayed another week to help another patient recover enough from the wounds in his legs to walk a few steps on his own."

"My, that is quite a tale." Mrs. Moore sipped her tea, eyes fixed over the brim of her teacup.

The servant entered the room to set down upon the parlour table the dessert tray which held freshly baked scones and left.

The china tea plates glistened in the warm glow of the table lamp. Yellow roses laced with greenery danced along the rims of the tea plates and cups.

"I've never seen her before, Mother." Evelyn indicated with a throw of her chin toward the doorway through which the servant had passed through.

"She's the newest addition."

"I'm glad to have found you safe in your home."

"You may stay a few days if you like. I lack the company."

"Thank you, Mother."

Her mother rang a little golden bell sitting upon a gorgeous mahogany table, exhibiting hand carved roses and thorns along the edging. The servant came swiftly.

"Take Mrs. Richardson up to the MacDonald room." Mrs. Moore had almost spit out her son-in-law's last name from her mouth.

Evelyn, enraged at the insult, balked.

You knew this was the treatment you would receive coming here.

She left the room and followed the servant upstairs.

As the servant was about to leave the room after having placed Evelyn's small valise of belongings upon the ornate bed, Evelyn cried, "Wait!"

The girl just stood there.

"Here." Evelyn opened the servant's palm and placed a dollar upon it. "Thank you."

The servant just bobbed her head as she curtsied and left the room immediately.

All night Evelyn tossed and turned as throbbing memories flooded her mind. Kissing Carl goodbye as he prepared to board the ship that would carry the troops to Europe, mailing letters everyday, seeing him return home, aching as his tears drenched her dress as she held him tight, the cold, the heat of their love—she prayed with a weak hope she hadn't lost him again. Although it was highly unlikely he would be in Dartmouth, she would scour the hospital and other first aid facilities tomorrow morning. Then she would visit the morgue.

***

She arose before her mother did, although she was fatigued because of lack of sleep. She told the servant where she was planning to go and set off. She went back to the Nova Scotia Hospital to start the hunt.

"Lucy, good day."

"Good day to you, as well, Miss."

"I'm looking for my husband, a Carl Richardson."

"Oh, pardon my ignorance, Ma'am."

"It's all right."

"Let's see..." Lucy hummed a tune as she flipped through patient records. "I'm sorry, but we have no record of his being treated here." She gave a sympathetic look. "When was the last you saw him?"

"Before he left for work...on the day of the explosion. And I don't know where he is. He wasn't accounted for as dead. So that must mean he still lives, doesn't it?"

Or maybe he was unrecognizable amongst the dead.

"I'm sure it does."

"Would it be possible for you to give me a list of all the medical faculties in Dartmouth? And perhaps the morgue?"

"Well, this hospital is the only one like it on this side of the Narrows, but I could give you a list of perhaps other...options people could have gone to for help. Could you come back, perhaps after lunch to pick up the list?"

"Of course. I'll return." She was hoping to start immediately and to delay seeing her mother for a precious few more hours. She could still do the latter by revisiting her old haunts. All her special places were to be found within her mother's estate. Mrs. Moore had taken many precautions to shield her young daughter from social evils. So Evelyn's only option had been to explore the lonely estate to its fullest.

As she trudged along, the pitter-pattering of the children's skipping and singing lifted her sinking spirits. The clusters of women enshrining together for their daily dose of gossip and the occasional motor car roaming its way through the streets were evidence to the fact that people's lives were starting to mend. Life went on through the sun and storms. Yet she didn't feel the stitching and mending for which she was crying out. Only more breaking and tearing took its place. There was hardly any good she could see or breathe.

She furtively checked to see if her mother loomed in one of the windows only to remember all the windows were boarded. She opened the gate taking great care not to let a creak escape its lips. In safety, she stole away into the rear gardens to which Mr. Thompson tended many hours of the day in the warmer seasons. She tip-toed through a maze of hedges to find the wooden bench still residing in the now slumbering rose garden. As she rounded a corner, her happy sigh flew into the sky as she sighted the haven. She sat down upon the bench and tipped her head back, eyes closed, drinking in the crisp cool of the day. Snowflakes started to drift from the clouds down to her anticipating hands. A small laugh emanated from her girlish parted lips. Evelyn stuck out her tongue to catch the falling stars, to taste the nectar from Heaven. They started to crown her head with sparkling dust.

She remembered a time long ago when she and Carl had stood there in that same place, hands bound together in the pouring rain. He had come to her to say goodbye, for he was going to New Brunswick over the weekend. Such a small separation seemed like a great chasm back then.

"Evelyn, you needn't worry. I'll only be gone for five days at the most. My father is dying. He needs me." Carl had cradled her face in his slender hands.

"I know. I want you to go. I just… I'll miss you so."

"I'll return, I promise. I'll never leave you for forever."

"Never for forever. I'll hold you to that promise."

Where was he now when she needed him most? Was his promise a petty romantic string of words? He now wounded her by not being by her side.

The wind, moaning and scorching, was starting to increase; so she returned inside to the comfort of her mother's home. Hanging her fur coat, hat, and mittens, she steeled herself for the sure to be unpleasant moment she would see her mother.

"Good morning, Mother." Evelyn entered the drawing room and sat near the crackling fireplace.

"Good morning. My, your cheeks are rosy."

"Yes, I was out walking with Old Mr. Chilly to keep me company."

"Walking? Where?"

"I..." There was no way to get out of the situation. "I went to the Nova Scotia Hospital to see if, perhaps, Carl had been treated there."

"You must face the fact, Evelyn, that Carl may very well be dead. And you...you'll waste away. How will you function if you're always pining? And there are other men that may come round..."

"Mother! Stop!"

"I'm just saying..."

"Enough is enough. I know how you felt about my marriage to Carl. He wasn't good enough for you, low birth, uneducated, and such. But, Mother, these days a man can reach aspirations with his bare hands and mind. He doesn't need a title to be someone. You may have a high opinion of yourself, but your backward notions bring you down."

Silence permeated the room until it stifled the core of Evelyn's soul.

"I'm sorry, Mother. It was wrong for me to speak out in that way."

"Do not treat me like a fool."

"Truly, I am."

"I never wanted you to marry him because he had notions of galavanting off into the war to serve his country and what rubbish instead of staying here with you to raise a proper family. Look at what has come of it all now."

"I'm proud of him and his service." Shame still flushed her cheeks.

"Yes, well, I would rather be proud of a husband who tends to his family than an unknown soldier whose name may very well be buried in the ashes of yesterday." Mrs. Moore rang her bell. "Tea?"

"No, thank you, Mother. I don't…feel well. I shall retire for now." As she started to go upstairs, she spied the maid near the doorway to the drawing room. "Please bring my meal to my room."

"Yes, Ma'am."

"Thank you." Her soul seemed to drain from the corpse it inhabited. She limply laid down once she returned to her bed. A couple hours later she was groggily aroused by a soft knock on the door. She arranged her tousled hair quickly and bade the visitor enter.

"Oh, thank you for remembering my meal."

The maid curtsied and left her presence.

***

She splashed some water onto her face and dabbed it dry. She returned to the Nova Scotia Hospital, picked up the list, and began searching. She visited two other private first-aid facilities where some of the explosion victims had gone for treatment. They gave their condolences saying they had never treated Carl. Her last stop was the morgue. There his body couldn't be found either. With an aching heart, she returned to her mother's home.

"Mother." Evelyn, suitcase in hand, stood in the doorway. "I'm leaving now. Thank you for the hospitality you have shown me."

Her mother looked up from her reading, "It was of no consequence."

The hurt her mother or she could inflict upon one another was always of great strength.

A tear slipped out of Evelyn's reach. "I must return to my home and continue searching there. Goodbye."

"Goodbye."

Looking back, the city seemed to be surrounded by a heavy-laden fog. There was no turning back; but the road ahead was daunting, unforgiving. She hoped she would have the courage to risk her heart and mind being battered over and over again.

Chapter 7

There was no home to go to. Her once classy house, paid by the lucrative means of her mother, was nothing more than a pile of uninviting rubble which had probably been removed long ago to make way for new development. Fleeting memories of wooden beams creaking in the moaning wind reeled past her mind; vestiges of the flames' attacks had scarred the once adorned walls. Where could she go? The only place which might render any comfort and opportunity was Camp Hill Hospital.

Returning to the whitewashed corridors, she let her right hand trail against the pimply grain of the painted wall beside her. Her home was here—with all the smells of fresh linen, carbolic acid, and…blood interwoven into one stream of familiarity.

Evelyn placed her hand upon a passing nurse's shoulder. "Excuse me, where may I find Nurse Randall?"

"She's down the hall, third door to your right. Wait…"

Evelyn overcome with excitement tuned out what the nurse had to say next and nearly ran to the room where she would find her beloved friend. "Betsie!" She opened the door leading into the desired room—but reeled back in horror as she realized her friend was in the middle of assisting a surgeon in a procedure. "Oh…I'm…I'm so sorry."

Why did that nurse tell me where to go if she knew Betsie was occupied? Oh...she tried to tell me. I have completely humiliated myself.

"Get this woman out of here, Nurse Denton," a doctor commanded. It was Doctor MacCrae. That same determined look, the knit brows and scowl overcoming his visage frightened her.

The man, Denton, led her out into the hallway.

What a fool she had been! What would they think of her now, her outburst. With as much grace as she could, she stoically sat upon a chair in the hallway, looking ahead, trying to shove her shame down her constricted throat.

Minutes ticked on, half an hour flew by. She heard a soft closing of a door, ambling footsteps. She shook her head from side to side. "Betsie, I can't believe…I did what I did."

"I know. It's all right. Come, let's take a stroll outside. I need some fresh air." Betsie helped her up, took Evelyn's arm in hers, and led her away from the scene of ignominy. "You had a hard time in Dartmouth, didn't you?"

"Am I that transparent?"

"I'm afraid you are…to me. Maybe I'm the only one who sees it."

"I hope so. I don't particularly want others to see everything. I have a hard time trusting others."

"You'll learn to give more of yourself in time. Letting others see who we really are—it's a gift to ourselves."

"Doctor MacCrae and his associates may never let me set foot in the hospital again!"

"Well, I know how you can wheedle your way back into Doc Mac's good favour."

"And that is?"

"Now, I'm serious Evelyn." Betsie put her hands upon Evelyn's shoulders. "We could do with a lot more help around the hospital. There are still so many long-term victim patients from the explosion to treat; and then we still must go on helping those who regularly come into the hospital with natural ailments. It would be…"

"I can help."

"But…"

"Listen. I attended nursing school a few years ago when I turned seventeen, but I never finished because I dropped out to marry Carl. I already have had some training. Please, let me learn even more under your tutelage. If I don't do something other than looking for Carl, I might go mad."

"Are you sure? The work can be quite taxing."

"Yes, that way I can perhaps show Doctor MacCrae that I not only make a buffoon of myself but I also retain some admirable and practical assets to my person."

Both women winked at each other in mischief.

***

Laughing matters put aside, the hard work was beginning. Evelyn filled out an application to become a nurse's assistant. Since the hospital needed many helpers to aid in the recovering process, it welcomed into its fold many who had had some experience in the medical profession. Evelyn had lost Carl and knew not where he was. She relished the idea of returning to the practice she wished to ameliorate.

Several doctors, who knew about her previous outburst uttered with firm tongues the hospital was an institution deserving of much respect, an institution in which tomfoolery would not be tolerated. The staff were required to command self-discipline and impose this virtue upon other staff members. Running or other such rambunctious actions were to be checked, and screaming or shouting eliminated. So fervent were these men declaring the rules of the establishment that Evelyn despaired even more over her previous foolish actions. She, after hearing the stern reproaches, steeled herself to regain their respect and perhaps later their admiration. Once she had been accepted into the medical force, she was told to begin her services on the morrow.

After Betsie had finished her shift, she and Evelyn took a stroll down near the newly refurnished docks. The dusk-lit waters lapped the cracked shore softly trying to lick its still fresh wounds with its salty kiss. Horns from incoming and outgoing ships blew feebly in the distance, as if they were the city's sole musicians trilling a wispy funeral dirge. The charred skeletons of the old wharf's sheds and the surrounding company buildings had been torn down and were now being replaced by spindly steel limbs, the framework of tomorrow. The two kindred spirits' footsteps ambled in synchronization, crunching pieces of already broken glass beneath the soles of their boots. Screeching screams from the seagulls occasionally disturbed the haunting symphony.

"Evelyn, how would you like to share a small apartment with me?"

"A small apartment?"

"Yes, it wouldn't be large. I believe, we would both be able to afford the rent with our pay. And you would be giving me the moon if you would grace me with your constant company." Betsie's eyes shimmered with hope. "What do you say?"

"You're an angel. Of course, I will. Thank you for being so considerate. I wasn't certain what I was going to do for lodging, but you have given me the answer I've been looking for. Thank you many times over." She sighed, feeling some burden float off her shoulders. "Where were you thinking of staying?"

"I don't know, to tell you the truth. We could start searching immediately."

"And where have you been living all this time?"

"I've been living in my uncle's spacious home on Seymour all this time. Some piece of metal from the *Mont Blanc* slashed his neck upon impact. I would continue to stay at his home; however, he left no will as to indicate who would gain all of his possessions upon his death."

"How odd."

"Yes, therefore, the bank has decided to repossess his home within the week. My cousin who works for the bank has persuaded them to delay the repossession so that I would have more time to find another suitable location."

"I'm sorry. Were you close to him?"

"No, I wasn't. He was a bit of a miser, God rest his soul." Breathing in deeply, she let out a soft chuckle. "Now we have each other. And what about you? Where have you been living all this time?"

"I've been sleeping at the Halifax Hotel these past few nights. I asked for their cheapest room; however I cannot keep the room much longer. It's becoming quite costly. I've only been able to afford living there because my mother had secretly placed a large wad of cash in the pocket of my coat when I visited her last."

"Then I insist you come stay with me."

Evelyn drew her near to give her an embrace. They were going to be all right.

***

Evelyn stayed the night at Betsie's deceased uncle's home. The home stood well enough considering the damage it had taken. All the windows were boarded up, and the sides of the house had been stained with the oily soot which had rained down upon Halifax's inhabitants during the explosion. There had been no effort to maintain or care for it. But what did it matter? Betsie would not be living in the house for long. It was somewhat dank and chilly. Loneliness pervaded its every crack. Despite all its decadence, it provided her with shelter for the night. Both women met each other in the gloom-infested kitchen before the dawn broke across the horizon. They set their tapers upon the crude wooden kitchen table. The chairs they sat upon resisted the weight of their frigid bodies.

"There's not much to eat in here, I'm afraid. I haven't been to the grocers in five days. A lot of mouldy vegetables did I find. Ah, here's some bread and cheese." She opened a small cupboard with one hand while holding her taper in the other to find the sole edible food in the house. "Here you go." She set the meagre breakfast in front of Evelyn.

Evelyn scrunched her nose. She was much more used to rich pudding with an orange and a glass of fresh milk. However, this friend was offering what little she had in stock. She briskly broke some cheese, placed it on some bread, and feasted upon it.

"Let us get ready for work." Betsie piled their plates and cups and laid them next to the sink.

As the women walked to the hospital, the clapping of the window shutters and the jingling of the storefront bells announced the beginning of a new day. Two young men, one brawny and tall and the other of medium height and pudgy, were carrying several large wooden planks stacked upon one another. As the pudgy one turned his head over his shoulder to shout some remark to the other, he bumped right into Betsie, sending her tumbling into a small newspaper stand, and then he stepped on the toe of Evelyn's boot.

"O!" Evelyn bent down immediately to massage her squelched toes.

Betsie managed to grab hold of most of the falling newspapers and right her apparel. She then neatly placed the newspapers back on the stand.

"Frank, stop!" The young man who had set the whole chaotic scene in motion set down his side of the load and started to profusely apologize. "I'm extremely sorry. We're late for work and we weren't thinkin'…"

"It's all right, young man. What's your name?" Betsie inquired.

"Joe."

"Joe, we accept your apologies. Just make sure you don't run over any other lovely ladies with your load this morning on your way to work."

"Yes, ma'am."

"Are you working on the reconstruction project? I'm curious."

"Yes, ma'am. Frank and me, we're headin' down to the North End. We're workin' with some new material called Hydrostone."

"Hydrostone?"

"Yes'm. It's compressed cement."

"You know, you young men are part of something great. Future generations will thank you for helping to rebuild this fine city of ours."

"Thank you, ma'am. You have yourself a good day." After they picked up the shipment, they ambled off.

***

Entering the hospital that particular morning…what could Evelyn say. Her previous visits had reeked of death, pain, hopeless despair. Now, she had the ability and the privilege to heal with her hands, to mop feverish foreheads, and to explore more of the profession she had given up years before.

"Nurse Randall, bring your protege with you to the case room," barked Doctor MacCrae.

No words were uttered as they bustled off toward the case room. Upon their entrance, they were ordered to lay out the necessary surgical instruments upon a glistening surgical tray. An older woman was moaning in pain, clutching at her intestines.

"Nurse Randall, prepare the anesthesia. Put her under gently, there. Keep an eye on her breathing."

"You," he nodded in Evelyn's direction, "will pass me what I need when I ask."

Once the older woman was under sleep, he sterilized the area of her stomach where he would make an incision.

"Scalpel."

Evelyn handed it to him and watched with intensity as he made the first cut. The blood started to slowly ooze around the groove in the flesh. She was extremely thankful that after all this time, she was still able to stomach the sight of blood. In fact, she began to relish it every passing second.

After a few swift strokes, he asked for the clamp. "Hold it here."

His cold commands chilled her heart as the raw metal instruments' frigidness seeped into her fingers.

"You're adequately knowledgeable," he said. After concluding the operation, he asked Evelyn to stitch her up.

"I'm sorry. I cannot…"

"Nurse Randall, please finish the job."

"Yes, doctor."

Evelyn's cheeks flushed red. She had never stitched a patient before on her own; therefore she determined to examine Betsie's actions closely so that the next time she would be able to perform when asked. What would Doctor MacCrae think of her wonderful capabilities now?

Chapter 8

Evelyn's work at the hospital busied her hands continually. She removed bandages, redressed wounds, fed those who were unable to feed themselves, and aided in several operations. Every week patients' families came to bring their loved ones home. She would sometimes stand by the entrance doors watching families and friends reunite. They would caress the marked hands of the hurt, kiss the rugged cheeks. They would fold them in their embrace and walk them toward freedom. Freedom to be loved, freedom to live. Every time she saw these rendezvous, she dreamed of seeing Carl again, of finding him by chance somewhere on a street. A pang of guilt berated her fortitude; for ever since she had returned to Richmond, she hadn't endeavoured to find him. Yes, she had tried to search in Dartmouth, but there was still the whole side of Richmond needing to be scoured. All those precious moments when she had time to search, she would run away into the recess of her fears, the fear that she would never see him again, the fear that he had perhaps escaped to begin a new life without her. She couldn't put it off any longer. She would renew her fervour.

"Evelyn, could you please fetch me a whole pile of bandages?" Nurse Jones said, breaking Evelyn's meditative stance.

"Yes, Nurse Jones."

Quite frankly, Evelyn enjoyed going to the linen closet to do some errand. The linen closets were one of the quieter spots in the hospital where she could go to satiate herself in the silence. The other rooms were either for patients or the doctors' own offices which, of course, she had never gone into. As she hummed a tune, footsteps approached.

"Ahem."

She swirled around while trying to balance her load and was surprised to see Doctor MacCrae standing behind her. Most of the time, he avoided her like the plague.

"Yes, Doctor MacCrae?"

"I'm sorry to disturb you, Mrs. Richardson, as I see you're busy. I don't know how to quite say this. There…is a patient…no, not a patient…someone who stays here at the hospital, a permanent resident of sorts."

"A permanent resident?" What was he talking about?

"Yes, a young boy named Clyde, Clyde Smith. I thought perhaps..." he stopped abruptly. His eyes grew wide then constricted as he wrinkled his forehead. Words would just not come out.

Clyde Smith? Sounds familiar.

"Yes?" She tried to goad him into speaking with as an encouraging tone as she could muster even though she was thoroughly confused.

"Perhaps you could find the time to give him some motherly care; he's an orphan, and he has no known living relatives."

"Should he not be reported to the committee responsible for finding homes for orphans?"

"Yes, he should. But you see, I cannot bring myself to do it. Please don't speak of this to anyone else. I trust you. Now, will you do this for him?"

She was taken aback by his earnestness and sympathy. "Why do you trust me? You hardly know me."

"I can't answer that question."

You can't or you won't.

Evelyn collected herself. "You're very gracious to ask this request upon his behalf. I'll find the time to see him."

A roguish grin sneaked upon his lips. "Good, now I'll leave you to your tasks, good day."

What strange behaviour he was exuding! How did he know she would be near the linen closet? He must have asked Nurse Jones of her whereabouts. She shook her head to dispel the odd thoughts running amuck in her head.

***

She greeted Betsie at the entrance doors once she had concluded her shift. "Go on without me this evening, Betsie. I have one last person to see tonight before I go home."

"All right."

"Betsie, is there someone you would like to visit this evening while I'm busy?"

"Now that I'm thinking about it, yes, there is. Our very temporary neighbour has asked me to come to tea sometime when I wouldn't be busy. She also wanted you to come along. I'll let her know you're indisposed for the evening."

"Thank you. I'll probably be home in an hour or so."

Not knowing where Clyde was, Evelyn asked one of the passing nurses if she knew where Doctor MacCrae could be found.

"Oh, you can probably find him in his office."

"Where is it?"

"Do you know where the maternity ward is?"

"Yes, I do."

"Go east of the main corridor on the second floor. At the end, turn left and then right at the first side corridor. If you go along there, you'll find his office indicated with his name plate upon the door."

"Thank you very much."

She followed the nurse's directions. After five minutes of searching for his office, she found it just where the nurse had said it would be. She smoothed down her uniform and knocked upon the door.

"Come in."

She opened the door.

The office was furnished with a large maple desk at the centre of the room. The exquisite beading along the rim of the desk complimented the leather-bound books which rested upon it in domino fashion. To the right of the desk was a small plain table cradling a microscope. The walls were white; a pleasant lightness pervaded the room.

"Hello, Doctor MacCrae. I was wondering if you could bring me to Clyde, the young boy you were talking about today."

He looked up from the botanical book he was reading. "Of course, I'll lead the way." As he was getting up, he noticed Evelyn was desirously eyeing the microscope. "Would you like to take a look at it?"

"Oh, I didn't mean to..."

"It's all right. Here, come." He waved her over. He opened a drawer, lifted a box housing some slides, took one out, and slid it under the microscope. "Take a look."

She approached the table cautiously, not knowing what to make of his generous offer. She centred her eye over the eyepiece, and what she saw took her breath away. The germ of a seed, designed for a special purpose. She remained spellbound for a few moments. "Thank you." She looked up into his ruggedly handsome face. The broad planes gracing his profile were smooth. His hazel eyes leered Evelyn's wavy brown hair and high-boned cheeks.

"May I ask you a question?" Her eyes darted around the room for something other at which to look.

"Of course."

"Why is your office located in the maternity ward?"

"Yes, I know it must seem odd given my practice doesn't usually include delivering babies. They did have another office for me to settle in when I first arrived at this hospital; however, in the end, it was given to another doctor who was higher on the seniority ladder than I was."

"The inconvenience isn't a bother to you?"

"No, there is less chance of my being disturbed for petty reasons. I enjoy the quiet and…being alone."

Alone! Hardly a suitable position for a woman to be alone in a man's company for too long. The room was hardly large enough to hold his desk: the close proximity of their persons was too close for her comfort. She stepped back, jabbing her lower back into the small table's corner.

"Oh!" She rubbed it tenderly.

"Are you all right?"

"Yes," she bit her lip. "Shall we?"

"Right, this way."

He led her to the end of the same corridor, adjoining his office, to a room somewhat run down. A lean mattress hugged a large part of the north wall, and a single book lay upon a thin pillow.

A young boy sat upon the crude wooden floor, hugging his knees with his head bent, resting in between them. He seemed to be crying; but it couldn't be. For there was no sobbing or even sniffling that could be heard.

"Good evening, Clyde."

"Good evening, Doctor MacCrae."

"A visitor has come to see you. Mrs. Richardson, this is Clyde. Clyde, Mrs. Richardson. She is one of the nurses at this institution."

Evelyn approached him with her outstretched hand as he turned his eyes to meet hers. She drew her breath in sharply. "Clyde? Is that you?"

"Mrs. Richardson, you know him?" Doctor MacCrae asked, doubt coating his voice.

"We've met; haven't we? Under very different circumstances…"

Clyde's eyes shimmered. "I remember you. Would you like to sit with me?" He gestured toward his bed.

"Thank you." She settled herself as best she could upon the mattress that hardly had any stuffing in it. It was as bad as sleeping on the floor.

Doctor MacCrae cleared his throat. "I'll leave you two alone."

Once the doctor had closed the door, Clyde turned his face toward Evelyn and smiled. Innocence enriched his already sweet visage. His sandy blond hair was long enough to cover a little of his ears.

She slowly covered his hand with hers. "I'm so glad to see you. Who knew we would ever meet again?"

"Yes, I'm still sorry for hurting your ankle."

"Tush, don't worry. Still…I can't believe it. Tell me, how old are you, Clyde?"

"I'm eleven. But I'll be twelve in three months, springtime. Spring always makes me feel as if…anything can happen. What's your favourite season?"

"Summer used to be my favourite season. Now I don't believe I have one anymore."

"Why don't you like summer anymore?"

"Well, summer used to be my favourite season because of all the memories I made with my husband. We would go to the park for picnics, and sometimes we would go fishing."

"I love fishing!"

"Do you? Most young boys like to fish."

"But you're not a boy."

"No, I'm not. When I was a young girl, I used to sneak out of the house and go fishing with the cook's son. He was about my age. Although we were good friends, my mother didn't approve."

"Is he still a good friend of yours?"

"No, he died when I was fifteen."

"I'm sorry. Did you still fish after he died?"

"No, I stopped. After I met my husband at seventeen years of age, he told me one of his favourite things to do was fishing.

When he started courting me, we would fish together twice a week. Summer stopped being my favourite season when my husband left to go to the war in Europe." She hugged her knees; her smile faded.

"I know I said I like springtime the best, but really every season is special. Springtime is when all the flowers and trees become green again. Summer is the time to play with my friends. Fall is when all the leaves change colours. And winter…it's easy. Snow. I used to go skating, tobogganing, and I made snow angels with my parents."

"What happened to your parents, Clyde?"

"My pa died from the blast. He was working at the sugar refinery near the docks that morning. My ma was crushed by the falling ceiling in our home." A few tears coursed down his freckled cheeks.

Evelyn took out her handkerchief and handed it to him.

"Thank you."

"It's all right to cry."

"I know. But I'm not terribly sad."

"Really?"

He shook his head softly. "No. I mean, I miss them very much. But they're in heaven; and one day, I'll see them when I die."

Heaven, the closest she had ever reached heaven was when she was blissfully married to Carl, when the whole world was moving in peace, before the war, before the explosion.

"You really think there is a Heaven?"

"Oh, I know there's a Heaven. It says so right in there." He pointed to the book on top of his pillow. Cracked and worn, the letters *The Holy Bible* were still visible.

Evelyn picked it up, cradling it in her hands. The book looked vaguely familiar.

Clyde continued. "Mr. Cox gave it to me. When he was here, I used to go visit him and talk with him. He was very kind."

"You've met him? How is he?"

"You knew him, as well? Was he not a jolly old fellow? He got better. But then he had to leave. So this was his gift to me. He sometimes still visits me."

"That is very kind of him. He's a dear old man. How did you know him?" Evelyn cradled her face in her hands, eager to form the connection.

"We met in the halls. He was practicing his walking, and I was just observing people. I started talking to him; and from there on, we grew quite close."

There was a long pause.

"Clyde, where were you during the explosion?"

"I was walking to school. The blast somehow threw me several hundred feet from where I had been. I had a broken leg. Two soldiers brought me here."

"And your leg now?"

"It's fine. I had a…uh, hairline fracture. I think that's what the doctors said. May I ask you a question?"

"Yes."

"Where's your husband now?"

"I don't know. He was working at the office of the *Halifax Herald* when the explosion happened. I haven't seen him since. I've tried to look for him."

"I hope you find him."

"I do, as well." She laid her hand upon his back. "I really should leave and go back home. Betsie, my friend, is probably waiting for me."

"Will you be back to visit me?"

His eagerness accompanied with a smile and clasped hands made it impossible for her to say no.

"Yes, I will come as often as I'm able." She rose from the bed and moved toward the door.

Before she opened the door, he had clasped onto her. She tousled his scruffy hair and gave him a peck on both cheeks. As she did so, roughly patched skin met her lips instead of downy baby skin.

The whole walk home, Clyde's words filled her thoughts. What joy she had seen in his face! Where did it come from? He was unlike any other child she had ever come across. She wanted what he had. Peace, joy, love. She would find out his secret. And Carl, she had become lax in her search of him. She would start tomorrow after her shift to find him.

You are a human boy, my young friend, A human
boy. O glorious to be a human boy!…
O running stream of sparkling joy
To be a soaring human boy!
Charles Dickens
Bleak House

Chapter 9

Evelyn softly shut the front door and hung her fur coat within the incommodious hall closet. "Ugh! This is so small and…Betsie!"

"I'm in here! What's the matter?" Her voice ejaculated from the far-removed sitting room.

Evelyn exchanged her outdoor shoes for her slippers and padded down the hallway. Her fists were balled by her side, her lips pursed.

Betsie, reading a novel, was lounging upon the divan, her feet resting upon a cushion. She shifted the open book to the side of her face. "What's wrong?"

"Every…oh never mind! Nothing."

"Really, tell me. It seems as if you're about to explode."

Only then did Evelyn realize the aching tension permeating her upper body. She concentrated on relaxing each flexed muscle and pasted an angelic smile upon her face. "Really, it's nothing."

"You're good, but not that good."

I'm too proud to batter myself in front of others, even Betsie. I'm already having a hard time admitting to myself I've failed to find Carl up until now.

"Should you not be studying some medical textbook?" Evelyn said with a smirk.

"Bah, we all need a little enjoyment once in a while in our busy lives." She laid the book down upon the coffee table in front of her, drew her legs into a proper sitting position, and patted the spot next to her. "Come, sit down."

Evelyn chilled, snuggled beside her friend, dropping her head onto Betsie's broad shoulders.

"May I ask who was your last patient?"

"His name is Clyde Smith. Doctor MacCrae unexpectedly came to me today while I was working and asked me if I would be willing to give this young boy some motherly attention."

"Really? Doesn't this boy have a family? And how is Doctor MacCrae involved with all of this?"

Evelyn's brows knit in frustration. "You know, I don't know much about the whole situation at all. I know he's an orphan; his parents were killed in the explosion. It seems to be Doctor MacCrae is somehow taking care of him. Perhaps next time I see the doctor I could inquire as to what living arrangements have been made for Clyde."

"Didn't you see Doctor MacCrae tonight?"

"I did. He's the one who showed me the way to Clyde. However, our meeting was…a short one."

"Well, Clyde is lucky to have someone like you looking after him."

"Yes, there's just something I don't understand. He's lost both his parents in the explosion, but…the sun…his face shines like the sun. He's oddly accepted the fact his parents are no longer with him. He believes one day he'll see them again. How can that be?"

"Sometimes a child-like faith is all one needs to be set free from the harsh reality confronting us daily. It truly is beautiful. But one day, he'll grow up, and circumstances will most probably change his rosy view. He'll realize hope is almost too good to be true. I think most of us realize this one day. Poor child."

If hope was almost non-existent, then what was the point of living? There must be something more to strive for, to gain.

"Betsie, what makes you think there is no hope?"

"I…something happened. When I was a young girl, my mother bore a baby boy. He was the sweetest thing I had ever seen in my life. His little hands and feet, his smile always gave me butterflies—I looked forward to waking up every morning to see him. At eight years old, he contracted the polio. My parents and I were devastated. My father told me to pray, to ask God to heal him. Believe me, I prayed every morning and night. If I could have willed him to be healed, I would have. But, he had polio until the day he died. My heart broke, and my hope…it faded away. I haven't seen it since."

"I'm so sorry." Evelyn placed her hand upon Betsie's hunched shoulder.

"Well, I think I'll go to bed."

"Goodnight, Betsie."

"Goodnight."

***

The next day at the hospital, Evelyn worked hard to finish her work as soon as she could. She was eager to see Clyde again. Something about him intrigued her. Perhaps it was his unwavering assurance of his eternal fate and the fates of those he loved. Or maybe it was his childish innocence that was the balm to her aching heart. He was the ray of sun when the day was done.

Evelyn dropped by Doctor MacCrae's office to thank him for the suggestion he had made concerning Clyde. She slowly poked her head around the frame of the slightly open door. No one was inside.

He must have forgotten to close his door all the way.

She cautiously ambled inside and shut the door behind her. She walked toward the microscope and fingered it, admiring its marvellous beauty. She drank in the bookish smells of the leather-bound medical textbooks all sitting in perfect order upon a pine shelf. Since Doctor MacCrae was not in his office at the moment, she decided to write a brief note upon a piece of blank paper sitting upon the top left-hand corner of his desk.

Dear Doctor MacCrae,

Thank you for re-introducing Clyde to me. He is a most enigmatic young boy. But his winning smile is easy to love. He's lucky to have someone like you watching over him.

Sincerely,
Evelyn Richardson

Satisfied, she folded the paper and laid it upon the centre of the desk. As she opened the door to leave, Doctor MacCrae entered. The force with which he had entered made Evelyn careen into a corner of a small square table behind the door showcasing a pot of fresh flowers.

"Oh."

The corner of the table jabbed her in the stomach. The pain was throbbing.

"Evel...Mrs. Richardson, are you all right?"

She offered the most convincing smile she could. "I think so. This seems to be quite a habit, isn't?"

He looked at her, eyes glazed over. He exhaled deeply while combing back his hair with his hand. "I'm so sorry. Please forgive me. I would appreciate it if I could have some time to myself."

"Of course. I'll leave you." She swiftly closed the door behind her. Resting her back against the door, her chest heaved up and down a few times until she could catch her breath. She glanced to her left then to her right a couple of times, apprehending any nearby footstep. She curled back a wisp of her hair. Why did she feel so guilty? She had gone into his study without permission to...?

Shaking her head to clear it, she righted herself and steered herself in the direction of Clyde's room. The door creaked open.

"You're back!" Clyde put down his book.

"Yes, you didn't think I would forget, did you?"

"No. I knew you wouldn't."

"And what made you certain of my character and intentions?" A playful smirk emerged from her usual serious countenance.

"I'm not sure…That's a good question. Maybe because I lost my parents and you lost your husband—maybe you don't feel so lonely anymore when you come visit me. I know I don't feel lonely."

"You're right. I don't feel lonely. May I come sit with you?"

"Yes, please."

She sat down beside him, adjusting her skirts. "What book were you reading?"

"I was reading Robinson Crusoe."

"That was one of my childhood favourites."

"You really were a non-typical girl! I like you!"

"I like you, too. I was wondering, how did you meet Doctor MacCrae? I mean other than your being his patient."

"I was never his patient."

"Really?"

"Yes, actually, it was by Providence he found me."

"How so?"

"Well, after having been on a bed for so long, the nurses said I could finally walk around the halls a little bit. I met Doctor MacCrae after I met Mr. Cox. I asked the nurse if I could be left alone just for a few minutes to pray. At first, she didn't want to let me out of her sight. I finally convinced her I would only be around the corner. When I found an empty chair in a more solitary corridor, I saw Doctor MacCrae sitting on a nearby chair. As soon as he saw me, he stuffed a piece of paper in his coat pocket and looked scared.

"How strange!"

"Maybe he wanted to be left alone, too. Well, I sat down next to him. He started talking to me. He asked me who my parents were and how I got hurt. He felt sorry for me. After I told him both my parents died and I didn't have any other living relatives, he said I could stay here at the hospital during the day while he worked and go back home with him at night. He said it would be our little secret. But now you know the secret, too."

"Yes, I guess I do." Evelyn mulled the matter over. "No one else knows your…situation?"

"I don't think so. I have a lot of fun sneaking in."

"Before the explosion happened, did you enjoy going to school?"

"I couldn't always go to school because sometimes I was busy helping my father run our farm. I love school. I miss learning."

"Which subject do you miss the most?"

"I miss arithmetic. I enjoy numbers a lot."

Evelyn reminisced upon how much she had enjoyed learning when she was in school. Now Clyde, an orphan in hiding, could not go to school with other schoolmates. He had no family. If he were to be discovered by the committee in charge of finding homes for orphaned children that was set up after the explosion, she might never see him again.

"Clyde, how would you like it if when I came to visit you that I would continue to teach you your numbers and perhaps whatever other knowledge I have on other subjects? I can bring some paper and writing tools."

"Really?" Clyde's visage beamed. His eyes twinkled as his mouth grew wide, ready to crack.

Evelyn bobbed her head up and down enthusiastically.

"Oh, yes, please."

"Well, then we shall commence the next time I visit you. I might not be able to see you for the next few days because…I'll be occupied searching for my husband. Do you think you can wait?"

"Oh, yes, I can."

"Good," she kissed the top of his brow. "Now, I must be getting back again."

"All right."

"Goodbye."

"Goodbye, Evelyn."

She turned to leave then stopped in her tracks. "How often does Doctor MacCrae come to visit you?"

"Not often, but he never forgets me."

"No, I don't think anyone ever could." His smile, stamped upon her mind, brought the warmth of day back into her chilled heart.

She bid adieu to those on the night shift whom she passed on her way out the door. At her locker, she removed her shoes to replace them with some fuzzy, warm boots.

The crunch of the snow was her only companion all the way back home. The dark did not intimidate her, neither the shadows lurking about. All she could think about was that she was alone. There was no hand slipped into hers squeezing in the comfort of another soul. Yet as she walked, her fingers lingered slightly apart, imagining and wishing for that hand.

Chapter 10

Slivers of rusty hued light penetrated Evelyn's bedroom through the cracks of the boarded window, painting a disarrayed flower upon the cold floor. The slight moaning of the wind's breath filled Evelyn's sleeping subconscious with screams, crying, shouting, mayhem. The draft drove her to tighten the covers around her neck and curl them up to her chin. Nightmares were her companions these many nights. She tried to count sheep when the nightmares berated her; but nothing helped. With a sleepy, heavy-burdened sigh, she uncovered herself slowly and grabbed her wool shawl from the foot of the bed. Reluctantly, she withdrew her hidden feet from the depths of warmth and padded down to the other end of her bedchamber to dress into her set out attire for the day.

"What is the use trying to sleep? I cannot get a good night's rest."

She peered through the tiny cracks in the boards to see the world lightly blanketed with snow. The crisp air stung her nose. In front of the mirror, her nightgown was shed, the material solitarily brushing past her goose-bumped skin. She could not move although she was cold. She reminisced upon a time when her eyes weren't the only ones roving up and down her body. She blushed at such…personal thoughts; she slipped into her day-clothes, buttoning them up and smoothing them down with her frozen hands.

Before she could start searching for her husband in the different locales of Richmond, she and Betsie needed to find another dwelling in which to live. They hadn't had much time to browse since their schedules were somewhat busy. They were due to leave the premises of the house in three days. What would they do if they couldn't find another place?

Although they were due to seek out housing early, it was not to be this early. It was five-thirty in the morning. Betsie would sleep for another two hours. Evelyn decided to go for a walk. Dressed warmly, she entered the streets. Some men were strutting along to work, humming or whistling merry tunes, tunes that could chase away any frigidity. Even though the streets hadn'tfully come to life with the city folk, she needed to go somewhere even quieter, more peaceful. She turned her gaze toward the Commons, a large expanse of urban park.

She came across Freshwater Brook and followed its frozen path southwest until she reached Egg Pond. She walked round its frosted embankment until she came to a crude wooden bench nestled under a ceiling of crystal branch work. She sat upon it and closed her eyes to listen, to feel, not to think. Thinking was the last thing she wanted to do.

The birds twittered happily, some stooping to the ground, their little beaks pecking upon the encrusted snow. The wind unfurled its delicate whispers into her ear, begging her to remain.

She didn't know for how long she had sat there. Perhaps it was half an hour or more. The sounds she had heard became adulterated by heavy, crunching footfalls. Her eyes opened to see Doctor MacCrae standing before her. His posture was a little off kilter, swaying back and forth between left and right. His fingertips came together, trembling.

"Doctor MacCrae."

"I'm so sorry to have disturbed you."

"It's no disturbance at all." She feigned pleasantness.

An awkward silence ensued.

Evelyn cleared her throat. "Would you like to sit?"

"Thank you, how very kind." He removed his newsboy cap from atop his head and moved toward her with slow, deliberate steps.

The sun's rising emblazoned him in an aura of white gold. His broad shoulders confidently held his head high. His curled chestnut hair complimented his hazel brown eyes, and his full pursed lips were an attractive accessory to his long-slopped nose.

He sat upon the one end of the bench while Evelyn tried to move herself more toward the opposite side without garnering too much attention to her action.

"Sometimes I like to come out here in the mornings or evenings after work and listen." His head was bent, an ear cocked to one side.

"To what do you listen?"

He inclined his head toward her, eyes flowing over her own. "I listen to the ocean."

"All the way up here?"

"Yes, I've practiced. At first, I would try to hear the whistling of the boats as they passed each other in the Narrows. Once my ears were accustomed to hearing the whistle, I moved on to a more subtle noise such as the waves crashing upon the shore during a storm. I like to think that I can hear the seagulls and the dockworkers shouting to one another. But it could very well be my mind is playing tricks on me. What made you come out here this morning? It's not even time for you to work, is it?"

"No, it's not." She quickly stole a glance his way, a small smirk breaking through her porcelain visage. "I couldn't sleep. There are many nights when I cannot sleep anymore. I wish I could."

"The explosion?"

"Yes…and more."

"I take it you're referring to your husband." His tone seemed suddenly reserved.

"Yes, my husband—I'm going to start looking for him later on today. However, it's been so long; it's probably impossible considering—I'm sorry. I don't know why I'm even bothering you with all of this."

"No, please, it's a…I mean, go on."

Unbarring her chapped lips, she watched as furls of hesitation floated away. "Betsie and I need to look at some options for a more permanent lodging. Presently, we are staying at her late uncle's home; but we can't reside there much longer as the bank will be repossessing the property in three days. That's why we won't be working today."

His head slumped down in between his shoulder blades, and his fingers interlaced with each other. "Down my residential street, I know someone who has opened up part of her house to rent to someone who needs a permanent residence." He looked forward, shielding his eyes from the rising sun. "Would you be interested?"

Evelyn put her hand to her throat, catching her breath. "Really? That would be so helpful."

His face contorted, trying to withhold a chuckle. "Yes, really. Now, if you don't put an end to your comically happy face, I shall be forced to make a spectacle of myself by bursting out in laughter."

"Oh, I'm…I'm sorry?"

"Oh, please, don't be. It's…quite entertaining."

"Doctor, you should be ashamed of yourself, jesting at the expense of a lady. But, oh, that's such good news. As long as the rent isn't too expensive and the owner doesn't mind our coming in and out at unearthly hours, Betsie and I'll be happy to take a look at almost anything."

"I know the residence has been refurnished after the explosion. The owner and his wife invited me once to see the renovations. It seems to be quite comfortable. I believe you and Nurse Randall will make a good match with the apartments."

"Thank you so much for this opportunity."

"Please, I…it's my pleasure. If perhaps you're not busy tonight…I mean you both…I could meet you at the entrance of the hospital after I'm done my shift. We can meet with the owner and see if the agreement is to your liking. I'll make all the arrangements." Some effervescence shone in his eyes like the April blooms thriving under rain showers.

"That would be most kind of you. Thank you again."

He nodded and fidgeted with his hat. "This, ah, new arrangement…would be most beneficial to you so that you are able to ensue your search sooner."

"Oh…yes, I'll definitely have lots of time to search today; the funny thing is, I don't want to leave. Why is that?"

"Perhaps you enjoy such fine company."

"What brash talk!" She moved a strand of hair from her lips. "Perhaps you're right."

His eyes met hers and held them captive for far too long than what was good for her.

"I should go." She rose from her perch.

"Shall I see you again tonight?"

"Yes, along with Nurse Randall."

"Farewell." He rose from his spot, as well.

"Goodbye." She gave him a curt nod and swooped off toward home to tell Betsie of the fortunate turn of events.

***

Since she had had no time to pursue her mission while she had been working at the hospital, she decided to start at home base, Camp Hill Hospital. She marched to the front desk and exchanged a few pleasantries with the receptionist whom she knew a little by having had some conversations with her over lunch. After having searched the records, the receptionist sadly informed her that her husband hadn't been treated there.

"Perhaps you could search some of the makeshift army hospitals that were installed here in Richmond. There are a few your husband could have turned to especially since he was part of the war effort himself. Also there are many boats in the harbour that have medical camps within. I don't know whether any of the ships that were here during the explosion are still here. I surmise most of them aren't. Yet there's no harm in asking around. Here's a map on which I have marked each hospital. These two…" she pointed to the last two places on the corresponding list, "…are some of the closest to the shore. I would say those two are your best bets," added the receptionist.

"Thank you."

The receptionist handed her the list and wished her luck. Receiving the single page in her hands infused new life into Evelyn's dull beating heart. Perhaps…someone had seen him. Then she would have some tangible evidence that he was still alive. She pulled out the dear photograph of him on their wedding day. It was as if she could still reach out and caress the contours of his handsome face. The photograph might help someone who had seen him remember him.

An agonizing twenty minutes of thinking, thinking, thinking—she tried to map out her route, but right there and then, she wished she could go back to this morning when she was only seeing…him. Somehow he was the simple balm to her tempestuous life; and yet, at the same time he aggravated her senses to the point that her conscious deliberations spun out of control. Only release from his presence would assuage such turbulence.

She arrived at the Victoria General Hospital, swarming with activity. Nurses, doctors abounded, heading in certain directions. She laid a hand upon a passing nurse.

"Please, I'm trying to find my missing husband. Is there someone who can help me?"

"I'm sorry. I can't talk right now. Just wait here, and I'll find someone who can help you."

"Thank you," Evelyn hollered.

The whole time the nurse had not relented from her course. From the tone and disinterest of the nurse, Evelyn assumed it would be a little while before the nurse would send someone to help her, if at all.

"Excuse me, are you needing some assistance? Pardon me, I overheard your plea with the passing nurse." An astute-looking doctor, with spectacles nestled atop the high point of his nose, looked to her expectantly.

"Yes, I need to know if this man was ever treated here or seen here," she said as she pulled out Carl's photograph and held it out for him to see.

The doctor curled his one hand around his chin as his brows knit together in concentration. With the other hand, he adjusted his spectacles. "Yes...yes, I've seen him before. Where have I seen him?"

To think that this awkward man was a doctor brought a smile to Evelyn's lips. "Perhaps you've seen him here."

"That's right. I have seen him...here! It was the day after the explosion. I saw this man—your husband—sitting there." He pointed to their right. "See, beside that room. He was sitting there. I was busy, of course, caring for the many patients who were coming in for immediate treatment. I saw him as I was passing by. When I returned, he had gone. I assumed one of my fellow colleagues had seen to him. I never saw him again."

What a revelation! A muffled cry was released, a single tear streamed down her cheek. A crazed urgency rose in her breast. She had to hold onto every ounce of her sanity; for she felt like clenching her fists upon his coat and shaking more information out of him. She felt so close to discovering her husband's whereabouts; yet she felt so far away. She was dejected, her head hung in near defeat. Suddenly, a thought dawned in her mind.

"Was he all right when you saw him? Was he hurt in any way?"

"If I recall correctly, he only had one leg."

"Was there anything else?"

"What else? You don't seem surprised! But…hmm…you must have already known about it since the stump had already recovered?"

"Yes, I did. Now, was there anything else?"

"He seemed to be covering his eyes with his hands. It could very well be that, from the impact, glass shards had cut his eyes. Many people were blinded from the explosion."

Evelyn gulped.

God, please don't let this be.

She never prayed, but she couldn't think of anything else to say. "Thank you so much for your time."

"My pleasure, is there anything else I can help with?"

"No, that's all, thank you."

He gave her a genuinely sincere smile and wished her all the best in finding Carl. All his kind words fell upon dumb ears. She turned away, crossing her arms to hold in the little warmth left in her heart. Her happiness dimmed.

Evelyn went to the Children's Hospital next door. Same routine. Different answer. They hadn't seen him at all. He was never treated there. One clue, one road. At least, a flicker of hope had ignited. At least *someone* had seen him.

Chapter 11

Evelyn scrambled back to Betsie to remind her of their evening appointment with Doctor MacCrae. "Betsie!" She burst open the door, causing the knob of the door to *bang* against the wall. Realizing what a raucous she was causing for no apparent reason other than the irrational flutterings stirring within her heart every time she thought of her night's appointment, she tried to walk calmly to the hall mirror to analyze her complexion.

"My, what in the world is this!" A bewildered Betsie came out of the kitchen with her hair in a tight bun, an apron snuggling her full body, and a floured rolling pin in her hand.

"I…I think we're running a little late. Don't you?" Evelyn pinned back a flyaway wisp of hair with her quivering fingers.

"Hmm," Betsie's eyes narrowed, trying to understand why her friend was so viciously animated. "Well, I'm ready. The biscuits are already baked. I believe the only one who's in an upheaval is you."

"No, I'm—biscuits?"

"One always brings a hostess gift when visiting others. Didn't your mother ever tell you so, dear?"

"Oh, but of course."

"I'll only be five minutes."

"All right." Evelyn swirled back to the looking glass. She straightened her skirt and pinned back her stray hair quickly. She pinched her cheeks, then suddenly stopped.

What am I doing? I'm not going to a ball. I've not acted this way since…Shame on me.

"Here I am." Betsie handed the plate of biscuits to Evelyn so that she could fasten the belt of her coat. "Ready?"

"Yes," Evelyn felt that a bit of a too cheery smile revealed her exorbitant amount of enthusiasm. She had hoped Betsie wouldn't notice. She was extremely thankful her cheeks cooled instantly as they stepped out into the brisk air.

"Is everything all right?" Bestie asked glancing sideways in suspicion.

"Yes."

"How did your search go today? Do you have any leads?"

"My search? That's right…no, I didn't find him. Nor did I expect to."

"Oh."

"However, there…was a doctor at the Victoria General Hospital who thinks he may have glimpsed Carl for a moment."

"What do you mean *glimpsed*?"

"He said he saw Carl sitting on a chair in the lobby on the day of or after the explosion waiting for medical attention. However, when he passed through the same area some minutes later, Carl was gone."

"Then perhaps Carl is alive."

"Betsie, you don't know how much I want to believe…that he still lives, that there is a real chance for us to be together again. But I'm so afraid that the more I crave this ending the more disappointed I'll be when it never comes about. Tell me plainly is there any chance this doctor saw what he really saw?"

"There might be a chance; I don't know what to say. The most likely explanation for all this is that this doctor only told you he saw Carl because this doctor has already had to tell so many others they have lost someone for good. Even I cannot remember most of the faces I cared for that day, except you. If I were in the doctor's shoes, I would have told you the same thing. I would have wanted to give you some hope. I wouldn't want to be responsible for keeping two loved ones apart."

"I thought you didn't believe in hope."

"I don't. But that doesn't mean others don't need it."

***

Once they arrived at the hospital, they saw a tall masculine figure waiting outside the doors, looking up at the clouded sky. A light-hearted Doctor MacCrae turned around with a bouquet of wax-flowers and greenery in his hand.

"Good evening, ladies, these are for you both." He bowed, swooping them into Betsie's open hands.

"Doctor MaCrae, how beautiful they are! I never knew you had such charm."

"I must admit the flower-shop girl arranged the flowers for me. I can take no credit other than picking the beauties and thinking about the gesture."

As Betsie toyed with the flowers, inhaling their citrus redolence, Doctor MacCrae leaned toward Evelyn and asked, "Do you like them, as well?" A glimmer of kindness brightened his dark eyes.

"Yes, they are most beautiful. Thank you for being so thoughtful." The last word fell from her lips as they trembled slightly. A single tear slid down to the corner of her mouth.

"Are you all right?" He laid a hand upon her shoulder.

"Evelyn?" Betsie's eyebrows rose in question.

"I'm fine." Evelyn turned her head to the side and angled it so that she could wipe off the rebel tear with one quick swipe. "Shall we go?"

"Yes, let's." He positioned himself in between the two women and held out his arms expectantly.

Each woman took his offered arm, Betsie on the left and Evelyn on the right. It was not a very long walk, about twenty minutes. During the whole walk, Betsie conversed with Doctor MacCrae about some of the different cases she had encountered recently. Evelyn kept quiet the whole time. Sometimes her interest was piqued by a certain case of smallpox or polio they were discussing. At other times her mind wandered. Stiffly did she walk; perhaps a little of this restricting action could be accounted for by the frigid air encircling her nylon-covered ankles which provided little protection but more so because of the fact that her arm was for the first time upon his.

Evelyn's arm was very sore once they arrived at the potential new apartments. Doctor MacCrae released the two ladies' arms to knock upon the door. As he did so, Evelyn inconspicuously massaged the crook of her left arm.

The door opened with a bang. "Oh, here you are. I've been expecting you. Come in," the corpulent female owner said in a heavy Italian accent. The lady did by no means retain any natural beauty. She was more plain and rough around the edges. The only softness she could boast of was the extra flesh surrounding the many joints of her body.

"We brought some baked goodies." Betsie held up the plate of biscuits to the circle of light shining from within.

"What a wonderful surprise! Oh, I am so happy to see you. Shall I show you around?"

All three of the visitors' heads bobbed up and down with mutterings of "Yes, please" and "How exciting!" She led the troop past her kitchen and down a wide hallway lined with paintings of

Italian vineyards and the countryside to a single door at the very end.

"This is where the house is peculiarly separated. Here is the key. Would you like to open it?" She held out the key to Evelyn.

"Oh, thank you." She took the keys from the beefy hands of the boisterous woman. She inserted the key into the keyhole and turned it.

They walked in.

"As you can see, my husband and I have decorated many of the rooms and replaced the broken windows. Most of the furniture is here, but I think you might need to purchase a new dining room table."

They viewed the spacious living quarters, admiring the simple yet cozy decorations and atmosphere. It was true. It was mostly furnished; it even had a double bed. The walls had been painted with pleasing pastels. A few of the windows had good enough views of the city.

"There is a separate entrance leading to these rooms. The key I have given you fits into the keyholes of both doors. The side entrance can be found on the perpendicular street to this one. Do you like it?"

Evelyn faced Betsie with a luminous smile. "It's perfect."

"Shall we talk about the particulars?" Betsie asked the owner, confident this was destined to be their new home.

"Yes, and then we can taste those delicious-looking biscuits of yours. Tea anyone?"

They left the solitary apartments and settled upon some comfortable chairs in the owner's kitchen.

The owner chuckled. "I believe I forgot to introduce myself. I am Hilda Rossi. But please call me Hilda. And you are?"

Betsie spoke out first. "I'm Betsie Randall and this is Evelyn Richardson. We work together at Camp Hill Hospital. Please call us by our first names."

"Wonderful! And Doctor MacCrae I'm already acquainted with. He has been an excellent neighbour to us. When we first moved here two years ago, he was one of the first to introduce himself. He helped us greatly while we moved our belongings."

"It was my pleasure, Hilda. And I can say the same about you and your husband. You both extend your hospitality to all your neighbours so gratuitously."

The tea kettle started to whistle, calling to its mistress.

"Please excuse me. Make yourselves comfortable."

Doctor MacCrae pulled out a chair for Betsie and a chair for Evelyn before seating himself directly across Evelyn.

Hilda and Betsie became instant friends. Both were outspoken and divinely full of life. They both laughed at a facetious joke Betsie told whilst Hilda brought the teapot to the table. Hilda also grabbed four teacups from a cupboard and poured the tinkling tea. The plate of biscuits sat in the middle of the breakfast table, available to all the feasting eyes.

Evelyn inclined her head toward the two friends' conversation, smiling a little here and there. More often than not her eyes were glazed over, looking at a tainted spot on the yellow mustard wall.

"No need to pretend, Evelyn." A deep voice swirled into her hollow ears, yanking her from her absent-mindedness.

Surprised and scared she had given herself away too easily, her eyes grew large. "Pretend? I'm not sure what you're trying to say."

"I'm sorry. Forgive me. I shouldn't have called you by your surname without your permission. It was quite unprofessional," Doctor MacCrae apologized.

"We're not at work."

"No, we are not."

"It's all right. I would prefer if you called me Evelyn."

"Yes, well we are friends, aren't we?"

"Yes, we are. What may I call you?"

"Gerald."

"Not Gerry?"

"No, never call me that, please." Amusing disgust overshadowed his face.

"Well, Gerald, if you don't put an end to that comically disgusted face, I shall be forced to make a spectacle of myself."

At this point, the pair were laughing while trying to stifle their ruckus. They realized the other two women's conversation had stopped and they were waiting for an explanation to this obviously humorous topic.

Gerald waved his hand. "I'm sorry, ladies. Please, go on with what you were saying."

Both women didn't seem to be entirely convinced but shrugged their shoulders saying young people would be young people, and there was no changing them.

"Really, what were you thinking of?" Gerald implored her to reveal her secret with his searching eyes.

"Thinking of what when?"

"Before I made a fool of myself."

"Oh, of course, before that."

She hesitated at first not because she didn't trust him; but she didn't want to seem to be a shell of a soul, less than she was. No more would people look at her for the woman she was but for the woman she had become, a victim of her circumstances. Thinking of their newly understood friendship, she decided to be honest. Was this not what friends did for each other?

Evelyn murmured, "I visited two hospitals today. One said they hadn't seen him…and…the other…. There was one doctor there who thought he might have seen my husband the day of the explosion. He had glimpsed him for but a moment and then he was gone. But one look…is that enough evidence to bade me continue further into the truth? Or am I just following an endless rabbit trail? One minute I hope and the next I despair." She cradled her aching head into her open hands. "I'm sorry. I probably shouldn't have told you all that."

"No, I'm glad you did. I appreciate the honesty."

"What do you think?"

"There is still hope. Don't give up on him, not yet. You deserve to know the truth, even though it isn't the truth you want to hear."

"You're right. I need to be strong. I must…press forward. Thank you for listening."

"It was my pleasure."

She breathed deeply. "I have a question for you."

"Ask and I will answer."

"What made you pick wax-flowers?"

"I have a soft spot for exotic plants. I don't think you know this. I study plants for a hobby. Actually I have in my home a small greenhouse in which I grow them. They are originally from Western Australia. I know they are small and not much to look at compared to other flowering plants, but they have a delicate frame. The bouquet I gave to you came from my own home garden. All I did was cut the stems and bring them to the flower girl down the street for her to arrange. How did you come to know of them?"

"I…while Carl was away at war, I used to go to a sewing circle every Saturday. We would knit socks, scarves, blankets, and all sorts of useful material for the men on the war front. One day one of the older woman who was a regular brought some photographs to show us of her trip to Australia the summer before. When it came my turn to look, I saw one of a wax-flower. I thought it was the most beautiful plant I had ever seen. My favourite flowers had been lilies until they were quickly replaced by wax-flowers. It's funny, you're the only one who knows this."

Feeling slightly self-conscious of the fact she had shared a piece of information of herself to Gerald that not even Carl knew, she fully angled herself toward the lively conversation to the right of the table and listened intently, unaware that Gerald continued to cast flickering gazes upon her statuesque profile, admiring her beauty.

Hilda proclaimed, "There it is all settled. Tomorrow, my husband will be in from work, and he will help you move your things here to your new home."

"That sounds wonderful! Thank you Hilda," Evelyn exclaimed.

"Well, we all better get going, including you Doctor MacCrae. We all have work tomorrow." Betsie wagged her finger toward the door.

As they all retrieved their coats and boots, they thanked the gracious hostess and said goodnight.

"Ladies, let me escort you back to your home."

"But Ge...I mean Doctor MacCrae do you not live but half a block from this place?" Evelyn asked.

"I do. But I insist."

"Thank you, doctor." Betsie plunged her arm into his.

Evelyn followed suit. The threesome leisurely walked the way back home. Betsie chattered on gaily about the good luck thrown their way. It was as if they had found their pot of gold at the end of the rainbow.

"Now, I can inform my cousin with this good news," Betsie said.

Gerald inclined his head toward her the whole time, politely listening to her blithe monologue. Evelyn rested in the sweet peacefulness which lit the night streets.

Once they approached their soon-to-be previous residence, Gerald deposited both women at the door.

"Thank you, doctor, for a fine evening." Betsie turned to go into the house, bubbling, "Oh, what a fine outcome this is!"

Both Evelyn and Gerald's gaze met, as their lips pouted into quiet laughter. After they had settled somewhat, Evelyn murmured, "Thank you, Gerald, for the time you have given to both Betsie and me. It was very sweet."

"It was an honour to escort you both. Please, let me do so in the future." He gave a quick bow.

"We shall see, goodnight."

"Goodnight."

She closed the door, humming a song to herself. She wandered into the living room where she found Betsie lying on the couch in a dramatic fashion.

"Isn't this wonderful?" Betsie exclaimed as she threw her hands into the air.

"It is. Did you have a good time with Hilda? You two seemed to get along quite well with each other."

"Yes, yes, we shall be good friends." She sighed contentedly. Then her brow furrowed slightly. "And what were you two talking about? If I didn't know any better, you were talking about books and medicine."

Evelyn answered not but gave a tired smile.

"You are tired. So am I. Let us go to bed. I'll see you in the morning?"

"Yes, goodnight, Betsie." She treaded across the room and gave her dear friend a large hug.

"Goodnight."

Evelyn floated back to her room. She exchanged her day-clothes for her nightgown and snuggled into her creaking bed. She blew out the candle on her bed stand, and darkness appeared at the whim of a wisp of smoke.

Books and medicine. They had in a way started to open up the books of her heart to find the medicine that would alleviate the numbness and dredge which infected every part of whom she was.

*Anger is never without an argument, but seldom with
a good one.*
George Saville, Marquis of Halifax
Of Anger

Chapter 12

The next day Hilda's husband Roberto and a couple of his friends brought over to Betsie's uncle's home a horse-hitched wagon in which they loaded a single load of goods; for Evelyn's and Betsie's belongings were of a meagre portion.

"We'll be going now! Pedro, Juan." Roberto intimated to his two friends to draw near.

The one who was called Pedro said, "Ladies, would you like our seats? Juan and I, we walk to new house."

"Thank you, Pedro, for your kind offer, but Betsie and I both enjoy walking very much. If you and…Juan go in the wagon, our belongings shall be put into our apartment sooner. Don't you think so?"

"Yes, yes, you are right, gracias." Pedro tipped his hat down and motioned to Juan to enter the wagon.

Once the two women had walked over, the last of their belongings were being placed neatly into their new home. Both Pedro and Juan were enjoying some refreshing water Hilda had poured for them. She had also baked some chocolate chip cookies. The ladies sat down with Roberto and Hilda at the table to sign their renter's contract stating they would rent from the couple for at least a year. The electricity and plumbing were included in the rent price. Once it was signed, all interested parties celebrated with a small toast. Congratulations were an order and so was extreme excitement.

The two working women retired to their new home. Although they had done much throughout the day, they still needed to unpack a few necessities they needed overnight such as their nightgowns, brushes, and baking soda with which they brushed their teeth. They did so without speaking to each other; for their lids were slowly falling over their eyes and their chests heaved with the rhythm of their slow motions. Both women lay down that night in peace, knowing what good fortune had been given to them.

***

Evelyn worked hard the next several days to do as much as she could at the hospital before she left for Dartmouth.

"Dartmouth? To see your mother?" Betsie's face scrunched surprisedly. "I thought you had parted ways under ill terms."

They were both seated on their new leaf-embroidered sofas. When they had first sat upon them, they delighted in the spiral textures titillating their fingers. Now, the two friends basked in its comfort and also enjoyed the warm teacups cupped between their numb hands.

"I know it doesn't make much sense. It's just…"

Betsie looked at her in a patient yet waiting manner.

"I owe…everything to my mother. Despite her prickly disposition and sometimes hateful demeanour, she has done so much for Carl and me. She bought us our first home, provided us with our own butler, and…. What do you think?"

"I'm sure deep down inside her there is a mother who loves her daughter. But to find it…you'll need a lot of patience, I think."

"I know. I don't even know if I have the patience or not, but I'm going to go. It's good I am going tomorrow. For if I were to wait another few days, I fear I might change my mind."

"Well, I wish you all the luck in the world."

"Thank you. I'll need it."

***

The next day Evelyn walked out the door early in the morning, bag in hand with a change of clothes and toiletries. Her mother always asked her to stay an extra day; therefore she would be prepared. She hailed a horse and carriage and ordered the driver to take her to the ferry. It was a damp morning, the fog invading the core of her body through the tight seams of her clothes. She shuddered and rubbed her gloved hands up and down her stiff arms, trying to bring little warmth from the friction to them. She briskly walked to the ferry and paid the fare for passage. She found a spot in the scarcely seated upper deck of the ferry and hugged her bag close to her chest, nestling her chin upon the handles. Shutting her eyes, she felt the swaying of the lapping waves. They were somewhat more vicious than she remembered them from the previous time. At times, their talons would strike Evelyn's hair, soaking it in their wake.

"Here, would you like a blanket, miss?"

Her eyes searched for a face in the mist. In a moment, the fog cleared and she saw the same old man who had ferried her across the first time. His strange cloaked companion was nowhere to be seen.

"Oh, hello, again."

"Do I know you, miss?"

"You ferried me over once before."

He inched his head closer to hers, trying to ascertain this supposed acquaintance.

"Oh, yes, I remember you. My friend accidentally bumped into you in the bakery."

"Yes."

"Well, nice to see you again. How about that blanket?"

"Yes, please. I would appreciate it very much."

"Here you go."

"Thank you. Sir, what is your name?"

"My name's Mister Cox."

Funny, it must be a prevailing name.

He ambled back to his post at the helm, and she wrapped the blanket around her hair and back. Covering herself with the blanket alleviated some of the shards of pain attacking her body. After a trying crossover, she left the boat, shuddering and chattering her teeth. She hailed a cab to bring her to her mother's home.

Walking up the path, she realized all the windows had been replaced to their former glory. She rang the doorbell while waiting upon the threshold. Mr. Thompson, her mother's handyman, opened the door.

"Please don't tell me Mother put the maid out on the streets."

"No, no, no," Mr. Thompson chuckled. "She's just in the kitchen. Her hands are full right now. So I've decided to…take her place." He mocked a cute curtsy.

"Are you lying to me?"

"Ha! Ha! Ha! Yes and no, miss."

"Well, I'll have to think of how I'll deal with you later." She jutted her chin out and attempted to threaten him with cold eyes, trying to act out her mother's condescending tone.

"You do that. You're very lucky your mother isn't here to see you impersonate her."

"Where is she?"

"Oh, visiting some high society friend of hers." He looked at her from head to toe. "You are dripping wet. Why don't you come in, get dressed. We'll feed you some luncheon. Your mother is expected to return soon after two o'clock."

"Thank you. I will."

Mr. Thompson removed her wet coat and splayed it upon the stone threshold before the roaring fire whose crackling sounds instantly warmed her from a distance. She lugged her bag up the stairs and barrelled into her childhood room.

The room she had once lived in had stayed the same. The rose pink walls accentuated by the white antique furniture dotting the sides of the walls had not been changed in the wake of her moving out. William, her brown teddy bear, still sat upon the large dresser. The large window overlooking the prettiest part of the gardens was still decorated by the frilly cream curtains. It was as if this room was always going to be set aside for her use. Did her mother still dream of living with her daughter? Had her mother let go the way she had, even before she married Carl?

She changed into her extra set of clothing and brought her soaked habits downstairs next to her coat. She returned upstairs to her room and removed all her hairpins in front of the gold-gilded mirror. Her chestnut brown hair cascaded down the side of her head like a raging waterfall, strands interlaced into one deep pool. She retrieved a towel from the linen closet and dried her hair by rubbing it between the soft mittens enveloping her hands, up and down. For fifteen minutes she brushed through the tangled hair until its usual sheen finally protruded. She left it down so that it would dry evenly.

Frankly, Evelyn was relieved her mother was not there. It would give her more time to rally her spirits before being in her mother's presence.

She went down to the kitchen, invited by the smell of shrimp bisque wafting through the house. "May I help you?"

A large question mark dotted the maid's comely face. Slowly, she bobbed her head then inclined it to the right where a recipe for biscuits rested on a stand.

Evelyn was disappointed with the maid at first. She was so quiet and meek, not venturing to make any conversation. As Evelyn kept observing her movements and quirky behaviour, she realized her quiet disposition drew out her beautiful personality.

Once the bisque and biscuits were complete, Evelyn invited both Mr. Thompson and the maid to dine with her at the table. Mr. Thompson and Evelyn bantered back and forth about her childhood ways and misbehaviours while the maid's eyes remained wide open and her ears always inclined to whatever the two were conversing about. After a hearty meal, Evelyn helped the maid wash and dry the dishes, and Mr. Thompson went back to…she didn't know where. Once the dishes were cleared and put away, Evelyn traveled to the sitting room to bask in the glowing embers. The tongues of fire wove an intricate dance, twirling, leaping, dancing hand in hand. The fire provided such a hypnotizing show that her eyes began to droop and finally remain shut.

It had been such a long time that she had had a peaceful rest. No dreams, just nothing. The clinking of a teacup as it was being set upon a small plate impelled her eyelids to groggily open. Her hand twitched to the side; and then she heard someone clearing their throat.

"You are finally awaking."

Evelyn wiped her hand across her eyes, trying to focus on the fire before her. "Good afternoon, Mother."

"Good evening is what it is."

Evelyn twisted to the side so that she could see her mother. "For how long have I been sleeping?"

"Oh, three hours."

"It was the best sleep I've had in days."

"I am…glad to hear it. So what brings you to my door?"

"I have come to see how you are faring."

"I am well, thank you."

"And how was your visit? Mr. Thompson informed me of where you had gone out."

"I tolerated it. The incessant chattering and giggling of the young lady brought a headache upon me; and her sense of fashion was dreadful."

"What was the purpose of this visit?"

"As you know I used to be the ladies' president for the Committee of Decor for the church's social functions. I tired of the work, and now that I am older I cannot do most of the work I was able to do in my younger days. So the committee agreed upon a new candidate Miss Candford. I don't believe she does half as well as I did. But what can I do? She asked me to visit with her so that I could give her my opinion on some ideas she has for the Valentine's banquet we are hosting at our church. They were…adequate. Of course, I had to give her glowing praise for her ingenious efforts else she would cry her poor heart out."

"That was thoughtful on your part. However perhaps…would it not have been better to tell her honestly what she could improve upon?"

Her mother gave her a disapproving glare. "You still have much to learn about the way one must socialize."

"Perhaps I do." Evelyn closed her eyes in frustration. "I see you have installed some new windows. I like the style."

"Yes, I do, as well. As you can see, I have changed the curtains to a rich hunter green; I started to tire of the dragging crimson red. Well, what have you done of late? Still looking for that husband of yours?"

Evelyn bristled under her mother's derogatory tone in which she talked of Carl. "I've been searching for him recently. I visited two hospitals. One had no leads to offer. The other…one doctor said he thought he had seen Carl."

"Thought?"

"Yes, he said that passing by a corridor the day after the explosion he had seen a man who resembled Carl sitting down waiting for someone to…see to his wounds. When he passed by again, Carl was gone. I want to hope, to believe he's still alive. I don't know what to think."

"My dear, don't chase after the ghost of your husband for the rest of your life. The doctor said he *might* have seen him. There is no certainty. Grieve for the necessary time. Afterward, move on with your life. You cannot always look behind your shoulder, waiting for a miracle to happen."

What her mother said sounded fine and dandy. It sounded so *easy*. But it wasn't. She wanted to be free, but at the same time she couldn't let go. And the game of playing tug of war was too painful.

"Betsie has been a good friend to me, sharing my burdens. She brings much happiness to my days."

"Who is Betsie? Do I know her or her family?"

"No, Mother, she doesn't…move in the same circles as you do."

"Ah, middle class I assume."

"She is a working woman."

"How dreadful!"

"She doesn't have a rich family or a husband to depend upon."

"I cannot believe my daughter would associate herself with someone like…well, like this woman."

"There are other worse women with whom to associate oneself such as criminals…"

"Good God, you're not...?"

"Of course, not, Mother. What wild ideas you have!" Evelyn decided to broach another subject with her mother; for she dared not start a risky conversation that would be a catalyst to a painful argument. "Mother…I must tell you about this wonderful boy I have met named Clyde. He is an orphan; his parents died in the explosion."

"Poor child."

"Yes, yet he is such a bright boy. And there is something about him; I cannot quite put my finger on it. He has such hope, such life even after the tragedy that has befallen him. Once I finish my work for the day, I visit him in his private room. He always shares with me a ray of happiness that…that makes me hungry for more."

"What kind of work are you referring to?"

"Did I not tell you? I work at Camp Hill Hospital, where I was treated from my burns. At first I was only doing volunteer work. Now I work full-time."

"And what does your job entail?"

"I change patients' sheets, feed them when they cannot feed themselves, change bandages…"

"It sounds like such filthy work!"

"It's not so bad, Mother, and I sometimes aid the doctors in operations."

"Are you not afraid of catching some sort of disease?"

"No, I'm not. There are certain precautions and regulations which all staff must follow to keep ourselves and the instruments sanitized."

"I do not approve of such work for you, Evelyn. Dirty…and what kind of socialization are you receiving?"

"Why do I always need to receive? Why cannot I give for once?"

"It is not your place to give. You have been raised with privileges. You are entitled to them until the day you die."

"No, Mother, that is not the way of life. The majority of people don't live the way we do…you do. You live in a fairy tale. I have chosen this path, and I will remain on it. Nothing you say can change my mind." Evelyn's knuckles had become ghostly white as she gripped the armrests of the upholstered sofa, her body leaning forward in frustration.

"I can see that. You should learn to compose yourself. It is not becoming at all." Her mother shook her head then sipped her tea.

Evelyn's anger skyrocketed. But unleashing her fury would only incite her mother to *tsk, tsk* her more than she wanted. She quieted the boiling inside of her for a few more moments.

"I work with many different, interesting people. Over the past few months, I have become good friends with Doctor MacCrae, Gerald."

"Scottish?" Her mother spat the word out of her mouth.

"Yes, he was the one who originally introduced me to Clyde and who operated on my burned arm. I didn't know he had such a caring heart. And when he performs the operations…his fingers seem to dance. I try to better myself by observing his methods."

"You? Become a surgeon?"

"I didn't say that. I mean, well, I'm quite happy, content actually, in the nursing profession. I don't believe I would like to further my career. I would someday like to bear my own children and nurture them. I wouldn't want to cheat them out of whole parental love because I'm too caught up with my own success."

"And how are you going to have children when your husband is dead?"

"I don't know. But maybe…I run out of hope so many times; Gerald urges me to continue on. Maybe he's right. " The words seeped in, fulfilling their true merit.

"Don't trust a Scotsman is what I always say."

"How can you so easily put people down? He has strengthened me more than you ever have. He is a good friend, but you are my mother!" Evelyn's face was livid.

"My!" Her mother clutched her throat. "You seem to be quite defensive on his part. I know, you have feelings for that doctor don't you?"

Evelyn's mouth gaped open. She then closed it, knowing what a fool she must look like. Was it true? It couldn't be! No, she didn't. They were only friends. "I believe your aged mind is playing tricks on you."

"Your sounding so noble, wanting to find your husband. Meanwhile, the whole time you're floundering with this…doctor. What a hypocrite!"

"How dare you! Me, the hypocrite? And you…pretending to be all kind to that poor girl earlier today. Your appearing to look all saintly is sickening! Do you ever wonder why I stopped going to church in the first place?"

Her mother's visage turned stone cold. "Get out of my house."

"What do you mean?"

"I said to get out now. Don't ever come back."

Knowing her mother didn't play games, she immediately packed her belongings and left, meandering outside in the cold rain.

Say, from whence
You owe this strange intelligence? or why
Upon this blasted heath you stop our way
With such prophetic greeting?
William Shakespeare
Macbeth 72

Chapter 13

Evelyn had no place to go. Ghostly hands appeared from behind several open windows and shut the shutters with a large *whack*. Lights from within the warm houses softened to an eerie glow, ebbing lightly across the windowpanes. The dry hours she had had were a luxury, for now she was soaked to the marrow of her bones. She didn't want to inconvenience strangers by asking them to take in a stray such as herself for the night. Although she couldn't see the state she was in, the strangling strands of her fallen hair and the clammy feel of her wet clothes sticking to her shivering skin were evidence enough that she wouldn't be welcome in any sane person's home. Therefore she decided to head back to the ferry and brave the sure-to-be perilous journey over the Narrows. In her miserable condition, she saw no need to hail a cabbie. She would only leave a puddle of water on their fine leather seats. Over what seemed to be an eternity, she plodded on until she reached the ferry.

As she drew nearer, a voice called out to her. "What in heaven's name are you doing out here?"

"Is it possible to bring me to the other side?"

"Sorry, miss. I'm not ferrying anyone over tonight, especially you. You look like a drowned pup."

"I need to get home. I have no place to go. I would go to a hotel, but I didn't bring enough money with me."

The old sea man looked hard and long at her, his breathing laboured from recently tying his ropes down. "I know somebody who will give you a warm meal and a bed for the night." He turned around, picked up the same blanket she had wrapped around herself earlier and deposited it upon her shoulders.

"Follow me. The lady lives just up the road."

Splashing through puddles for ten minutes down the main street, they turned onto an inconspicuous side road; they walked a few feet forward until they came to the promised place.

"I thought you said it was near by."

"Well…it seems like it…sometimes."

He rapped the rough heavy oak door with his bare knuckles. There was some shuffling noise coming from within; a woman's greying head popped outside.

"What are you doing here, Mr. Cox, at such an ungodly hour?"

"Now, now, Jane, you told me I could come here anytime I needed to."

She muttered under her breath. "'Tis very true, indeed."

"But it's not for me, I'm here for her. She came to me tonight…"

As he pointed to Evelyn, the haggard visage melted; and she swooped them inside and put some water in the kettle to boil.

"As I was saying, she needs a place to sleep for the night and…" He put his finger to his chin. "Don't you have any family here on this side?" he asked Evelyn.

"I do. But I'm no longer welcome."

He nodded his head as if he himself understood the hurt sentiments. During a few moments of silence, Evelyn viewed her temporary surroundings. They were all standing in a small cottage-like cozy room. There was about one foot in between the ferryman's head and the ceiling. Because of the illusion that he was too tall to be, let alone, live in that home, he tended to hunch over and duck down halfway to the floor when he passed under the main doorway. The room was lit by tall and short candles alike, their flames flickering to and fro in synchronization. Trinkets such as gnomes, porcelain dolls, and crafted wooden boxes lined the three shelfs upon the wall opposite the front door. The smell of camphor pervaded the room.

After Evelyn drank a few sips of tea, the old lady led Evelyn to another small room on the eastern side of the home and gave her additional linens from a hanging cupboard outside Evelyn's room. Despite the strange aura which blanketed the home, her head touched the pillow, and she fell into a deep sleep.

***

The next morning Evelyn awoke and remembered the odd happenings of the evening before. The ghoulish dolls welcomed her from her slumber as she wandered back into the main room. What little light filtered through the grungy curtains was subdued by the suppressing atmosphere of the woman's home.

"Good morning, dearie."

Evelyn gasped and slightly reeled backward at the unexpected voice which loomed from a dark corner of the room. "Good morning to you, as well." She cleared her throat. "Thank you for your hospitality."

"Did you sleep well?"

"Yes, I slept sufficiently well. Now…I really must set off for home. I shall just retrieve my bag and…"

"Wait!" The woman's hand slapped her small round breakfast table. She slipped from her chair and slithered to Evelyn's side. "I sense…that you have lost someone dear to your heart. Your husband? Yes, yes that's right."

"How did you know?"

"There are many answers yet to be revealed. You will not listen until it is too late."

"I don't understand."

A sinister smirk crawled onto Jane's face. "Goodbye, dearie, I'll see you soon."

"Goodbye," She quickly grabbed her bags and exited the superstitious home. What a strange individual that woman was! She had not understood a word the hag had said.

***

All the violent and threatening weather from the day before had passed and had become a sweet mesh of white cotton-candy lazily floating upon the azure blue river hanging above. Sweet air oozed from the frozen ground bringing a sense of promise to the new day.

As Evelyn gazed into the dark abyss of the Narrows, the fact of the seaman's name being Mr. Cox suddenly seemed to be ingrained in her mind. Mr. Cox the man who had lain next to her in her same recovery room at the hospital and now there was another. The two men were close in age, and the family resemblance was striking now that she had made the connection. Could it be they were brothers? As she mulled over this possible new information in her mind, the ferry was nearing the shore of Richmond. Once docked, others departed and paid their fare. As she paid hers, she asked Mr. Cox, "Would you happen to have a brother?"

His hand trembled slightly as he took the money. "Why do you ask?"

"I met another Mr. Cox, while I was recovering at the Camp Hill Hospital. You both bear a similar resemblance to each other."

"I used to have a brother."

"What happened?"

"Same thing that happened to you last night. I was no longer welcome. Haven't seen him since..." He pocketed his money. "You have a good day, miss." His lips pursed in a sour fashion.

"By the way, my name is Evelyn."

He had turned away, not hearing her share her name.

She immediately veered off to the direction of her new home. Once she arrived at the apartments, she bathed in some hot water, changed her clothes, and napped. Being in a strange home the night before and being caught in a storm had brought upon a necessity of more sleep. She slept until she felt someone shove her shoulders.

"Good afternoon, sleepyhead," Betsie fuzzily stood above her, slowly being focused more clearly.

"Good morning," Evelyn stretched her arms and yawned.

"You mean 'good afternoon'."

"Oh."

"I have some fun news to tell you. But first you must rise up and have a cup of tea with me."

"Gladly."

As Betsie readied the tea and procured the biscuits she had baked the day before, Evelyn crossed her arms over her chest and asked, "So, what is this news you're so excited to tell me?"

"All right. Oh—we're going to have a banquet and a ball!"

"You and I are hosting this…banquet and ball?"

"No, no, no! The hospital is hosting a banquet and ball to raise some funds for those surviving patients who need extra care. We're going to have a ball! That means I'll be able to meet some eligible men. Or we can try to find dates before it…"

"Dates?"

"Yes, of course, that means you, as well."

"I'm not sure…"

"Evelyn, it would be good for you to forget about all your worries for a night and have a little fun."

The prospect sounded exciting enough. Evelyn hadn't gone to a ball in years. And food…There was so much good to be had out of this event.

"When will it be?"

"In two Saturdays from now, and we're both going!"

"I guess I have to or else you'll probably drag me out of our home anyway."

"You bet I will."

Both women laughed and revelled in thoughts of the upcoming event. Once their tea was ready, they sat down in their sitting room, stirring in their sugar and cream.

"And how was your visit to your mother's?"

"Terrible."

"What happened?"

Evelyn recounted to Betsie the strange going ons of last night all because her mother had cast her off into the pouring rain and chill of Winter's bite. But she did not tell her friend of the hag's haunting words which floated in her mind like a wisp-like thread. "What do I do, Betsie, to make this better? How did it ever come to this?"

Betsie sipped her tea quietly, her eyes overlooking the rim of her teacup. "I don't know what to say. What can you do?" She shrugged her shoulders. "Let your mother be for a little while. Perhaps thinking about what happened between the two of you will make her want to reconcile. Are you going to work tomorrow?"

"Yes, I missed it and you and…everyone."

Her mother's pointed words about her having feelings for Doctor MacCrae hounded her. What kind of wife was she? Her husband could very well be alive and in good condition, and she…she was entertaining thoughts of another man. She was appalled by her own self. A tempest brewed in her heart, making it pound with such a force as the waves in a storm beat upon the rocks of the shore.

"Evelyn?"

"Mmm."

"I asked if you had any dates in mind for me."

"Oh."

"And?"

"Uh, lets' see. Why don't you wait for someone to ask you? I'm sure one of those fine senior doctors will ask a wild one such as you."

"Don't entertain such ridiculous notions. They always have their heads in their books, or they always only think about their work. I mean, of course, their work and books are all really important—you really think so?"

"Yes, you're very special. Any man would be lucky to have you as his date."

At this comment, Betsie's cheeks reddened as she gasped a willy giggle.

"I've decided I won't go back to work tomorrow."

"I thought you just said you would."

"I did. But I need to use the time I have tomorrow to find any vestige of my husband's whereabouts at any of the local hospitals I haven't searched yet."

"You still think he might be alive?"

"I cannot in good conscience have a date for the banquet and ball if there is any glimmer of hope that my husband is still alive. It's the last thing I can do."

"Is it Doctor MacCrae's attentions that trouble you?"

"What do you mean? I'm sure there is nothing…"

"He dotes upon you. The way he looks at you—it's not the same way he looks at me." She fiddled with her hands for a moment. "I deduce you have some feelings for him, as well."

Evelyn's heart almost seemed to jump out of her mouth. Her eyes frantically searched for some consolation or guidance from her friend.

"We many times cannot help feeling a certain way for someone who is agreeable to our tastes. What you had with your husband I'm sure was very special, but there has been no sign of his existence. You have a right to move forward with your life and find love again."

"Then why do I feel so guilty?"

"I don't know. Perhaps the guiltiness will pass with time."

"I…don't know if it will. Perhaps I'll go see Clyde," Evelyn sighed. "I miss him."

"All right."

"Goodbye, Betsie," She rose from her seat to give her dear friend a sweet embrace. "Thank you for listening to me."

"Go."

***

Before she went to see Clyde, she stole away to Egg Pond to listen…to the sound of her heart and to hear the sound of her husband's. She wished she had some supernatural sense to feel his breathing, to feel his movement. Yet she was a simple being with simple functions that could do no such feat. She watched the dusk and reminisced upon the times when she and Carl would go to the park, especially right after they were married, and watch the sun set, finishing its course for the day. Night fell and the stars commenced their performances of brilliance. She forced her body to awaken from its emptiness. She found her way down the corridor leading to Clyde's room. Just as she was about to reach for the door's handle, out came Gerald. Surprise flooded his face and a twinkle in his eyes immediately shined as he closed the door.

"Evelyn."

"Gerald, how was your visit with Clyde?"

"It was good. I was just informing him I would only be half an hour more in my office. However…"

"What?"

"He has the measles."

She made a move toward the door, but Gerald's firm hands stopped her from her course.

"Evelyn, Clyde is fine. It's a mild case. He should recover in a week or so."

"You're sure? Forgive me. Of course, you're sure."

"It's all right, I understand. You know I would do all I could to make sure he makes it comfortably through."

"Yes, I do." Suddenly aware that Gerald's hands still held hers in their grasp, she looked down at them feeling their warmth spread across her skin.

He let go, slowly. "Have you had the measles before?" he inquired.

"Yes, I have."

"Then you may visit with him as you wish,"

"Thank you."

"Where have you been these past couple of days?"

"I went to see my mother. However, it was not the kind of visit I had intended to make."

"I hope it has not caused you too much distress."

"I'm all right now that I'm back."

"I'm glad you are. We all noticed your absence."

"I've missed…all of you, as well."

His eyes held hers. "Did you hear we are to have a banquet and ball?"

"Yes, I did hear of it."

"It should prove to be a splendid evening."

"Yes."

"I wonder if you would do me the honour of escorting you to the occasion."

"May I give you my answer tomorrow?"

His struggle of masking his disappointment was somewhat evident upon his face. "Of course, take all the time you need to think it through."

"I *will* let you know tomorrow. There's just something I must do first before I can know myself."

"I understand." He opened the door to Clyde's room. "Mrs. Richardson has come to see you, Clyde." He motioned to Evelyn with his head to enter the room. "I shall see you tomorrow?"

"Yes."

"Then goodnight…Evelyn."

"Goodnight."

Chapter 14

"Good evening, Clyde, how are you faring?" Evelyn lifted the inside of her wrist to his forehead. "You have a fever."

"I'm not feeling my best as you can see, but I'm willing to bear this small burden for a little while."

"Your stoutheartedness amazes me to no end."

"Providence reminds me of the joy I possess even when I'm ill. Reading my Bible daily provides me with all the encouragement I need to keep going." He crossed his legs and laid his chin upon his fists. "You seem sad, Evelyn."

"I am. I didn't have a good visit with my mother. We don't have the best relations right now. There has always been tension between us ever since I could remember. All my life one thing which has upset me to no end is that she doesn't approve of half the things I do."

"Have you forgiven her?"

"No, I've never thought of it before. I guess I've been constantly preoccupied in trying to bear her reproachful disposition." She thought upon the idea more intently. "No, I don't believe I have, and I'm not sure if I can."

"The Bible says to bless those who persecute you. This is one of those times you have the opportunity to do so. When I've forgiven someone, I always know that I've done the right thing. All the anger I had stored up goes away; and then I feel free." Clyde took her hand in his. "Maybe that's what you need to do."

"Maybe," She *was* holding unto frustration, anger. She could no longer reminisce upon the good times with her mother. All Evelyn could think of were her mother's vices. It continued to eat away at the fabric of her ability to love; but she didn't want to admit this disconcerting truth to herself lest she hurt her own pride and self-conceit. "Doctor MacCrae says you will soon recover from the measles."

"I hope so. When I get better, do you think you could continue to teach me mathematics?"

"Of course. I'd love to. I was wondering, what do you do in your room everyday? Do you not feel somewhat trapped?"

"Mmm, I guess I miss playing outside. I do feel trapped at times. Then I become upset because I think I deserve better. I want what I used to have, but I can't. I need to learn to be content."

"I want better for you. I'll make sure your circumstances change for the better."

"I don't know if you should make promises you can't keep." He sighed. "I read a lot of Doctor MacCrae's medical books and learn a whole lot of interesting facts. I sometimes don't understand everything I read or the images I see, but I try very hard to. Once in a while, he brings me some toys to play with. Such as…here…I'll show you." He scuttled off to a dark corner where there was a small hope chest, large enough to store several quilts. He dragged the chest to the middle of the room. Just like a little boy opening presents on Christmas Eve, he opened the chest. Inside were a few pieces of a train set. "These are my favourites. I've never been on a train. When I hear one…oh, I just want to board and ride it forever."

"Would you like it if we went on a train ride one day?"

"Oh, yes, I would."

"Then I promise that one day we will do so, together."

"I can hardly wait!"

"I see you're missing a few pieces such as…"

Clyde handed her the parts he had as she examined each piece.

"You're missing…the caboose and the tracks, of course."

"Yes, I am. One day I'll save up enough money to buy the rest of the pieces."

"If you work hard, you can attain anything."

"Evelyn…" He leaned his head toward her ear.

"Yes?"

"I love you."

She had never heard whispered in her ear those tenderest of words leap off the lips of a child. Her heart enclosed them in its bosom, never to let them go. This is what it was like to be loved by such innocence.

"I love you, too." She pulled him close to her chest and embraced him, playing with his straight dusty blond hair. "It saddens me that I'll not be able to see you for a couple of days."

"Are you going to try to find your husband again?" he asked.

"Yes, tomorrow, I will check the remaining hospitals on my list. If I cannot find him…I fear…I must move on."

"Don't lose hope."

"I know…it's just that…I cannot keep living like this. I'm holding my breath constantly, waiting for a miracle that isn't going to happen." She looked away in pain. "Please forgive me for prattling on about my woes. I will return soon, goodnight."

"Goodnight."

She drifted out of his room and down the hallway. She neared Doctor MacCrae's office and stopped before it, biting upon her lower lip. What should she say? Should she say how wonderful he was to provide Clyde with a beautiful train set? Was she seriously trying to find an excuse to see him? Glancing right and left without espying another soul, she put her right ear to the wooden door. She heard no footsteps, no shuffling of books' pages, no humming.

He must be somewhere else in the hospital.

She departed homeward to go to sleep where she would be free from the shadowing amorous thoughts which beset her mind.

***

The next morning, Evelyn had her breakfast with Betsie, informing her friend of her own plans for the day.

"Your last try, huh?"

"Yes, my last try."

She put on her boots and coat and began her trek to discover her husband's whereabouts. Door after door she entered, asking the receptionist to check their records to see if her husband had been treated there. Every time, the receptionist would shake her head, give her apologies and move on to her other duties. Sometimes a nurse or doctor would pass by as she had been given the unwanted answer. She would plead with them to give her a moment of their time. Some doctors would gruffly shake her off and say they were too busy to deal with her sad circumstance and kept walking on. Most of the staff were sympathetic to her plight. Hoping they would recognize his face, she would show them her husband's photograph. Yet again each of them said they didn't or they couldn't remember. She even went to Rockingham and inquired there, having heard that many of the injured had been carted off by train to that certain town. Her efforts were to no avail; for he was nowhere to be found, nowhere to be seen. Her last hope was the harbour. She traveled there, having barely enough energy to put one foot in front of the other.

The carpenters were diligent in constructing an au courant Richmond, a different Richmond. One where the houses faced tree-lined boulevards, one where each house looked similar; yet each had unique features. Would she one day see herself through a lace-curtained window surrounded by bounding children and held by another man? Could she ever let herself forget?

"Excuse me, sirs."

A group of dockworkers she had addressed halted all movements.

"Yes, miss." A darker-skinned man with his arms crossed upon his chest stepped out of the crowd and waited for her to speak.

"Do any of you know whether any of the ships which were present during the explosion are still here in the harbour?"

"Miss, ships don't stay here that long. But...let's see. I think one of 'em that was here has returned and is down a few docks. Am I right, men?"

"Yep," they all muttered.

"Which one was it again?" He looked to each face of his crew.

"USS *Old Colony*," a young man piped.

"That's right, just walk down a few piers. You'll not miss it," the head dockworker said.

"Thank you, sir," Evelyn replied.

She did as she had been told. Yet even the USS *Old Colony*'s records showed no sign of Carl ever having been treated there. All avenues had been searched, and not one produced some chance that she could ever have restored to her the love and life she once knew.

She dreaded visiting the morgue, prolonged the need to see a gravestone marked with his description; but it had to be done. The school with its clinging stench of death and misery came into her carriage window's view. The carriage wobbled a little as the horses slowed to a sloppy stop, the movement making her sick to the stomach. Before opening the carriage door, she endeavoured to take in large breaths of air so that she would not faint whilst she stood to exit. The *clacking* of the departing horses' hooves and wheels made her want to run back to it, to beg the driver to let her back in. Would she be able to handle the possibility of seeing not only her husband's grave but also the hundreds of others?

The creaking of the entrance door sent a small shiver down her arms. She walked a few steps and stopped. Another woman was walking down the hallway toward her.

"Good evening, can I help you?" The woman asked in a firm tone.

"Perhaps you can. I know you probably don't have the unidentified bodies still in the morgue…"

"No, we don't. The bodies were buried on December 17 last year; the burial of the dead continued on until Christmas Eve."

"Last year…"

"Yes, it's hard to believe how much time has passed. Professor R. N. Stone and another by the name of A. A. Schrister embalmed the bodies to preserve them as long as possible. After a time they needed to be buried."

"Of course. Where may I find the graves?"

"Well, the dead have been buried in several cemeteries. It would take a long time for you to visit all of them."

"If that is what I must do, then I will."

"There is an easier way to find your loved one. A chart of the graves was made. On it has the number assigned to the deceased and any description of what they looked like, their personal effects, and such things."

"Where is this…list?"

"We have a copy of it here. Let me retrieve it."

"Thank you."

The woman returned five minutes later with a few papers in her hand. She pointed to a desk at which they could both sit.

"Here are the markers. Take all the time you need."

Evelyn handled the papers, reading each description. Many only had one or two pieces of information such as the unidentified person having had three children and a pocket watch. Another woman had a whole paragraph dedicated to what she was wearing, her personal effects, and so on.

And still no one claimed her. How can that be?

There were some descriptions of men which were similar to what Carl's description might be if he were really dead. But she couldn't say with certainty that anyone one of them was he.

He might not have been brought to the morgue. What if his body is a pile of burnt ashes, carried away by the wind? Or he wandered so far into some woods and is now rotting away without a proper burial place? Nothing is certain.

"Thank you so much for your time." Evelyn recruited all the papers into a neat pile and put them into the hands of the woman. "I must go now. You've been very helpful."

***

She returned to her apartment, hair all amuck, body slumping. She couldn't think of a good reason why she should see the end of the day and the beginning of another. She sat upon the sofa for what seemed like hours staring at…the green wall. She tried to remember the memories of Carl, but all they seemed to do was evade her. After a while her mind gave up; and so she sinked into a lower pit of despondency. The creaking of the door did not stir her, neither did Betsie walking into the room.

"Evelyn?"

Evelyn had to reign in as much willpower as she could to even answer her friend. "Yes."

"Are you all right, sweetie?"

All right? Feeling all right was the wish she would ask for if given only one. "I didn't find him, nothing, not a trace." A single tear escaped her stoic stance.

"I don't know what to say. Tell me how you feel." She sat down beside Evelyn and hugged her shoulders.

"I feel…emptiness. I haven't told this to anyone, but before the explosion happened, after Carl came back from the war, the atmosphere between us was stifling. There was a chasm that neither of us could cross. The day of the explosion, Carl changed. He was loving me the way he had used to. Then he left. And then it happened."

"I'm sure your love for each other was a beautiful thing, something to always be cherished. What are you going to do now?"

"I'm going to move on. What else can I do?"

After receiving some hugs and comforting words from Betsie, she left to go to the hospital. The entire way there she felt a lightness and guilt. Every time she tried to free herself from the past, guilt entrapped her in its snare.

Knock, knock, knock!

A voice from inside called out. "Come in."

As Evelyn swirled inside, Gerald's pen came to a halt and his head snapped up to look upon this beautiful woman he esteemed so highly. Her long, wavy hair piled atop her head framed her heart-shaped face perfectly, endearing its attractiveness even more to his eyes. Her slightly parted lips were so enticing in their soft frame. Somewhat flabbergasted, Gerald stood up. "Tell me, what happened?"

She glanced a look at him and then stepped toward the bookshelves. She fingered their worn bindings. "I looked everywhere, searched all the hospitals in Richmond and Dartmouth. I even went to Rockingham. Many of the injured received medical treatment there as I'm sure you well know. But I couldn't find him. I also went to the Chebucto Road School where they used to store the bodies. There was a woman there who gave me a list of the deceased and their descriptions, but I couldn't be certain of...anything." She looked up into his deep hazel eyes, cheeks trembling. "Finding him is what I needed to do. And yet after all my efforts, I couldn't. There is nothing else I can do." She took a step forward. "Thank you for asking me to the banquet and ball. I would love to go with you."

"Really?"

"Yes."

"You quite surprised me. I was mentally preparing myself for rejection."

At his effusion of relief, they both laughed.

"You won't look for him anymore?"

"I cannot. I'm now holding on to a ghost of a memory. I need to move on. Thank you again for being such a wonderful friend to me."

"You're welcome. May I escort you back home?"

"Are you not working?"

"I'm done most of my paperwork for the day. As for practical medicine, someone else is covering me."

"In that case, yes, I would enjoy that very much."

He quickly put away some papers which sat upon his desk into the right-hand drawer, grabbed his coat and hat, and walked out the door with Evelyn. As they withdrew outside, flurries danced all around the air, pairing into couples. In a few seconds, Evelyn's hair was coated with them.

"What?" Evelyn asked, moved by his shimmering pools of amber.

"You look beautiful. The finest diamonds in the world could not grace your hair so well as these."

"They are beautiful." She gazed up into the dark sky, admiring the cool feel of the flurries falling upon her face with such soft elegance.

"Yes, shall we go?" Gerald murmured into her ear.

"Oh, what about Clyde?"

"Clyde is already settling into bed. Before you came into my office, I had just returned to my work fifteen minutes earlier after having had brought Clyde home."

Evelyn linked her arm with his, this time enjoying the warmth which radiated from his strong arm.

"Have you had any dinner, yet?" Gerald asked.

"No, I haven't."

"I would love to treat you somewhere. Where would you like to go?"

"Oh, let me think. Mmm, I quite like the Green Lantern."

"The Green Lantern it is."

They were served quickly since the restaurant was somewhat empty.

"I've never been here before. I didn't even know it existed. The truth is I don't eat out much. I'm always so busy with my work," Gerald said admiring the quaint decor.

"You cook?"

"Of course, I need to eat something, don't I?"

"Yes, yes, you do. Whenever my mother and I used to come to Richmond for small holidays with my aunt, I would sneak out to visit some of my friends who resided on this side of the Narrows. We would all hatch a plan to eat a meal here while I was in town."

"Even then you didn't have a good relationship with your mother. Do you not long for some true familial connection with her?"

"It's more complicated than it appears to be."

"It may be more simple than you think. I didn't have the blessing of growing up with a substantial amount of motherly oversight."

An awkward silence ensued while their plates arrived.

"I don't know much about you, Gerald. Tell me, where do you come from? I know you're Scottish. Were you born here?"

"No, I'm an immigrant from Scotland. I grew up working my father's sheep farm nestled in verdant hills. Every long labor's day I knew I wasn't destined to remain where I was the rest of my life like my father did before me. On a sheep farm, one learns some veterinary skills for cases when sheep are giving birth or they receive a broken leg because of their stupidity. I became interested in the dynamics of caring and healing the sick and injured sheep. But I didn't want to just work with animals. Animals are animals. Humans are so much more..."

"Ah, I see you're not a fan of Darwin are you?"

"I don't care much for his theories, not because I don't approve of them. I'm only disinterested. As I was saying, the human body is such a passion of mine. I went to the local doctor who resided in our town. I made such a convincing case that I would be a most diligent apprentice; he took me in. Once I had a taste of it, I wanted so much more. After a few years of being an apprentice, I told my father I wanted to go to Berlin to study medicine. I chose Berlin because I had some relations who lived there. I'm so thankful my father didn't estrange me from himself but gave me his blessing instead. I resided in Berlin for seven years, practicing on my own for two."

"What made you come here to Nova Scotia?"

"Work." His eyes were subtly evasive. "I was offered a position here at the hospital. I thought a change would be good for me."

"How long have you been here?"

"A year after the war started."

"How do you like it so far?"

"I like it very much."

After they had eaten their fill, Gerald paid the bill, and they left. Evelyn's apartment was only ten minutes away. Snow was still falling from the heavens as they made their way to their home street. Laughter escaped their lips every few minutes. So much were they enjoying each others' company that they seemed to disturb their fellow journeymen on the streets.

"I had a wonderful evening, Gerald. You helped me think of…better things. Thank you."

"The pleasure was mine." As he said so, he stooped down to pick up her hand and kiss the top of it lightly. "I'll see you tomorrow, Evelyn."

"Goodnight."

He jogged down the flight of steps and called out to her from a distance. "Remember Saturday." He then turned, walked past a few houses, then went into his own.

Saturday, the Valentine banquet and ball. She wasn't sure if she was ready quite yet.

Chapter 15

"Should I choose this one or this one?" Evelyn held up two beautiful long silk gowns in front of the hanging mirror on the north wall of Glube H on Barrington Street. One of them was a baby rose pink, embellished by a crocheted bust sweep, complete with a shimmering purple ribbon tied around the waist. Another was an emerald empire waist gown with a sweep train. At the bottom of the train were embroidered light green ivy leaves. Its sleeves were a shimmering gossamer, a rose petal's silk. "I'll try them both on."

The pink gown hugged her body comfortably while bringing out her naturally rosy cheeks. And the way the emerald gown's sheer cap sleeves fell mimicked the way her hair did when it was let down. A handful of fabric was pinned to the side by a delicate flower brooch with two moderately sized emeralds embedded within.

She showcased each dress to Betsie. "What do you think? Which one?"

Betsie tilted her head to the right with one hand clasping her cheek. "Oh, dear, they're both lovely. Which do you like better?"

"If I knew, I wouldn't be asking you, Betsie. I like the pink one because it is soft and elegant, but the emerald, I believe, would match my green eyes a lot better. It exudes a type of fire, a brilliance which I find mesmerizing."

"Well, then, your heart seems to have settled on the emerald gown. Buy that one."

"Oh! Here is the perfect accessory to go with it." She held up a peacock feather attached to a headband.

"Exquisite! You'll be the belle of the ball."

"Me? I think not. You'll take on that role flawlessly."

"Nonsense, what do you think of this canary yellow dress?"

"It suits your sunny disposition very well."

The women made their way to the counter, gabbing on about how excited they were.

"All our hard-earned money spent," Evelyn sulked. She reluctantly handed over her dress to the salesperson.

"This is a special occasion. The whole city is invited to this event. We'll get the money back. The hospital cannot do without us."

After the women swiped their purchases from the counter, they banded arms and skipped out of the store.

"I hear you're going with the good doctor."

"And what of it? He's been such a good friend to me."

"Oh, well, call me blind, but there is more than friendship on his mind."

Evelyn's mouth twisted in confusion and surprise. "Betsie Randall, what a scandalous thing to say! I don't know what you're talking about."

"You must have said yes right away. I know if I were twenty years younger I would have."

Evelyn stopped in her tracks and laid a firm hand upon her friend's arm. "I did not say yes right away. I couldn't. Before I gave him my answer, I searched for Carl in all the hospitals and medical institutions which were on a list given to me. I went to the school they had used for a morgue. My love for Carl…no one can take that away. Now that it seems Carl is…gone—it's time for me to move on."

"I understand. I'm sorry if I seemed to make light of the situation. I'm sure it's hard for you to do this, to take a chance at a new beginning."

Evelyn smiled meekly, knowing her friend was trying to help, trying to be positive.

***

Having had a goodnight's rest, Betsie and Evelyn went to the hospital to work their last day before the following grand evening. Evelyn was busy all morning doing her usual chores and duties as nurse. As she hummed a childhood lullaby to herself, a *bang* aroused her from the mundane routine. Betsie's strained face appeared before the slowly swinging doors.

"Evelyn, Doctor MacCrae is wanting our immediate presence."

Evelyn deftly put away a pile of clean sheets and followed Betsie into the operating theatre. Crying and moans of pain rang in her ears as she beheld a poor man who had been shot in the chest near his left lung. Blood soaked rags covered the wound. At the sight, Evelyn wondered what had happened to this man; but this was neither the place to think of it nor her job to pursue it.

"Nurse Richardson, stand across, here. Hold this."

Doctor MacCrae handed her the clamps. His movements were sharp, precise, beautiful at which to look.

"Nurse Randall, anesthesia."

"Yes, doctor."

Once the man had been put under, Doctor MacCrae and Evelyn had a hard time catching the bullet. It would not relent escaping their grasp, but soon after, their perseverance won over. Both were thankful the man's lung hadn't been punctured. He would be weak for a long time; but they had an optimistic outlook for his recovery.

"Nurse Richardson, please stitch him up."

Evelyn was now confident in her abilities to stitch a wound, unlike the first time Doctor MacCrae had asked her to. She had done it several times after watching others do it countless others. She cradled the needle between her fingers and started to sew. In and out, tightening, pulling, her fingers owning the practical magic which flowed through their tips. Once she had finished, she looked up to see Gerald's eyes piercing her own, roving over her face.

"Well done."

She smiled in reply, heat rising up her neck.

"Thank you, everyone." He congratulated all the staff in the room. He then turned to talk to a senior doctor who had just entered, relaying to him what had transpired.

That was the only real excitement which happened during Evelyn's shift. After her work, she went to visit Clyde to teach him some arithmetic. She brought some paper and a pencil and wrote down her own problems for Clyde to answer. At the end of their session, she left the tools with him so that he could practice even more. Every trace of the measles was gone and in place of sickness was a glowing face of a young boy, carrying in his heart all the hope of the world.

After a long day's work, Evelyn went home, ate a quick supper, and laid her head down to rest for the night, dreaming of the possibilities that could appear tomorrow night. Possibilities of what…she wasn't sure.

***

Betsie and Evelyn worked only the morning the next day. After their shifts, they almost ran home, for the excitement bubbling inside them was almost unbearable. They napped for an hour and then commenced the beautification process. They, one by one, bathed in oatmeal, rubbing their skin all over with the natural exfoliant. Evelyn eyed her emerald gown draped over the chair in front of her mirroir. As she carefully placed it over her undergarments, she revelled in the slick glide of the fabric. The shimmer of the silk basked her in an ethereal, fairy-like glow. She sat down and shimmied the feather hairpiece into her long hair. Wavy tresses adorned the nape of her neck. She put on bare minimum rouge and powder, indulging in a more natural, fresh look. Content with the way she looked, she sat down upon the sofa and started to read a novel.

"What do you think?" Betsie came out of her room, bright and beaming, wearing her dress.

"You look stunning!" Contrary to Evelyn's look, Betsie had doubled the coverage on her face and had opted for a pompadour.

"My..." Betsie's eyes started to glisten. "I feel as if I'm watching my own daughter at her debutante." She wiped away a tear.

"You're more a mother to me than my own mother ever was."

"It's an honour to hear you say that. Thank you."

"No, thank you."

The women didn't have to wait long until Gerald, clad in a fancy evening suit, rang the doorbell and sashayed them into the carriage. Although it was somewhat cramped, the three fell into easy conversation, shooing away any awkwardness.

"Who's staying at the hospital, Gerald?" Evelyn asked. A need for medical services would never sleep.

"Well, all those senior doctors who don't have a taste for a grand evening such as this have huddled together, bunkering down the fort."

"Oh, there's a few like that whom I know," Betsie added.

Such delight was being passed around the three friends. Smiles were bright and laughter never ran empty. They arrived at the entrance of the Halifax Ladies' College, masses of people being escorted into the building. Gerald brought both ladies inside and insisted on getting them some punch to drink. While Gerald was fetching the drinks, both women looked at their surroundings in awe. A grandiose chandelier hung in the centre of the gymnasium turned ballroom. Flowing dresses and men's dashing suits created a kaleidoscope of wonder. Huddles of young girls whispered to each other and pointed at the young men they fancied. Some even seemed to take a liking to Gerald. A pang of jealousy swept over Evelyn as she watched them dish flirtatious glances his way.

I don't understand. He's not even mine. Why do I feel this way?

She held her head up a little higher and cast down her eyes at her rivals. Trying to ignore them, she continued to glance around the room. Many of the older women held onto their husbands' crooked arms, listening to either a political or work-oriented conversation. The musicians' fluid movements of their arms and bodies as they swayed to the music they played created beautiful lines in a dance of their own.

Gerald finally advanced to where they stood with their promised punch glasses in his hands. As soon as Betsie took a sip from hers, an older jovial fellow asked her to dance. She gave Evelyn her glass and accepted the offer.

"Did I say how beautiful you look tonight?" Gerald whispered in Evelyn's ear.

"No, you didn't. Are you sure you're not thinking of any of those young women over there ogling you in a very indiscreet way?" She jutted her chin toward the babbling group of girls.

"Ah, do I sense a hint of jealousy?"

"Well, it seems as if you're the expert. What do you say, doctor?"

"I don't believe it's very gentlemanly of me to reveal your secret."

"If that's the way you want it."

He beamed a handsome smile which made butterflies flutter madly in her stomach. "I did really mean you."

"I must say you look quite dashing yourself. I didn't know you could dress so lavishly for an occasion. I've long seen you in your medical garments; I couldn't imagine your wearing anything else."

"Now you are jesting."

"Yes and no."

"Would you give me the pleasure of this dance?" He bowed with his hand outstretched to hers. Couples were starting to dance the foxtrot. The beat was impelling Evelyn to tap her foot.

"I'd love to!" She placed her hand in his strong clutching fingers.

Gerald and Evelyn swept through the floor, each playing off of each other's rhythm and movements. After the dance was over, both were perspiring a little. They sat down upon some chairs, commenting on the other dancers' techniques. Throughout the night several young men came to Evelyn and asked to dance with her. Loving to dance, she could not refuse. Several upbeat songs were played. When the music slowed to a lower tempo, out of the corner of her eye, Evelyn saw Gerald waltz with Betsie, twirling her about the room. A minute later he excused himself from her and walked out of the room with a look of extreme frustration. What had he seen that made such an impression on him that he would have to leave the room in such a fashion? Ten minutes passed. Evelyn was constantly being asked to dance by bachelors and old married men alike. When she finally had a moment to herself, she sat in a secluded corner and watched the evening's magic unfold before her eyes.

"Good evening," A familiar voice touched her ears.

"Good evening," She turned her head to the left to see a face she slightly remembered but could not place.

"Have you found some of the answers you were looking for?

Now she remembered where she had seen this distinguished face before. It was the woman who had housed her that stormy night on the Dartmouth shore.

"I…How…? You don't look the same."

That haggard face had been washed clean to be a blank canvas for a drastic transformation of rouge and powder. "Yes, it's quite different isn't it?"

"What do you want? Why do you tell me these words? I don't understand."

"I see you are with a special someone tonight."

Evelyn's nerves were pricked by such personal games this woman played.

"Excuse me, may I?" Gerald's voice resonated to the right of her, as he firmly asked her present acquaintance to relinquish her to himself. "I was starting to think I wouldn't have a chance to dance with you again." He whisked her to the centre of the room.

"You dance quite well. I'm surprised. I wouldn't have imagined a doctor to be so accomplished in the arts."

"I have many hidden secrets."

"Do you?" Evelyn giggled. "Well, I'll tell you a secret. This song 'You Made Me Love You' is one of my favourites. Ever since I heard it a few years ago, I fell in love with it."

"And why is it one of your favourites?"

"It talks about falling prey to passion, that other person who cannot help but resonate in your mind constantly. Yet at the same time, it's falling into a trap you've helped make. It's so tantalizing."

"You have a darker side to you I didn't know about. Have you ever helped create a trap you eventually fell into?"

"When it comes to love, not yet. One never knows what's around the bend."

Fully relaxed and at ease, Evelyn and Gerald fell into perfect step with each other, listening to each other's slow breathing.

"When you were dancing with Betsie, you seemed to be upset. Is everything all right?"

His eyes snapped to hers, a wide-eyed scrutiny ensnaring her curious gaze. "Yes, everything's all right. I did see someone who I thought I wouldn't see. I had to speak to them for a few minutes on some matter of…private business."

"Oh, I didn't mean to pry."

"Please, don't apologize."

The night, full of gaiety, was coming to an end. Everyone's feet were starting to ache and the music started to fade around eleven o' clock at night. Gerald escorted Evelyn and Betsie to their apartment.

After Betsie giddily floated inside, Gerald and Evelyn stood out in the cold discussing what a wonderful evening it had been.

"Thank you for procuring a carriage for us. I had a wonderful time. I almost don't want this night to end."

"I had a wonderful time myself all because of my engaging date." Gerald picked up her hand, held it between his own, and kissed the top of it. "Have a good night."

"You, as well."

Evelyn's heart fluttered as he strode onward to his own home. What a spirited night it had been! She had enjoyed the dancing so much, especially when Gerald had asked her to dance. Something inside her was igniting. She was afraid, unsure. For now she had no need to think about it. She was wondering at the sudden change of mood she had seen occur for but a brief moment. She had never seen him that way before. So she decided to ask Betsie to see if she knew any additional information. She knocked on Betsie's bedroom door. Betsie was sitting down on her bed, combing her tousled hair.

"Betsie, did you notice Gerald acting differently when he was dancing with you?"

"Yes, the occurrence was all very strange. Wasn't it grand? I'll never forget this night."

"Betsie, please concentrate."

"What?"

"Gerald's strange behavior…well, go on."

"Oh yes, where was I? Oh, he asked to be excused. Of course, I said he could be. Because he left, I decided to go fix my toilette a little. I sat down upon the sofas in the outer room, east of the ballroom. Once I had touched up my rouge, I spied him thirty yards away from me standing in front of the large window near a side door. There was another man much smaller in stature than Gerald talking with him. I didn't stay long, but it seemed to be that Gerald was very angry. He raked his hand through his hair rather fiercely, whispered something, then stomped off. But when he was dancing with you afterward, he seemed to be normal again, even glowing."

Evelyn's mind was racing trying to understand what had happened. "That's all you saw?"

"Yes."

Evelyn would continue thinking in her own bed. "Have a goodnight, Betsie."

"Evelyn?"

"Yes?"

"Have you thought about the possibility that…Gerald might have feelings for you?"

"Yes."

"All right. I just thought I would ask you so you won't be surprised when the time comes."

"I don't know if I'll ever be ready."

Youth is a blunder; Manhood a struggle;
Old Age a regret.
Benjamin Disraeli

Chapter 16

A green flash of silk, dress skirts swirling to the right, to the left, aromas of expensive perfumes, the crests and troughs of each musical note—these were the erotic senses which pervaded Evelyn's and Betsie's dreams that night. They didn't wish to rise from their sleep lest they shatter the perfect images playing over and over.

Looking into the mirror, Evelyn saw the lids under her eyes impoverished by a purple hue. She spent some time righting the damage which had undertaken its work during the night with a light powder. She let her hair fall loosely upon her back to warm every inch it could. She found herself drifting toward the hall closet and putting on her coat. Unlike the other times Evelyn had woken up rising with the sun, last night's festivities had taken a toll upon her so that she could not resume her routine. Betsie was still sound asleep in her bed. When she walked out to be welcomed by the sounds of the busy world around her, the kaleidoscope of energy in the busy streets lifted her spirits. She made her way toward the Commons to think of...? Why had Gerald become so evasive when she had asked him about his quick interruption from the dance floor? Or perhaps…he was telling the truth. Men's thoughts were so hard to determine sometimes. She had grown up an only child with no brothers to analyze. When she did get married right before the war, she was only starting to comprehend her husband's masculine reasoning for only a few short months. Most of the men she had known throughout her lifetime were fleeting spectres or highly established older gentlemen whom her father had worked with the short time she had known him. Her father had died of pneumonia when she was eight.

Gerald…did she really have feelings for him? Did he have feelings for her? He seemed to enjoy her company exceedingly. Could she let go of the past love she had shared with Carl for a future with another man? She wondered at the prospect for several blissful minutes but then bit back her tongue.

She walked east along Gottingen St. to see a strange looking building north of Kaye St. There stood a tar paper building. Was that a church? Yes, yes, it seemed it was. The reverend bowing his head and smiling with a sincere sparkle to a little girl whose crimped hair flowed over her navy blue dress coat, the small groups of women gossiping with their heads all bent together trying to hear every incriminating word flowing from the tattle tale's lips, some young boys playing tag, the men exchanging pleasantries and discussing the faults and merits of the previous sermon—these were the sights on a Sunday morning which she had not seen for months. Everyone looked so happy, joyful. It seemed as if the past, the explosion were…behind them; they were moving on with their lives making the best of every day which came along. Maybe it was her time to do so, as well.

As she watched the dispersion of the crowd, she recognized a familiar face. She looked both ways up the street, then crossed it, waving at…"Mr. Cox!"

His eyes searched for the voice which had called out to him.
"Here, Mr. Cox!"

Once she reached him, he grasped her hand in his, firmly pressing it between his hands.

"Oh! Your hands are like ice! Here take my gloves," she pleaded.

"No, no," He pulled out his own gloves. "See?" He held them before her to touch. The gloves were lined with rabbit's fur, a sweet blanket for one's aging fingers. "I'll be all right with these." As he put them on, he was interrupted by a hacking cough, making him double over. "This dreadful cough…I've had it for weeks."

"Would you like to go to the hospital?"

"Oh, no, I know it'll go away soon. I have had something like this before. It always goes away. You know why?"

"I cannot imagine."

He leaned over, cupping his hand over the space between his lips and her bent ear. "It's afraid of me." He chuckled, bringing another fit into place. Once he recovered, he stood still, gazing fondly at her pink-cheeked face. "What have you been doing all these long months? I've not seen you since you left the hospital after your recovery."

"I now work at the same hospital."

"Camp Hill Hospital?"

"That's the one exactly; oh, I have thought of you at times, wondering how you've been faring. And now we meet again. It's so good to see you. I don't even know why I came here in the first place."

"You were meant to find me. I've been praying for you, hoping you would find your husband. Did you ever find him?"

"No."

"My condolences."

"Thank you. Shall we go somewhere warm? The wind is biting."

Mr. Cox followed her gaze to a far off corner cafe, warming at the sight of the cozy building.

They both sat down upon floral-padded chairs, soaking in the warm ambience. Ivy decorated wallpaper embellished the walls while being accessorized with large candleholders nailed into the wall. Fresh flowers neatly bunched into petite vases sat upon each wooden square table.

"Mr. Cox, I hope you don't mind my asking, but would you happen to have a brother?"

His head sidled to the left, away from his view of the menu. "Yes."

"I believe I've met him."

Silence was the only reply.

"He looks so much like you."

"Are you sure? It could have been anyone else. I have a common-looking face."

"I'm sure."

"How old would you say he is?"

"Well…" She put her index finger upon the tip of her chin. "I would say about fifty."

"Where did you see him?"

"At the ferry."

Surprise crossed his face. "So he is retired. He used to be in the navy."

"Oh, but you didn't know where he was?" Then she realized the reality of the situation. "You and your brother are not on speaking terms, I gather."

A worn sigh escaped his lips. "We have not been on speaking terms for about thirty years."

"Thirty years? How could that be?" She couldn't imagine not being on speaking terms with flesh and blood for thirty years. And yet, could it be that unbelievable?

"So much time has passed, indeed. I don't even know why it has been so long now. An offence can be held against for someone for so long…and for what?" He rubbed his aged hands up and down his face. "I remember when my brother was first born. I was proud to be his protectorate. I would help my mother change his diapers and feed him. When he grew older, I would bring him to the park to play along with my sister and me. One day, we were sword fighting with sticks we had sharpened ourselves. We slashed through the air and cried out, 'War!' We each chose to be a certain admiral we admired. At one point, my little sister ran up behind John telling us to stop our foolish play. I put down my stick saying we would play only when Clara wasn't present so that we wouldn't egg her on. But John didn't listen. He swung around with both of his sticks pointing straight out and accidentally gouged one of Clara's eyes while the other stick punctured her eyelid."

A gasp escaped Evelyn's lips; she could picture the atrocity happen before her.

"I was…so scared. My knees faltered. I screamed for help. And John…stunned by what he had done stood frozen in place as if he had been turned to stone.

"Because of the accident, Clara immediately lost sight in her left eye while being partially blind in the other. I could not forgive John for what he had done, whether it was intentional or not. No more did I want him to be my shadow; but I didn't have to worry about that. He constantly sat with Clara, describing the wonder of the outside world from inside our front windows.

"One day, there was a large market held in town. My mother was busy with housework. We begged her to let us go. She eventually conceded, holding us to the promise that we wouldn't let Clara out of our sight. We all dressed smartly and headed toward the fair. At one of the horse pens, both John and I stood, mesmerized by the stunning beauties. But I let go of Clara's hand. Once I realized what I had done, we searched everywhere for her. Then we spotted her at the corner of the street. We shouted her name. She inclined her head, trying to find the source of our voices. She then stepped out onto the street just as a swift carriage came clattering down…killing her. We rushed to her side, just to see her eyes glazing over as Death stole her from us.

"I'll never forget that moment, my tears silently rolling over her lifeless body. John just stood there, limp. After the whole commotion, I urged John to rouse from his stupor and get Mama. The agony which pierced my very soul—I was to blame this time. Losing Clara to death was a hundred times worse than having her lose her eyesight. I stood there, until the shuffling of the crowd's feet aroused me from my own cowardly stance to see my mother cry her grief.

"John never forgave me after what happened. My mother said she still loved me; she forgave me. But every time she looked my way, all precious glint was drained from her eyes."

Mr. Cox, folded his hands together and placed his trembling head upon it. As he lifted it, Evelyn's hand enclosed his fingers. She nodded, her eyes penetrating to the core of his heart and touching its depths to heal the opened wound. There were no words needed, only love from one sincere heart to another.

They sat there in silence for more than five minutes, as statues in peace. Strangers still bustled around, chairs scraped the wooden floor, orders were written, taken to the back. But they were in the land of healing.

"What will you do now?" Evelyn asked, as she gave his fingers a little squeeze.

"I don't know. I'm not sure if…if I have the courage to see him again."

"And your mother?"

"My mother died ten years ago. I can only pray she has truly forgiven me."

"I wish I could have half the certainty you have. But my mother isn't dead."

"You still have time to fix what has been broken."

"But I don't know if I have the courage either." She clenched her fists.

"I will pray for you."

"Thank you. I cannot say the same for you, but…I'll be thinking of you."

"I know you will."

"May I walk you back home?"

"You don't want to walk home a humbug like me."

"You're no humbug. You are a dream."

"Come, come. Don't waste your words."

She linked her arm in his, while making sure he put on his rabbit fur-lined gloves back on his hands. After she deposited him in his humble abode, she took a ride to the ferry. When she arrived, she was told by a young man that the ferry was on the other side and it was expected to return at four o' clock. She had half an hour to wait. So she sat upon the dock, gazing into the shallow ice water.

The ferry returned precisely when it was expected. All on board waited for the ferry to dock. They finally disembarked; and Mr. John Cox stepped out last, carrying the heavy sea ropes in his arms. After he deposited them, she stepped into his view.

"Mr. Cox?"

"Oh, well, hello, miss!"

"Hello."

"Have you recovered from the storm's haggish effect?"

"I have, thank you." She shakily stepped closer. " I've seen your brother, Mr. Cox. He told me…everything."

He cast a spiteful eye her way.

"It was hard not to see the brotherly familiarity which I see in both your faces. Do you not miss him?"

He swirled around in agitation. "I don't want to hear another word about my brother. He…he's dead to me."

"How can you say that?"

"Have you ever lost a sister?"

"No."

"Then you have no right to spout your unwanted opinions."

"He is hurting, as well."

"Then let him hurt." He wiped his hands down his face, and exhaled roughly. "I'm sure you mean well, but there is no fixing what's been broken. Please, leave me be."

She had hoped he would see…that through her, he would see his brother's hurt, that he would hear reason and change. Dejected, she walked away. How dare she try to bring two hurting brothers together when her own relationship with her mother was in shambles. He was right. What right did she have? She wished…no…Carl was not there. The sooner she faced this truth, the easier it would be to move on.

Chapter 17

A month passed. The snow had melted into the earth, allowing the tender grass shoots to breathe fresh air yet again after such a long slumber. The sweet singing of the birds each morning compelled Evelyn to always leave her window open a crack during the night so that she could hear the melodic symphony swell her heart into song at the appointed time.

Every morning on the way to work, she would see the young children play hopscotch and ropes; the little girls would sing and the young lads would shout at the top of their lungs as they walked, hopped, or ran to school. Winter coats had been put away in favour of spring coats which didn't consist of so much fur and layers. Today the streets were quiet; for a torrent of rain splashed upon the roads like the sound of thunder crackling across the sky.

"What a dreadful mess we'll be today!" Betsie prepared to cover herself with a heavy coat for the watery onslaught.

"What shall we do?" Evelyn pulled back the lace curtain adorning the front window, looking at the sight in despair.

"Well, there's no use getting out of it. We'll have to make a run for it until a cab comes along our way. If we wait for one on the streets, we'll be soaked through."

"All right. Ready…GO!" Evelyn flung open the front door.

"Wait! I'm not ready! Evelyn!"

Both ladies scrambled outside as fast as they could. Evelyn closed the door. Then Betsie's feet slid while she jostled down the front steps, making her fall flat on her back.

"Betsie!" Evelyn gasped while laughing at the same time. "I'm so sorry. I don't mean to be ru…"

She stopped suddenly as Betsie's furrowed brows flew her way. She felt terrible. Soon the angry eyebrows gave way to a hearty laugh as Betsie asked to be helped up.

"Are you all right?"

"Well, my back is a little sore. But…" She laughed her way up to a standing position. "It was fun."

"Can you run?"

"Yes! I'm not an invalid!"

"All right. Let's go."

They cautiously ran for five minutes before a cab finally pulled around the corner. They flailed their arms around in desperation and were rewarded by warm cushioned seats which they wet very quickly. Evelyn tried to blow a piece of hair from her face but failed to do so miserably. She swiped it to the side with some frustration.

"At least we have extra dry uniforms at the hospital," Betsie piped.

Evelyn felt Betsie's eyes upon her when she turned her head to look at the mess outside.

"Someone is going to be waiting for you."

Evelyn nodded her head.

Once they arrived, Betsie headed off to chat with some of the nurses while Evelyn slipped away to first put on a dry uniform and then to bid good morning to a dear face.

She flitted down the familiar corridor. She stopped at her right and turned the doorknob.

"Good morning, Evelyn," Gerald's voice rang as he saw her delicate frame slip through the doorway.

"Good morning."

He rose and walked around his desk, warming her with a luminous smile. He took her hands in his own and kissed them both lightly. "I'm glad you came to see me anyway despite the weather."

"Of course, I would come to see you even though we couldn't meet in the park."

"The place where we listen."

"Yes."

"Your hands are cold." He took them gently and placed them upon his chest whilst enveloping her in a sweet embrace.

A week after the ball, Gerald had asked Evelyn if he could have the pleasure of courting her. With some hesitation, she had found herself accepting his wish. She did warn him he would need to be patient with her. He readily accepted her one request.

She had found that being courted by the good doctor was guiltily easy. His courteous manners and vivacious spirit endeared him to her heart so effortlessly. He was a close mirror of the man her husband used to be. The more he became dearer to her, the less conscious she was of the guilt, whispering its persuasions to not indulge in such fanciful romances. He was winning her heart piece by piece; she was smoothly falling prey to his charms. However, she still held back what little she could, fearful of what others would think of her good character and fearful she would lose something precious all over again. She appreciated the fact he was honest with her, open. But a nagging thought in the back of her mind taunted her that he was still withholding something. What…she couldn't say. But the thought was continually being pushed farther and farther into the back of her mind as she drew closer and closer. His arms around her like a fortress, all her worries couldn't bring her shield down.

"Gerald?"

"Yes?"

"I should go."

"Of course." He let her go an arm's length away. "You have work and I do, as well. Oh, before you go." He turned her to face him, "Did you enjoy the present I left for you at your doorstep?"

Her eyes suddenly brightened as she realized the box of chocolates had been from him. She had heard the doorbell ring two days ago, announcing the goodies' arrival.

"That was you?" Glowing with gratitude, she caressed his right cheek with her left hand as she gave him a kiss upon the other cheek. "Thank you."

"Your welcome."

"Goodbye."

"Until later."

She closed the door softly and rested against the wall outside his office. She could hear their two hearts beating as one. She knew not what had possessed her to kiss him in such a manner. Gratitude? Love? Gratitude could have been shown a thousand other different ways, but love…She was slightly afraid to say the word. She brought her fingers up to her lips, letting them dance across her smile. After a moment of bliss, she exited the corridor and headed straight to where she was needed.

Gerald and she were diligent in making sure their courtship wasn't known to their co-workers. Even when they were thrust into working together, they didn't glance at each other longer than necessary or didn't relay to each other any terms of endearment. No chitchat of a possible romantic entanglement between them was heard among the batches of nurses working together; and Evelyn liked it that way. Other's disliking looks and haughty words such as her mother's would weaken her morale. She knew the breaking of mourning regulations could seriously damage one's reputation. But the times were changing. War, with so many deaths, made one realize that so many people had lost loved ones; and there were still so many that yet lived. The concept of moving on was becoming more public. Yet there were still many who held fast to the old tradition. Evelyn had been raised to adhere to regulations which had been set in place, had been raised to please the public. But their secret affection for one another was feeding her the courage to break out of the mould which had been formed around her for so long. She was starting to embrace a small sense of freedom.

***

Knock, knock, knock.
"Who in tarnation would brave such weather to come visit us so late in the evening?" Betsie bellowed.

"Well, we should let the poor soul in, not harangue him on his poor timing." Evelyn arose from her seat at the table, setting her spoon upon the rim of the large bowl. She opened the door to see an already drenched Gerald from only a few houses down. "Gerald! What are you doing here? I mean, come in. Please forgive me for my poor manners. Here, would you like a glass of water?"

"Yes, thank you. It would be much appreciated."

"What brings you here, doc?" Betsie gawked at him, her fists on her hips.

"Betsie, forgive me for the late night intrusion. I'm here to invite Evelyn to a dinner party tomorrow evening to be held on the HMCS *Niobe*. The captain is a personal friend of mine. I've told him much about you; and he relishes the prospect of meeting you. Will you come, Evelyn?"

"I would love to. Thank you for inviting me. For when should I be ready?"

"I'll come fetch you at six o'clock in the evening."

"It sounds splendid. Would you like to share our meal?"

"You don't know how famished I am."

***

The next evening after work, Evelyn held up her emerald silk dress in one hand and another less formal dress in the other.

Well, I'm not going to a ball; I'll wear the other.

The other was a white silk chiffon dress, embellished with a wide bright yellow ribbon at the waist. She easily put it on, buttoned the front, and tightened the sash. She placed upon her neck a string

154

of pearls. Because she had worn it upon her neck the day of the explosion, it was her only belonging to survive.

She used to wear extravagant clothing and jewels every day because she knew the act befitted her high station. Now, the humble uniform of a nurse was the clothing which graced her form daily, and her jewelry was only put on sparsely. Life was no more about parties, rank, and social status. It was more…it was about others' needs and how she could provide for them in what little way she could.

She bobbed her hair into a low bun, pinning back different strands of hair to create a smooth texture. She held her perfume bottle a few inches away and spritzed herself with vanilla rose aromas. Finally, she put on her cream coloured heels and covered herself with a crocheted white shawl. Suddenly, a hazy shadow caught her eye through the small window of their front door.

"Gerald!"

"Evelyn, how are you?"

"Good."

"Ready?"

"I'm so excited! I've never met the captain of a ship before."

"Well, you will tonight. I must say, you look beautiful."

"Thank you."

They boarded a carriage and arrived at the awe-inspiring *HMCS Niobe*.

"She weighs 11,000 tons and is 466 feet long. She's a lovely cruiser," Gerald said as they stepped out of the carriage.

"Is it not bad luck for a woman to board a ship?"

"Ah, well, there are some men who still hold to that…thought; but the general consensus is that you females are fully exonerated from that curse."

They entered the ship by the gangplank. Gerald was familiar with many of the officers he encountered. Many of them he embraced as dear friends. A man named Wilbur took his jacket and her shawl and hung it upon hooks on a wall. They were led to the captain's quarters. There spread before them was a feast. Roast pork, oven-baked potatoes, green vegetables of all sorts whet their appetites. The wall was lined with many naval paintings. One was *The Storm on the Sea of Galilee* by Rembrandt van Rijn; another was *The Fighting Temeraire* by J. M. W. Turner. There stood in the corner a man of a distinguished nature. His posture was perfectly erect. In his left hand, was a glass of red wine.

"Uh, hum," Gerald coughed his greeting.

The man in the corner turned around suddenly with a large jovial smile upon his face. A dark mustache fit his stern features perfectly so as to soften them somewhat. "My good man, come in. I've been looking forward to seeing you again."

"I have, as well. Captain, please let me introduce Evelyn Richardson. Evelyn this is Commander Holme. We have known each other since I immigrated here."

"I must say, Commander, you have quite the collection of naval paintings. Are they the originals?" Evelyn asked, admiring one up close.

"No, no, good God, sadly, they are only replicas."

"Nonetheless, you may still admire their beauty and the prose within the art."

The Commander's smile grew. "I like her very much Gerald."

"I thought you would."

"Commander, you said you knew Gerald since he immigrated here?"

"Yes, it was quite an unusual way in which we met was it not?"

"Yes," Gerald said, looking down at his boots.

"Shall I tell Ms. Richardson?"

"Oh, please do." She eagerly listened with bright eyes.

"Well, the terrible truth is is that I was shot in the chest somewhere in the streets. That hooligan, whoever it was, will never want to see my face again. I was shot and lying on the street bleeding. I tried calling for help, but I believe I was in shock. A minute later this good doctor comes running to my side and sees to my full recovery. Ever since then we have become good friends. We try to see each other whenever I come into port. But…enough of that, shall we eat? Wait! Where are all the other officers? Wilbur, are they ready?"

"Yes, commander."

"Good man, bring them in."

Gerald immediately pulled out Evelyn's seat; and she sat upon it with ease, being in such high spirits with such entertaining company. Gerald then walked round to his spot opposite her and waited for the other men to arrive. All the officers came in with laughter, jostling one another, frolicking about. But as soon as they saw Evelyn, the only beautiful female in the male-dominated room, they quieted quickly and bowed their heads in respect to her presence as they passed her. At the commander's orders they all sat down and said grace.

"Bon appetit! Eat your fill!" The captain raised his glass and toasted, "Here's to the men and women from the bravery of their hearts to help raise up a new Halifax and an end to this Great War!"

"Hear! Hear!" Every man cried with heartfelt sincerity, showing a great love for his country.

The room was full of gaiety. Many of the officers had their eyes fixed on Evelyn half the time and on their plate the other half. But she only had eyes for one man in the room, the one whom she listened to with rapture. She enjoyed seeing him with a friend, whom he got along with very amiably.

"Commander, what damage did your ship receive from the blast last December?" Evelyn waited for the captain to finish sipping his drink.

"We received damage in the upper works of this ship, and some of the men were killed while they tried to rescue those in the Narrrows. The upper decks have been mostly repaired. Actually, I only came in possession of this ship December 22 last year."

"It's truly a great sight! It took my breath away when I saw it moored in its place, here."

"I would like to thank you Ms. Richardson for gracing us with your meek presence this evening. It's good for my men to have a touch of femininity in their lives now and then."

"It's my pleasure."

"And how did you and Gerald meet?"

"He patched my burnt arm a day after the explosion. I quickly left after my recovery to inquire after my mother in Dartmouth. I returned to work at the same hospital at which Gerald works. We became good friends after that."

"Gerald…he is so good to those around him. I've never known a man who is so deserving of blessings."

Gerald dipped his head. "Thank you, commander, for those fine sentiments which you so easily place upon me. But I am an average man who makes as many mistakes as any other and who only tries to do what he knows to be right."

"Stuff and nonsense! I say what you are and that is that."

"All right. I bow to your superior insight."

A deep roaring laugh erupted from the pit of the commander's stomach. "Gerald, you always know how to humour me."

"Yes, would you please excuse me for a moment? I left my cigar in my coat pocket, and I would like to fetch it."

"Oh, but Wilbur can fetch your jacket for you."

"Yes, but you know how fond I am of traveling the ship's corridors. I'll be back within a few minutes."

Cigars? I never knew he smoked cigars. I've never seen him smoke cigars.

Although she had misgivings over his errand, she busied herself with talking to the sailors closest to her, asking them questions of their sea voyages and exploits. They were very willing to share with her, and so they did with animated faces and voices. A few soldiers started to quiet down because of the excessive drink they had.

After what seemed to have been much longer than a few minutes, Gerald returned with a large cigar in his fingers. He stuck it in his mouth and held it near a candle to light it. The brim started to smoke. He breathed it in but then sputtered. He quickly grabbed his glass of wine to quiet his ruckus. He again brought it to his lips and inhaled the smoke smoothly and puffing it out comfortably.

The rest of the night was delightful, although Gerald's disappearance for those interesting few minutes left Evelyn's curiosity running at full speed, wondering what had he done other than retrieve his precious cigar.

Chapter 18

Ever since Evelyn confronted the seaman Mr. Cox, she had not been to or gone near the docks. The more she thought about the two brothers the more her heart ached to see their reconciliation come to pass. Though tragic the events were, healing could restore what had been broken for so many years. So one day after her work at the hospital, she followed the enticing of her heart to restore her own friendship with Mr. Cox, the brother in charge of the ferry.

She strolled down the dock to where Mr. Cox fiddled with his ropes. "Mr. Cox, good, morning, how are…"

"Great Jehosephat, Miss, what are you doing sneaking up on me?"

"You didn't hear me? The heel of my boots made quite a bit of noise."

" Ah, pay no mind to me, it's nothing," he said as he dug the heel of his palm into his temple.

"Mr. Cox, are you all right?"

"As I said, pay no mind. Now what do ya want?"

"I know we parted under less than favourable circumstances the last time we saw one another…I came to apologize."

As she said so, Mr. Cox's face angled upward to see her.

"I had no right to meddle in your affairs when my own are in disarray."

He continued to tie his knots. "Apology accepted. I know you're right. I've been thinking about what you've said. I'm so tired of being upset at my brother. I have been bitter for thirty years or so. Thank you for…your help."

Evelyn nodded to acknowledge his thanks; she was surprised by the difference of his sincere demeanour. She thoroughly enjoyed seeing him happy, happier than she had ever seen him before. "What will you do now?"

"I suppose I'll go see him. Tarnation! I don't even know where he lives!" He raised his hands in frustration.

An idea came to Evelyn's mind. "I cannot recall the way to your brother's home, but I know where we can find him. Meet me here this Sunday around eleven o' clock in the morning."

"All right. I don't know about this…"

She left, feeling quite pleased with herself; therefore she decided she had to share her good news and excellent plan with someone. Gerald still didn't know anything about the two brothers' past, but she decided it would be a good time to tell him. She also wanted to ask him about…cigars. She raced to his office, but when she arrived, he wasn't there. It really was quite odd. She always found him in his office reading, or studying, or musing two or three hours after work. She stepped in and inhaled deeply some traces of his presence. She let her fingers glaze over his shelves, microscope, desk, papers. Thoughts of him left her somewhat giddy, prodding romantic thoughts to surface from their weak jail cell.

He treated her with respect, admiration, and care. She had been left in want when Carl left her the first time and then again when he died. Now Gerald had taken his place. Both men were so different. Carl…had been sensitive, intelligent, full of energy and life before it had been taken away. On the other hand, Gerald was a leader, somewhat fearless, nimble with his hands, and steady. How could she ever reconcile the fact that she loved two different men in such a short span of time? Was she fickle? She didn't want to believe so. She had always thought she was constant, faithful. She had never during her marriage to Carl ever thought of another man in a romantic way, even when he had gone and she had been all alone. Most of the time when she thought of Gerald, she had no qualms; however, there were times like these when she doubted her own good character.

She left his office spotless, untouched. She walked down a few more steps to Clyde's room.

"Hello, Evelyn. I'm so glad you came tonight. See…" He jumped up with a piece of paper and set it into her hands. "I've been creating my own mathematical problems and solving them."

She studied the problems and was consequently amazed at his ingenuity. "Clyde, these are…well, these are wonderful. You have such a fantastic mind. Where do you get it from?"

"Well, perhaps, I received it from my mother. She was a schoolteacher, you know."

"Was she? Come, sit. Tell me about your parents. Oh, first before I forget, where is Doctor MacCrae?"

"Is he not in his office?"

"No."

"Well, wherever he is, I know he'll come back to bring me home…I mean to his home." Clyde started to play with his laces. "You wanted to know about my parents?"

Evelyn enthusiastically nodded.

"My father—he wasn't particularly smart like my mother was. He worked in the sugar factory which used to overlook the harbour."

"The Acadia Sugar Refinery?"

"Yes, that's the one; he was hardworking, and he used to tell me stories just like Doctor MacCrae does sometimes. Did you know Doctor MacCrae reads his medical books to me sometimes? I really like listening to all the complicated terms."

"Do you intend to study medicine one day?"

"Maybe, I think it's a very honourable profession."

"It is."

"Anyway, what was I saying again?"

"Your father worked in the factory."

"Oh, yes, he was gruff, but he loved us very much. He would teach me to play baseball and we would go fishing. He also loved my mother very much. Sometimes when she was in the middle of cooking supper, he would wrap his arms around her waist and twirl her around the kitchen. He never hit my mother like some of my schoolmates' fathers hit their wives. And my mother, she was beautiful. She had golden hair and green eyes. And whenever I was sad or mad, she would say, 'Clyde, never look down but up.'"

"You paint them with touching words as wonderful parents."

"Yes, they were."

"Do you remember the Cox brothers I told you about?"

"Yes, I do. They sounded like a sad pair."

"They won't be very soon. This Sunday I'm bringing Mr. John Cox to his older brother Mr. Cox. Mr. John Cox has decided he wants to reconcile their sad past and see his brother."

"I am glad but…"

"What is it? You don't seem to be too glad." Evelyn touched his arm.

"I just wish you and your mother would do the same."

What truth were in his words; but her fear that the situation would become worse continually held her back. Her walls were up and they would not so easily be let down. "I know. But it's not that easy."

"Why not?"

"When you grow into a man, things will not be so simple. They will become more complicated."

"I cannot see why. Everything is simple now. How can it not be when I'm older?"

"That's just the way life is."

"Well…I'm going to try my hardest to stay true to what I know."

"Then you do so. Are you sad being here by yourself most of the day?"

"Sometimes, but I'm not alone. Providence is always with me."

He showed such fortitude; but he couldn't stay in that forgotten room day after day. Someone could adopt him, bring him under the wing of a real family home setting. She could adopt him. But, of course, not in her present situation. Perhaps in the future when her circumstances changed, she could become his mother.

"I must leave. It's getting late." She kissed the top of Clyde's head. "I will see you soon and let you know the results of Sunday's meeting."

"Please, do."

***

Sunday morning's bright sun filtered through the partly open curtains. She stretched her arms over her head. Her mind was a little groggy, but it snapped back into awareness when she thought of the potential reunion between two lost brothers she had come to hold dear to her heart. She had brunch with Betsie, whilst sipping on hot lemon tea. After a relaxing morning of lounging on the sofa, reading the newspaper, and chatting about goings on in the city, both Betsie and Evelyn started to get ready to go out. Betsie was going out for a walk with one of her beaus.

"And which one is this?" Evelyn called out to Betsie as she was primping her hair.

"Rupert."

"And what are you going to do with your string of beaus? After that banquet, a whole lot of men showed up at the door asking for you."

"You know," she stood under the frame of Evelyn's bedroom door, twirling her lock of hair, "I really like this one."

"The bookworm?"

“Yes.”

“I’m so happy for you and I approve.”

“Really?”

“Yes, he seems like an amiable gentleman.”

“I think so, too.” Her cheeks coloured instantly.

“Have a wonderful time, Betsie. I’m going to go now.”

“All right.”

“Is Rupert coming for you here?”

“Yes.”

“Good.”

She strolled out and arrived at the docks half an hour later. “Good morning, Mr. Cox, you look rather fine today.”

“You like my scarf?” The scarf was a green and red checkered pattern.

“Yes, I do.”

“I only wear it for special occasions.”

“Well, you picked the perfect day for it. We’re going to see your brother.”

Mr. John Cox was excited though he carefully made sure his features would not divulge anything; yet he almost trotted rather than walked. Evelyn had to work hard to keep up her pace with his.

“So where are we going?”

“We’re going to the tar paper church north of Kaye St. That is where your brother attends church.”

“Church? Well, what do you know. Really, I’m not that surprised. He was the one who really held to tradition. The first Christmas we spent with my sister being blind I suggested that she open her presents first, seeing that well...she could not see. But no, he was so pigheaded in staying firm to our tradition that the eldest open his presents first. I thought that was one of the most selfish things he had ever done.”

“I don’t think he goes to church just because it’s tradition. It seems he is quite sincere in his actions.”

“Humph.”

They walked the whole way to their destination; for it was a brisk warm day. How could one not want to walk in such weather as it was! Evelyn planted herself upon the exact same spot where she had seen Mr. Cox the first time since she had seen him in his confinement. She held Mr. John Cox back, insisting with some pressure that he stay back and wait with patience. They had arrived a little earlier than what she had been aiming for. In a few minutes people filed out. And then…there he was. Evelyn had no need to hold back Mr. John Cox. The subtle shock of seeing his brother after so many years rendered him frozen, speechless. After a moment's time, a gulp slid down his throat.

"That's my brother."

"Would you like to go see him?"

He nodded in reply.

She walked but he…he was at the rim of the parishioners' circle in seconds. And from afar she saw two estranged brothers beholding each other, slowly walking up to one another in wonder, and finally embracing each other, both frames heaving like mountains shifting from the pressure which had been building beneath the earth. Change was happening; to Evelyn it was a miracle to see. She stood there in place until both brothers looked at each other and then to her. Once they did, she neared them with her heart brimming full of happiness.

Mr. Cox's eyes were full of wonder. He raised his hands to the heavens and breathed out, "God has done this; He has used you, Evelyn, to help two old codgers reunite despite their cowardice."

"I'm happy for the both of you. I believe I'll leave the two of you to rediscover who each of you are after so many years of separation."

"Thank you for your help," Mr. John Cox said.

"Your welcome, goodbye."

The two brothers waved her off, as she meandered back home through the sea of people.

Chapter 19

The next few days Evelyn repeatedly thought of that wonderful reunion which had happened on that bright Sunday afternoon. Yet her joy for them metamorphosed into guilt she bore daily. Would not a reunion with her own mother provide the same results?

Not necessarily.

She knew her mother and she could be unbending in their ways if it meant their own hurt could be exposed. Clyde ever telling her it was going to be all right, their relationship could mend, it was not so complicated…she thought it to be a bit too sunny of a thought for reality. Her conscious torture was building day by day until at last she could take it no longer. She rushed up from the couch she had been pondering upon, swiped her shawl from the hanging hook and marched out toward Gerald's home, frustrated with herself. She needed him to help her decide. She was so confused by her conflicting thoughts. She was scared she would have to do a hard thing. Her life had been…easier before this blasted war commenced.

Knock, Knock! Gerald opened the door, his hair uncombed, and casually dressed with the first two buttons undone. "Evelyn! Are you all right?"

She looked at him with pitiful eyes.

"I'm sorry. Please, come in." He drew her inside and slipped the shawl off her shoulders, brushing his hands against them.

She had never been inside his home before. She had thought it would not be proper to be in his home without a house party there. But she was desperate for him to listen to her burdens.

Everything was neatly placed. The furniture and decor boasted of a tolerable salary, although it could use a feminine touch. A gramophone was sitting upon a small table in a corner of the living room, the first room one entered in the home. A disc was spinning upon it, belting out one of Beethoven's symphonies. A coffee mug half full and a newspaper underneath it were the only items sitting upon a long table situated between the two chocolate leather love seats.

"I hope I'm not disturbing you."

"Evelyn, really. I'm very glad you came. I was missing you. I haven't see you for days." He fingered one small curl resting on her cheek.

"I've been quite busy, thinking."

"Oh?"

"May I sit down?"

"Why, of course, please do." He gestured to the love seat behind him.

She sat down upon the seat and looked down upon her lap. "Clyde?"

"Clyde is in his room praying. He does so for an hour every day around this time at night. He has such a faith in God! Do you know he said he would pray especially for you?"

"How sweet he is! However, it's hard to imagine how one can dedicate a whole hour to talking about me. I would say hello, but I don't want to disturb him. Do you remember my telling you I discovered from observation that two men I was acquainted with were brothers?"

"Yes, I do remember. I believe you told me quickly last Monday before work."

"When I asked the both of them separately, they each admitted to the truth. Their past relations with each other were far from favourable." She strung along the whole story, not sparing any detail. Evelyn felt special with Gerald listening so intently to her tale. His eyes dampened when she relayed the more horrible sentiments of what had happened, and at times his eyes would gleam with such intensity into hers that she had to look away for fear she would not help being drawn closer and closer to his person.

"This past Sunday they were reunited after forty-five some odd years."

"That is wonderful."

"And I've been thinking about my own life, me, my mother. I don't want to go through the same pain they did for most of their life. Yet some part of myself is telling me that going to my mother and talking to her won't do any good. I...don't know what to do."

Gerald stood up and paced the room for a few minutes, hand to his chin, brow slightly furrowed. Sometimes, an idea would arrive and his whole face would brighten to relay to her the solution; but then his face would darken yet again, and he would shake his head. At last he stopped, walked toward Evelyn and raised her up from the sofa. He cupped her hands in his, looking down upon them. "Evelyn, I want to tell you what to do. I keep thinking of what good or harm will come of it. Every time I think of a solution, a barrier rises up. I cannot tell you what to do."

She was opening her mouth to say something, but he put his finger to her lips. "Please, let me finish. You're right. Nothing might happen. But something might happen. You have nothing to lose save your pride. It might hurt, but I'll be here for you if you need me. I will comfort you. But you must decide." His sincere speech defused the tension which had been bubbling within her.

"Thank you."

"Your welcome."

And then it happened. The catch she was dreading and yet anticipating the most succeeded in taking root within her. Her gaze couldn't leave his. He lowered his head so that it would touch her forehead and rest upon it. They stood there breathing the same still air, chests lightly heaving up and down. He bent his head down a little further, caressing her mouth with his. A small dangerous kiss. He pulled back as she soaked in all the sensations which flooded her inhibitions. His head moved down again to plant another tender token, but her fear drove right back into her mind. She turned her head so that his mouth touched her cheek instead. He held both her shoulders and searched her eyes.

"What are you afraid of ?"

"I…I don't know." She felt hot with shame and pain for his hurt.

"Evelyn."

"I must go. I've decided to go see my mother. Thank you." She unentangled herself from his already desirous grasp.

"Will you come back to me?"

"I promise." She gathered her shawl and gave him a kiss on his right cheek. "Please, forgive me." She opened his front door and looked back at the man who had kissed her. She turned and closed the door suddenly wishing that perhaps she shouldn't have ended that spellbinding kiss.

***

She forced herself to head in the direction of the ferry the next day after work. Last night she had told Gerald she would see her mother. If she didn't go today, she would never go. She had to keep her word.

It was a chillier day than usual for the end of April. She wrapped her knitted scarf, which she had been given at the hospital right after the explosion by those involved with the relief committee, tighter around her neck. She tucked her chin inside and watched the weathered grey cobblestones pass beneath her feet. She only glanced upward occasionally to make sure she was going in the right direction. She didn't know why she didn't take a cab most of the time. Perhaps it was the money; it could be put to better use elsewhere. Or perhaps it was the fact that walking provided her with a few moments to herself to really think and to listen to the beating of her own heart.

Gerald had shared with her the night before that Clyde was praying especially for her. She knew it couldn't be of her own merit; for she was unworthy in all senses. Time and time again she could find many instances in her interactions with others which could be less selfish on her part. The self-seeking thoughts of her heart shocked her to no end. So what was the good that upheld the deed? Perhaps it was his sincere love for her, a love which gave and never asked in return. Perhaps it was the fact that he believed God would actually hear his supplications and aid someone like her, someone who might not return the favour. Was that true unconditional love? And how could unworthy she respond to such a love?

As she neared the harbour and veered toward the docks where Mr. John Cox had his ferrying business, she saw both brothers each eating an apple, chatting and laughing away.

"Good evening, sirs."

"O! Miss, I'm so glad to see you," said Mr. John Cox, nearing her with an open hand and leading her to an empty overturned crate. "We were just reminiscing over the old days, especially over our days of fishing."

"Yes," said the elder Mr. Cox, "we were talking about one particular time. It was a hot summer day. We boys were getting mighty fidgety in our seats so we decided to sneak out of the house. But let me tell you though…we got into a lot of trouble about it. Well, we ran to the small river which wound near our childhood home back in Quebec. We rolled up our pants and nearly fell into the river. We were so excited. So there we were talking and shoving when John here caught a really big fish. He could barely hold on to his pole. But Winifred, a young girl who lived in our town turned up just as he was reeling in his catch. Well, John was so startled that the girl he was sweet on noticed him and called to him that he tragically lost his catch. He was in a sour mood after that. None of her consoling words could make him happy. She eventually left. And the whole way home I laughed and laughed. It was one of the most enjoying times we had together. But you know what? He was never sweet on Winifred again." He slapped his hand on his knee and doubled over in laughter. "However, when we got home our sis…" He fell silent and cast his eyes downward. "Our sister scolded the both us for acting shamefully. She was right. She usually was."

Mr. John Cox confirmed this fact by nodding his head up and down. He caught Evelyn's sympathetic gaze. "It's all right. We…we're able to talk about our sister. We're at peace with the past."

"I'm relieved."

Mr. John Cox piped, "Tell me, what can I do for you?"

"I was wondering if I could catch a ride to the other side."

"Well, now, it's very late. We both insist you come and have dinner with us tonight."

"That's right," Mr. Cox reiterated.

One more night without seeing my mother will do no harm.

"It would be my pleasure. Shall we go?"

All three agreed to leave for Mr. John Cox's house in the country. They borrowed an automobile from one of Mr. John Cox's friends who lived nearby. They chugged along for half an hour.

Mr. John Cox informed, "In the morning I usually walk from my house to the crossroads that we just passed back there and then hail a buggy. Since we are three, I thought this would be a spiffy treat."

The sky's ominous skin hung darkly over the fields. In a few minutes, it seemed there might be a downpour; so low were the clouds hanging. Only a thin string of force withheld them from opening up their contents. Thunder rolled overhead and lightning flashed in the sky. It started to pour as they drove down the quarter-mile lane leading to John's home. The automobile was driven into a small shed big enough to hold only one such beauty. All three friends ran up the porch steps and into the tight entrance. The house though old was not inefficiently run down. Although it looked to be more than half a century old, the owner had taken care to upkeep it by giving it a new coat of paint. It hardly had a spot on it. The shingles were a navy sea blue.

Mr. John Cox opened the creaking front door. "Welcome to my humble abode."

As they entered, they immediately saw a hunched cloaked figure sitting upon the sofa. His head snapped up as soon as he heard their voices. He nearly tumbled out of the room, knocking his knee against the corner of the crude centre table. He uttered a small gush of moaning while grabbing his knee. Evelyn walked around the doorframe to see the stranger once more. She watched him pass through two small rooms and then open a door that she conjectured led to his own room or haven.

"Is that…?"

"Yes, he's the friend I had with me in the bakery that day."

When he had been startled and shown his face, she could not see it because of the darkness he had been sitting in.

Mr. John Cox sat on the couch and explained, "Poor man. He suffers blindness in one eye. I encountered him on a road leading out to the country. Actually, I was driving the very same automobile we drove in today. I was driving into town to see myriads of people walking down the roads in search of a place to live. I picked up many people that fateful day bringing them to relatives' homes or places where they knew their friends would take them in. But this man…had no place to go. He mumbled only a few words. He didn't even ask to be taken in. I took pity on him and have had him under my wing this whole time. I asked my town doctor to treat his wounds. He recovered well, all but his eyesight. I've been taking care of him ever since. He mostly keeps to himself. He's said very little to me."

"What a shame! Has he no family?" Evelyn's heart thudded dully.

"I don't know."

"Well, it is very kind of you to take care of him."

"He's a good samaritan." Mr. Cox proudly put his arm around his brother's shoulders.

"Well, shall we eat?" Mr. John Cox went into the kitchen. "I am starving!"

Both guests of Mr. John Cox sat at the kitchen table while he cooked up a quick meal of fresh fish, potatoes, and carrots. Evelyn asked her host where all the utensils, plates, and cups were and then set the table. Mr. Cox lighted several large candles and put them upon the centre of the dining table. They sat down and ate.

As they ate, Evelyn asked Mr. John Cox how he had become involved with the navy. He relayed some of his adventurous stories. Others were mediocre. He suddenly became very animated about the subject as he informed his guests about the present debate of the explosion.

"There have been many rumours that German spies were responsible for the explosion."

"Yes, I have heard that, as well. Is it true?" Mr. Cox piped.

"No, no, no, the Huns are not intelligent enough for this sort of thing."

"What makes you say so?" One of Evelyn's eyebrows moved upward in curiosity.

"Because…well, the reason why they joined the war in the first place was because of their alliances and what not. It's a whole lot of rubbish to me."

"I'm sure there are intelligent politics involved that neither you nor I could understand," Evelyn countered.

"Humph! Anyway at first, they did think that Johan Johansen, a Norwegian helmsman of the *Imo*, was a German spy. The doctors who had treated his wounds at one of the relief hospitals reported him to the authorities because they thought he was German. After he was arrested, they found a letter on his person that was supposedly written in German. But they soon found out that it was written in Norwegian. The whole story was given a lot of talk for the sake of stirring up nonsense.

"But a judicial inquiry occurred a few days later. Aime Le Medec, the captain of the *Mont-Blanc*, Francis Mackey, the pilot, and Frederick Wyatt, a Royal Canadian Navy officer, were charged with manslaughter."

"How terrible!" Evelyn effused.

"I think the decision seems unjust," Mr. Cox added.

"What do you think?" Evelyn asked Mr. John Cox.

"I think the whole fiasco was a mistake, an accident. Really I don't think anyone is to blame for it."

"Why do you think so?" his brother asked.

"A lot of things can go wrong on the waters, especially when maneuvering in the Narrows. With all the war ships' activity going on, something like the explosion was bound to happen."

"I hope those poor men…I hope they receive proper justice. It would be horrible for them to pay for something which was no one's fault." Evelyn concluded.

She then relayed to the men how many funds were garnered at the banquet for those who had been injured. Night soon fell as the small dinner party continued to converse. Mr. John Cox drove both his brother and Evelyn back to their homes.

As Evelyn entered her apartment, she glanced at Betsie lying upon the sofa reading some magazine.

"And how was it?" Betsie asked.

"I didn't go."

"But I thought…"

"I know. I was supposed to, but the Cox brothers invited me to dine with them for the evening. Their offer was very tempting. It seemed to be more promising compared to the meeting with my mother which I was not looking forward to."

"When will you go?"

"Tomorrow and nothing on earth will deter me from going."

Chapter 20

Evelyn arose early before the sun made its usual appearance. This time she didn't pack an overnight bag, knowing the remnants of her relationship with her mother might all go up in flames. She put on a simple day dress, neatly put up her hair in a curled bun, and slipped on some slipper-like shoes. She grabbed her small satchel and tied up its long drawstrings. She slipped it into a secret pocket existing beneath the folds of her dress. After her preparations, she pensively sat upon the sofa staring at the wall in front of her. What help could she ask from anyone? She was to do this alone. This was one of the scariest ordeals she thought she would ever have to go through. No one had ever crossed her mother, and she was about to do just that.

Oh, God, please help me. I don't know what to do.

She could hardly believe she was pleading to a God whose existence she knew to be true but whose involvement in human affairs she thought to be dead. But she was hanging on at the end of a string, and she was desperate to reach onto any ledge presenting itself.

After a suitable amount of time had passed to allow her mother to wake and dine, she stood up and left with a shallow prayer floating on the wind.

She arrived at the docks to find Mr. John Cox just about to leave. "Mr. John Cox!"

"Oh, come on in." He waved her over.

"How are you today?"

"Good, by the way, from now on you may just call me John."

"Thank you. It will be easier for me, my not having to say your full name."

He left her side to write in his log. He returned shortly. "So you're going to see your mother today."

"Yes, but I'm not looking forward to it."

"You'll be all right."

"I hope so. How is your companion?"

"To tell you the truth, not so well. He hasn't even left his room since you and my brother dined with me last night."

"That isn't normal?"

"No, he always comes out for breakfast."

"Have you ever seen his face? Every time I have ever seen him, I haven't seen a smidgeon of his features."

"No, I haven't either. He always does a very good job of hiding himself. He must have gone through an awful lot to always want to conceal himself from other people. Let us hoist away."

Not much was said between the two. Partly because Evelyn was too distracted with her own thoughts; she would not be able to utter any intelligent conversation and partly because John knew the struggle which existed within her mind. He did not want to interfere with any such turmoil. At the end of their course, Evelyn readied herself to leave.

She turned from the side of the railing overlooking the mighty ocean. "Goodbye."

"Goodbye." He watched her steps, full of trepidation, slowly walk away. "Wait!" He waved her over.

She came back.

"Evelyn, I just want to say that…it is worth all the pain."

She nodded her head. "I'll try to remember that."

***

She arrived at her mother's imposing house. She opened the gate and walked through, brushing past the out turned hand of an angel statue. Once again she asked for help from above. She rang the doorbell. The door was swiftly answered by the maid.

"Miss?" The maid's eyes widened in fear. She took a quick glance behind her back.

"I'm here to see my mother."

"I—I am sorry, she is…indisposed right now. She cannot have any visitors, good day."

"But…" the door was quietly shut in her face. The maid had seemed to be terrified of her presence. Her mother had probably threatened to dispose of the maid if the maid had even thought of letting her in. She left dejectedly, head hung low. As she walked around Dartmouth, she thought that if she couldn't see her mother through the front doors, she would sneak into the house unnoticed and talk to her mother then. She did not travel all the way here to have the door slammed in her face. During these pensive moments, she had not noticed that she had strayed into the uglier side of town where most of the poor lived and where the macabre stayed vigilant. As a lady of good status she immediately turned to leave the area, but a slithering shadow to the left of her vision caught her attention. She hid behind the corner of a building as she strained to see what had caught her attention. The street was fairly deserted; so no distractions were about. The man looked vaguely familiar; therefore she decided to move in a little closer, her curiosity piqued. The man swivelled his head to the right, looming into full view. Gerald! What was he doing here? He furiously knocked on the door in front of him.

The building was quite run down. Some of the outer shutters were hanging at odd angles on their hinges, and the house didn't seem to be well insulated. It almost looked as if any large gust of wind could knock it down to the ground.

When no one answered, he banged upon the door. The door was opened cautiously. She could not see who stood within the threshold of the building. Gerald reached his hand into the outrageously large overcoat he was wearing and revealed some sort of package. He and the mysterious person exchanged some pleasantries. Then Evelyn heard a woman's laugh. He nodded his head as the door closed. Once it did, he left quickly almost running toward the better side of town.

What was Gerald doing here of all places? She knew a woman had secretly met him behind the door. Was he in a secret relationship with another woman? Her cheeks were becoming hot; she slightly trembled at the thought that he could betray her in such a fashion. He knew she was supposed to have seen her mother yesterday, and that is why he came today. There would be no way of her ever finding out. He had planned it perfectly.

She memorized the details of the building's looks and where it was located. She then went to follow her beau. The path he was taking was absurd. He wound through the streets, entered random shops for a minute or two and exited them. He continually glanced behind him as if he knew he was being followed. Evelyn made sure to keep herself far away so that he would never notice her face in a crowd. However, at one point he entered a very crowded area. She lost sight of him for a second, and he was gone. She panicked for a minute, knowing that if she were not careful she could be found out at any moment. She was determined to know what he was doing. She craned her neck, trying to find him through the cracks of people's linked arms. But she couldn't find him. Suddenly, she saw him coming her way. She quickly grabbed a newspaper off a stand and opened it up to cover her entire face. After a few moments, she had the courage to peek around her disguise. He had passed her and was now continuing his journey to wherever he was headed. He left the central part of town and stole his way through a side street.

I've seen this place before. But where?

A rough oak door, the smell of camphor—it was the hag's residence! She remained at her post around the corner of the side street until she saw Gerald enter the preternatural house. Once the street was clear, she slinked her way down the row of homes and halted at the open window from which she heard two voices straining against the other.

"Please tell me." The intensity and clear desperation which coated his raw voice almost compelled Evelyn to save him from certain hurt. But she remained at her post, her curiosity governing the eavesdropping in which she indulged.

"What do you want to know?"

"Has my oldest sister received the money I sent to her?"

"Of course. All of our dealings are honourable. We haven't intercepted any such correspondence if that is what you fear."

"This wretched business!"

"This business will come to an end shortly. 'Tis only for a little while longer."

"Yes, yes it will be. My family, are they well?"

"Well as can be. Does she know?"

"No, no she does not. I intend to tell her sometime. But…I don't know when." He fiercely pulled on his hair. "Is there ever a good time tell her such a secret as this?"

"It is your burden to bear. Tell me, do you really think she will continue to care for you, even love you after she knows…this. Your large heart is your weakness. More likely than not, she will leave you and never want to see your face again."

"Quiet, you hellion! I don't wish to hear any more spiteful words fall off your slippery lips. I have faith in her, faith that she could still love me despite these circumstances, faith that she will understand the moral reasons why I have committed such crimes."

"Do not be fooled by blind love! Now leave me and aggravate me not with your delusional fantasies of…unconditional love."

"True, my business is concluded with you. I will leave you. Forgive my intrusion, good day."

Panic flooded Evelyn's body as she realized there was no crevice in which to hide herself. She was open bait in a barren street. Just as Gerald opened the door, Evelyn suddenly spied a stack of crates five feet away. She swooped down around it and pressed her hand upon her chest lest she let out a gasp of alarm. The door banged open, and she heard his shoes clack upon the cobblestone street. A pause, no sound. Then the clacking of his footsteps neared her hiding place.

Oh God, please spare me.

She could hear his laboured breathing beating in time with hers. She then heard his footsteps fade away; and only then was she brave enough to peer around the crates. His posture usually poised and gentlemanly ached with pain and frustration. Once he exited the small street, she left her hiding spot to continue following him. She followed him to the ferry which he boarded. In a minute, the ferry disappeared into the fog, swallowing into the mist the man she thought she knew inside out, the man that she knew she still loved.

What a conundrum! Why all the running around? And that...woman, the woman, she decided to go back to see just what kind of a place he had just visited. She eventually after some trial and error found her way back to the place where she had first seen Gerald. Some anger had started to settle in her mettle; she marched up to the door and knocked. The door opened almost immediately. There to greet Evelyn was a woman in her twenties with black curly hair tied halfway up. She had smeared red rouge all over her lips, and one of the sleeves of her dress was half falling off, exposing some part of her breast.

"Yes?" Her breath reeked of alcohol.

What could Gerald have had to do with her?

"I saw Doctor MacCrae pass by here about forty-five minutes ago."

"Oh, you mean Gerald."

She knows him on a first name basis?

"May I ask what business he had here?"

"Well, I…he—you need to leave."

"I want to know what he was doing here."

Just then she heard a man call down to the woman as he descended the stairs behind the front door. "Roberta, get back up here." In the shadows, Casby's face appeared.

Casby?

Roberta started breathing heavily. "Goodbye."

"Wait!" Evelyn protested as the door slammed shut in her face. She was stunned by this strange experience. Casby—what was he doing there? What ever had happened? Was there some connection between Gerald and Casby? Nothing made sense. She would clear her head with a long walk to her mother's home. She was so surprised at the courage and determination she had shown in wanting to know Gerald's business, yet did she have any right to snoop around?

***

She figured it would be about the time the maid would start preparing a dinner for her mother. She would not enter through the front door but sneak around the back. She huddled the side wall of the house and intently listened for movement in the kitchen. She had no need to. Pots and pans were clanging around; the maid was busy. She then sidled around the corner toward the back door when she ran into Mr. Thompson, the manager. She gasped. Her heart sank as she realized she had failed in her attempt to enter the house unnoticed. She expected him to escort her off the premises immediately.

Instead, he put a finger to his lips. "It's all right. I know you mean well." He gently led her to the back door, poked his head in first to make sure the way was clear, then motioned for her to enter.

She cautiously stepped past the doorway which led to the kitchen and crouched around various rooms until she entered the living room where her mother sat upon the divan reading a book of poetry.

"Hello, Mother."

Evelyn's heart nearly burst as the *thwack* of her mother's shutting book sounded as a gong, its reverberations penetrating any chinks in her armour.

To err is human, to forgive, divine.
Alexander Pope
An Essay on Criticism (1711), 1.525

Chapter 21

"Evelyn?!" Her mother stood up quickly and assumed a posture of stone-still superiority. "I thought I told you never to enter this house again."

"I know."

"Well, then, if you know, then I demand you to leave the premises."

"No, Mother, I will not."

"Are you ever going to defy me over and over again?"

"I came not for the intention of defying you but of seeking reconciliation with you."

"I want no reconciliation. I have washed my hands of you."

"Is that truly what you want?" Although Evelyn made sure to keep her gaze and stance composed and somewhat forceful, a single tear left its prison walls. "I don't want to live the rest of my life without a mother. Can you imagine not seeing each other for the next thirty years of our lives?"

"Yes, I believe I could." However, her mother's upper lip quivered; her facial muscles strained to recover their control.

"Why do you keep hurting me like this? You have been doing this to me my whole life."

Suddenly, her mother's brows bent together in surprise, her lips pursed. She took one step forward. "What on earth do you mean? You don't remember any of the good times we had together when you were a little girl?"

"Ha! What good times?"

"We…used to have picnics in our garden. I also used to hold your little hand while we strolled along the streets near our home."

"I vaguely remember such dreams. Those happy moments have been clouded with years and years of my never being good enough for you, of always falling short in your sight." Evelyn bit her bottom lip.

"Come, sit." Her mother gestured to the chair across from her.

Evelyn hesitated at first, keeping her distance from the one whom she thought would bite without warning.

Her mother did not speak for several minutes but blankly stared at the wall behind Evelyn. "After your father died, I…I felt as if my whole world had been ripped away from me. Contrary to what you may think, we did marry for love although his having status and riches didn't hurt either. Every time I looked at you, whether we were having a conversation or you were just playing with your porcelain dolls, you reminded me of him so much. Your sweet yet headstrong disposition, I almost…resented you for the fact that you were still alive and he was not."

"I was only a little girl…with little comprehension of how my actions could affect…"

"You foolish girl, hiding in some covert room of the house. We called your name so many times, but you did not answer."

"I meant no harm. I was only playing, wanting you or Papa to find me."

"Well, he did not find you the way you had envisioned it. Instead, he waltzed out into the winter cold wearing only a thin jacket and looked all over the streets for you. You know the end of the story."

"I'm sorry that…that Papa died of pneumonia. Do you not think my own guilt berates me in the middle of some nights? I blame myself as much as you blame me. Please forgive me. Unshackle the fetters of your hate toward me."

"I…do not hate you. This particular topic always heats my passion to the point I can hardly control it. There is nothing for me to forgive. I was the one who changed."

Evelyn's head slumped downward toward her folded hands, not caring whether it was not proper etiquette to slouch on a social call. "Why did you never approve of my getting an education, of marrying Carl?"

"My story had a happy ending until Providence took your father away; but I had seen many other girls my age who had done the same as I and suffered…such horrible fates. I wanted to protect you from something I knew I could not control. Women who go off to college get such incredulous ideas, and women who marry for love sometimes die because of lack of it or worse—they sell themselves so cheaply. I thought that if I trained you to be a wife in the home and set you up with some nice young man who would have plenty to share with you, you would be happier."

"Mother, I am not like all those other girls. I have a sensible mind, able to determine my own future."

"I know that now and have known for quite a while. My bitterness seized my logic when I saw I was wrong about your future. I did not want to accept it."

"Listen, Mother. I have come to reconcile, not to dredge up the past and inflict more hurt than necessary. I do not want any more bitterness to abide between us. I want us to be friends." She took the next moment to consider what she would say next. "I have come to ask your forgiveness for the way I have treated you and for the contempt I have shown you at times. I have been hurt, but I believe…you have been hurt, as well."

Her mother's hands inched up to cover her trembling mouth and tears started to stream down her face.

"Do you forgive me, Mother? Please, say you do," she fiercely whispered.

"Yes, yes."

Her mother's trembling form in contrast to her superior stance shook Evelyn's heartstrings to the point that they would not stop ringing until she showed her mother the affection she had wanted to for years. She thought it would be so hard to let go of the anger, and at first it was. Yet every look she cast at her mother slowly tore down the wall which surrounded the dusty room crying for a cleansing. She arose from her seat, sat down next to her mother, held her, and quieted her sobbing.

"Do you forgive me?" her mother asked, pointing all fingers toward herself.

"Yes, I do."

"You should have demanded this reconciliation sooner, tied me down with ropes until I would listen."

"No, I was a foolish girl not to hold on to some faith that you would see, not with force and brutality, but with the opening of another heart."

The air which once was soiled by malevolence was now clear, scented by true charity. She could not remember the last time she had hugged her own mother. It had been too long. No words could they say which could describe the elatedness they felt. So they sat there saying nothing but rejoicing in their union.

Her mother was the first to pull away. "Would you like some tea?"

"Yes, that would be lovely."

"I will also tell the maid to bring in some biscuits."

Instead of ringing her bell like she always did, she got up from her seat and went to the kitchen to tell the maid herself. She came back after a few minutes and sat down once again. "I have been so foolish, so unloving. How did I ever become like this?"

"You have the chance to change."

"Yes, I do, but now, enough about me. Tell me what has happened to you over the last few months."

"There is so much to tell. I don't know where to start."

"Tell me anything."

"I've been thinking a lot about Clyde of late and what has happened to him. He is an orphan I care for some days after work."

"How old is he?"

"Eleven, but even though he is young, he has an extremely bright mind. He loves numbers. I believe he has a bright future ahead of him. Right now no one really knows of his circumstances except Doctor MacCrae." She paused. "I've been thinking more and more of how wonderful it would be to adopt him. There is no one to claim him."

"But Evelyn—you have to be married to even consider the option."

"I know."

"There is something you are not telling me."

"For the past few months, Doctor MacCrae has been courting me."

"Evelyn?!"

"The affair has not reached the public's ears. No one knows except Betsie. We do our best not to make a show of it even when we work together."

"It isn't proper."

"I know."

"Yes, I know you know. I'm very concerned. Are you sure of his good intentions?"

"I thought I was until today."

"What happened today?"

Evelyn related to her mother how she had followed Gerald close behind his footsteps, how she had found herself and he at the worse part of town, how he had seemed to be evasive the entire time, and how she had returned to the dilapidated building and saw the…prostitute open the door. What was she to think?

"Oh goodness, I don't know what to tell you."

"Please do not chastise me."

"No, I will not. But you must do something about this."

"I will. I must talk to him. However, I'm scared that…well, that all of what we had wasn't… real. What if I make a fool of myself?"

"You will remain the fool if you stand by and do not act. I know this is a sensitive topic with you. I surmise that your being involved with Doctor MacCrae…that you have given up on finding Carl."

Evelyn clenched and unclenched her fingers when she heard his name. A small tinge of guilt still resided deep within the pits of her soul, and she thought she had rid of it. "I…I have. Every day I would look at the newspaper and skim the lists of the missing or the dead; it seemed as if he ceased to exist after the explosion. Maybe he did. There was really no trackable trace of him. I decided it was time to move on. I cannot live my life hanging on to the images of a ghost. And Gerald—I knew he had feelings for me. He said so himself, and I started to feel something for him, as well."

"Well, I hardly know what to think of all this. Really, Evelyn, you have gotten yourself into quite a mess."

"I have, indeed."

"You will need some time to think. Would you like to stay the night?"

"The time when I least expect to be invited to stay is the time I do not have my overnight toiletries."

"I am truly sorry."

"I am, as well. It was just as much my fault as it was yours. Now I'm glad it is over."

"I will have the maid polish your old room while we dine."

"What is her name?"

"Mmm? Whose name?"

"The maid's."

"Oh, I believe…it is…well…I don't quite know."

"Would not now be a good time to ask her?"

"Yes, it would be. You're right. I will go right now and ask."

As her mother made her leave to start a more friendly relationship with the maid, she warmed at the thought that perhaps her mother was capable of change after all. She had commenced upon the road to starting anew. This brought Evelyn much happiness.

Both mother and daughter sat down at peace with each other for this evening meal. They shared memories of the man who had been part of their lives for a too short time. They laughed, and they kept gushing with delight that now they were able to talk with each other as they were now doing.

"Her name is Martha." Her mother said.

Evelyn replied, "It will be wonderful to call her by her name instead of awkwardly asking for something from someone whom one knows so little of. A name says much of whom that person is. It puts one with another on a more intimate ground if they know each other's names."

After conversing for five more minutes, her mother sighed. "I will be retiring for the night. I'm quite tired. I will see you in the morning." She walked to Evelyn's seat, kissed the top of her head, and left.

Evelyn entered the kitchen and saw Martha, the maid, tackle the dishes. "Martha, would you like some help?"

"Truly, miss, I'm all right."

"Here," Evelyn grabbed a towel. "Let me dry the dishes."

They went on in this fashion for a few minutes.

"Martha, where do you come from?"

"Well, miss, I must say I don't know. I mean I know I was born around here somewhere, but I don't know who my mother was. My father, well, he was a drunkard, always cursin' and shoutin' at me. I have three little brothers who have no true parents except maybe me. I take care of 'em. I bring in the money to feed 'em."

"That is very noble of you. It must have been so very hard to grow up in such a household."

"It was. A few years back, I took on a job of entertaining men at bars. The pay was real good, but..."

"I didn't know."

"Mr. Thompson, though, he found me one day. Not that he was in one of those places, mind you. He found me cryin' on a patch of grass on a rainy day. I can't even remember where. I don't know why he risked getting wet or where he was going. He found me and told me the missus was needin' a maid. Ever since then I've been here, and the pay is just as good."

Evelyn's eyes started to water as she heard this girl's tragic tale. However, her life had to climb upward even a little. "You must love your brothers very much to have gone through…what you have gone through."

"That's right. I do. I would do anything for them."

"Thank you, Martha, for telling me more about you. I enjoyed our chat. Good night."

As she traversed the hallway, she was beckoned by the moon's eery glow, shining through the front window. She passed the staircase and leaned upon the curtains, basking in the night's light. She marvelled at the stars in the heavens. Her eyes roved downward to the light of the street lamps. Nothing could compare to the beauty of nature. Suddenly, a movement caught her eye. There it was again! A man stood at the front gate, fearlessly staring at her. His hypnotic glare planted her in place. She swallowed hard. When she was finally able to move, she shut the curtains close, hoping the man would go away. She didn't have to have the curtains open to feel the reach of his gaze.

Chapter 22

Throughout the night, Evelyn did not sleep well; she tossed and turned. Images from the day before haunted and disturbed her. When she awoke the next morning, she discovered that black crescent moons had taken home below her eyes during the night. She rubbed her hands down her face.

What a night!

Slowly she descended the stairs, pausing every three steps. She met her mother at the breakfast table for some tea, bacon, eggs, and fruit.

"Good morning, oh, dear, what happened to you?"

"I couldn't sleep."

"I hope it was not upon my account."

"No, no, it was something…oh, never mind. It was nothing." She decided to not tell her mother about the unwanted stalker she had seen. Perhaps it had been Mr. Thompson.

"Are you sure?"

"Yes," She tried to engage her mother with her brightest smile. However, her brightest smile turned out to be a lopsided weak line. "I must be going after breakfast. I am due back at the hospital this afternoon."

"I do not think that's such a wise idea."

"Why not?"

"You seem to be…tired, worn out."

"I must work. I'll be all right."

"Take care you get proper rest after your shift."

"I will."

After breakfast she wished her mother and Martha a good day and exited the house. As she walked down the short path to the front gate, she noticed Mr. Thompson pruning some rosebushes.

"Mr. Thompson?"

"Oh, yes, good morning, miss."

"I know this is such a strange question to ask you but…"

"Yes?"

"At what time did you retire last night?"

"Well, let's see. I think it was about nine o'clock."

"Are you sure?"

"Sure as the sky is blue."

"Of course."

"Mind if I ask you why you asked such a question?"

"Mr. Thompson, this is a delicate matter that I prefer my mother didn't know about. Can I trust you to keep the knowledge I am about to impart to you to yourself?"

"I can keep secrets."

"Last night at eleven o'clock I saw a man standing near the front gate watching the house. I had the wild idea it might be you, but it seems you have disproved that idea."

"A man you said?"

"Yes, I couldn't see his features…or anything really. Although it was quite light outside, he was standing in the shadows beneath the boughs of the maple tree over there."

"Are you sure he wasn't just some man strolling outside on a lovely evening?"

"I'm quite sure. Regrettably, I will be going now. Please, watch over my mother, and do not tell her about this; it will rattle her nerves. I do ask you to make sure no harm comes to her."

"I promise you, miss. Nothing or no one will touch her. She'll be safe with me."

"Thank you. Now I must be on my way, good day."

"Good day, miss."

Confident that Mr. Thompson would keep his promise of seeing to her mother's safety and well being, she opened the gate and strolled out.

***

When she arrived at the ferry, John wasn't there. Instead another man was managing the transportation.

"Hello, there. Ready to board?"

"Why, yes" She entered the ferry. In a few minutes, they set off. She ambled near the front. "Pardon me?"

"Yes?"

"I was wondering if you can tell me what has happened to John today."

"Are you a relative?"

"No, a friend."

"Well, he had to stay home today because the man he has been taking care of is getting worse."

"He hasn't exited his room at all?"

"Yes, he has, but he's not eating. He occasionally drinks water or milk during the day."

"Poor man!"

"Yes, indeed, so John decided to stay with him and bring the village doctor to him. He thought perhaps the doctor could talk some sense into him, tell him just how it is."

"I see, and you are?"

"I'm a close friend of John's. My name's Walter."

"Are you by chance the friend from whom he borrows that beautiful automobile?"

"Yes, I am."

"Oh, I must tell you your car is splendid."

"Thank you."

She and Walter chatted on gaily until they reached the other shore. Their simple conversation lifted her spirits a little. She bid him adieu and hailed a cabbie to bring her to North Park St. where she could enter the Commons. She strolled to Egg Pond yet again and sat upon the bench she and Gerald usually shared. As she sat down, she could almost feel his presence beside her, his arm cradling her. Now she was glad she had their bench to herself so that she could think about yesterday's events. She was thoroughly confused. She wasn't so sure if she wanted to see her beau yet. She ached for him; yet the thought of his seeing another woman was repulsive. Her thoughts stormed and whirled. Eventually she left to go to work.

***

Almost as soon as she entered, Gerald asked her to follow him to the operating room.

Oh, no.

He was the last person she wanted to see at the moment. She was not sure how to act around him when she knew his secret, yet she answered his beckoning by doing as he asked.

She arrived at the sight of a woman under anesthetics. She heard Gerald tell all the staff they had to remove her appendix. She went through the motions of preparing herself and helping Gerald by handing him each surgical instrument he requested. As he moved his hands, she could hear her heart pounding alongside his. She didn't dare look up for fear she would freeze and stare at his dapper features, be held captive, and consequently make a fool of herself in front of the present staff. So on and on they went working together yet separated by unsaid words. After Gerald dismissed everyone, she made sure to fall into single file with all the other staff so that he couldn't lay his hand on her arm, reach out to her, and ask to talk about her silence. He would not dare touch her in front of everyone;

so she was safe. She continued to busy herself throughout the rest of the day, making sure she wasn't alone for too long. She met Betsie in the main hall after her day's work. Evelyn wanted to leave immediately, but Betsie was finishing a quick chat with the receptionist. Just as the two were saying their goodbyes, Gerald strode into the main hall.

"Nurse Richardson, may I please speak with you for one moment?"

So formal, yet that is how they agreed to address each other at work, the way it was supposed to be. She neared him and then gestured him to step away from the few single people standing around so that no one could really hear her response. She did not want to disrespect him in public.

"I'm sorry, I cannot right now. Betsie and I are quite tired and need some rest, goodbye." She then left his side to leave the building with Betsie as he tilted his head to the side and shook it.

"Well, what just happened?" Betsie asked Evelyn with genuine concern.

"I'm not sure what you are talking about."

"You know you do, Evelyn. What happened during your small trip to Dartmouth? And why did you just leave Gerald standing there? It is not like you to act so, even if you were merely friendly acquaintances. I thought you would have been happy to reunite with your mother after a few months."

"I was and am."

"Something else happened, didn't it?"

Evelyn did not need to confirm. Her sunken eyes and grim-lined mouth said so. She recounted to her friend everything she had seen before she had gone to her mother's home.

"That's why you've been avoiding him."

"Is it that noticeable?"

"Quite from my perspective, of course. I don't think others notice. You two have done good work keeping your courtship *hush, hush*."

"I just…do not know what to say to him."

"Have you thought that maybe he had a good reason for his strange behaviour?"

"What good reason could there be?"

"Oh, you never know with men. I know they say it is hard to read women, but sometimes it is hard for us to read them, as well."

"I need some time to think."

"Just make sure you don't take all the time in the world to think. You might lose a good thing. Dear Evelyn, tell him the honest truth. Don't try to hide yourself from him because the truth is going to come out sooner or later."

"You're right. I will talk to him…in the morning."

When one relationship had been mended, another was in danger of breaking. She was not sure if she could go through the same pain and agonizing mental exhaustion again so soon.

Once they arrived home, they cooked a good meal and enjoyed it very much. However, Evelyn's creme brulee suffered terribly from having been burned. Feeling quite down and not knowing what to do, she decided to return to the hospital to speak with Clyde, whom she had missed dearly.

***

She tiptoed down the hallway, not wanting to alert anyone of her late night presence. As she neared Gerald's office door, movement from within stopped her in her tracks. Her body froze in place for fear he would know she was there and would want to talk to her; she heard his steps approaching the door. She sucked in a sharp intake of air. For a minute she didn't move because he had not. When she had produced no sound for a while, she heard his footsteps retreat to his desk; and she quietly escaped her precarious spot. She smuggled herself into Clyde's room and ran to give him a large embrace.

"Hello, there." She caressed him immediately, craving to show the sweet child the love he deserved.

"Hello, Evelyn. I've missed you."

"And I have missed you."

"What is the report on relations with your mother?"

"All is well."

"Thank the Lord. I've been praying for you ever since the last time I saw you."

"Thank you. I know you care." No longer did she spite the idea of others praying for her. She had come to appreciate this gesture. She still wasn't sure if any good came out of it, but she hoped that one day she would find out.

"Tell me everything, please." He clasped her hand.

She wove the true tale of how mother and daughter had finally put aside their differences for something greater; but she left out the part where another worry had started to infiltrate her mind. She did not want to incriminate Gerald; for she knew he had a close bond with this same boy, as well.

"When do you and Doctor MacCrae usually return home these nights?"

"Very late and I don't mind so much. I usually fall asleep, and then he wakes me up to let me know that it's time to go home."

"Oh," Evelyn had to leave soon. What awkwardness would come if he found her in here!

"I must leave, Clyde. I need to sleep for tomorrow's work."

"You know...he spoke much about you. He admires you very much. He told me how I was lucky to have such a good friend as you."

This confession closed in around her and almost brought about suffocation. Did he really think that highly of her? The thought was flattering to the least, but she was not sure what to do with that kind of information.

"Goodnight, Evelyn."

"Goodnight, sweet dreams."

She fled from the room and the hallway and out into the starry night. What a turmoil of thoughts and feelings residing within her! She wanted to come through alive, intact, yet she was almost certain she would sport some battle scars and wounds. What was she willing to risk to find love? What was she willing to risk to keep love? Although the thought scared her, she could not hide it or lie to herself anymore. She had found love again in a place where she had least expected it. Even though she was in danger of getting hurt by this love, she wanted more.

She prayed Gerald would have a reasonable explanation for his actions which he had exhibited two days ago because she truly believed her heart would break if…he did not.

Chapter 23

The next day she decided that throughout her day's work she would mentally prepare herself for what she would say, do, and think when she would go to Gerald's home after dark. When she was in one of the patient's rooms redressing a wound, she caught Gerald's eye as he walked in with a clipboard. He stood over another patient and discussed with him certain conditions of his case. Just before he left, they stood there looking at one another. Evelyn gave a hint of a sad smile. His eyes brightened in return. She then returned to her work, still feeling his gaze of care over her. She was lucky, blessed to be linked to a man like him.

After work, she went home. She bathed, put on a simple clean evening dress and a locket around her neck. She didn't fuss over her appearance too much; for Gerald had several times mentioned the fact he found her beautiful without her trying to be. Betsie was not home yet. She had gone on a date with Rupert, the one she had chosen out of her three dashing suitors to woo her. So Evelyn slipped out into the quiet of the night. The damp warm air tingled upon her skin. She soaked in the sea smells, listening to the seagulls' chorus above her head. She tried to look inconspicuous. She rapped her knuckles upon Gerald's door and waited for her love to bid her enter.

"Evelyn."

"Gerald."

"Please, come in. I have been waiting for you."

"I needed some time before I came to see you."

He nodded. "I understand."

"Do you?"

"Yes, I needed some time myself."

Perhaps he did feel remorse over what had happened. He cleared his throat. "Shall we?" He motioned to the sofa.

She nodded. A warmth started to spread over her body; she hoped he would hold her in his arms and tell her everything was going to be all right. Sometimes it felt as if nothing could breach the protection she felt underneath his wing, but she was wrong. She had to focus and not be waylaid by her swirling emotions.

"Clyde?"

"He's asleep. I drew the covers over him half an hour ago."

Just as soon as they sat down, Gerald rose from his seat and brought his hand to his forehead. "I'm sorry. I forgot to ask you if you wanted a drink of some kind."

"Water would be pleasant, thank you."

"Of course."

She needed a glass of water to quench the dryness of her lips. She watched him reach into a kitchen cabinet and pull out two glasses. He brought them to the faucet and filled them with water. Every movement of his entranced her. "Thank you." She reached out to hold her glass.

"Your welcome."

Immediately she quaffed half the water she had been offered. "I came here to talk to you about some…things that have happened recently."

"And I have something to tell you."

"Please tell me what you have to say first." Perhaps he would confess to her what he knew to be wrong in his heart; and she wouldn't have to accuse him of anything whether it was true or not.

"All right. If that's what you would like."

"Yes."

"I…I know we haven't been courting for long. It has only been a few months; but I must say what my heart truly feels. I love you, Evelyn. No words can express what I feel. I always want to please you when I am with you."

She could not believe it! The moment she had dreamed of and…dreaded was here. "Ger…"

"No, please, let me finish. My heart aches for you when I am without you. Your good is always foremost in my mind. Do you not know it?" He reached for her hands.

"I do not doubt it."

"I love you, and I want to spend the rest of my life with you." He reached for a small velvet black box from behind a cushion. "Will you marry me? None other will suffice." He opened the lid to showcase a beautiful diamond, the planes around it encrusted with small sapphire stones. He gingerly lifted it from its place and softly slid it down her wedding finger, which had been void of its previous ring for two months.

"Oh, Gerald, I…"

"I know we cannot get married immediately. We would at best have to wait perhaps another six months to announce the engagement, but I want this commitment. I am more than willing to commit to you."

"I…" She gazed at the gorgeous ring embellishing her finger. Breathtaking was its beauty. She had never received such a costly gift from another other than her parents. "It is beautiful."

"I'm glad you like it."

"Gerald, I love it. It's just that.…" She turned her face away. Even though she was hurting, she did not want to hurt him in return. "I think I should tell you now what I came here for."

"Go on. I am listening."

"My attempt to see my mother three days ago failed. You see, I found John at the ferry, and he and his brother were so happy for the service I had done them that they asked me to dine with them that very evening."

"That must have been very pleasant."

"Yes, it was. As you now know I did not visit my mother that day as I had intended to, as I had told you I would. So I went the next day." She stopped and tried to gauge his reaction. Nothing, his face remained open, ready for her to continue her story.

"I went the next day to my mother's house. I knocked on the door, and the maid Martha answered. She was fearful my mother would blame her for my entry into the house, therefore she denied me entrance. I left and wandered about town, trying to come up with an idea of discreetly entering my mother's home. My mind was so preoccupied with hatching a plan that I did not notice I had arrived at a lewd part of town. Something, someone caught my eye. I saw a gentleman knocking on a door, talking to an…immodest woman, and handing her a wrapped package of some kind."

Gerald's face betrayed a sense of doom. His mouth was set in a grim line; but infuriation did not make an appearance.

"I was so surprised to see this man there that I followed him around town. He always seemed to be looking over his shoulder, scared someone might find him. He then took another odd turn to an old woman's home where he and she talked of his family, dealings, and so on. I followed him all the way to the docks, and then he left the shore. I decided to go back to where I had seen this man. So I knocked on the same door, and the same woman answered. She was a prostitute. I demanded her to tell me what this man had been doing there, but she refused. Another man called to her from the top of the stairs just as he was descending them. I recognized him. He was the butler who was in my service before the explosion. I asked myself what kind of connection did this mystery man have with Casby the butler." She finished and stared, waiting for him to shed light on these past happenings. "Gerald?"

He let go of her hands and crossed his arms. The muscles in his face eased their tension. He took in a deep breath. "Now you know."

"Know what? Are you referring to your lascivious relationship with the prostitute?"

"What?" He drew up his posture and imposed upon her a most frightful glare.

"Yes, I saw it before my eyes. You met her. You handed her…perhaps a gift!"

"No! No! Evelyn, I promise you I have no such relationship with another woman. I would do no such act to dishonour you. Evelyn, you have to believe me!"

"Then explain everything to me, no more secrets, Gerald. I cannot accept your proposal when you hide things behind your back from me. How can I trust you?"

"You're right. I suppose that…I really must tell you everything."

"Gerald, I'm not demanding you to do anything. If you tell me whatever it is you need to tell me, I might have some peace of mind. I would be able to trust you. It is extremely important that I can do so. I was able to trust Carl when I married him."

"Yes, I'm sure, but I am not Carl." His words became heated.

It was her fault. It was not right for her to compare him to Carl. They were both so different from each other, and Gerald knew he had a lot to live up to.

"No, I know you're not. Please forgive me. I should not have said that."

He drew his head near hers and enclosed her hands with his. "I understand. I know, as well, that I cannot hide these things from you. You are right. You need to trust me."

She kissed him on his left cheek. "Please tell me."

"Evelyn, this is very difficult for me to say. I don't know how…"

"Please. I am listening."

"The day you saw me, I was delivering a package, yes, but not to the prostitute, to Casby. I have no relationship with this prostitute. She entertains Casby. Now, you are probably asking yourself the question, how do I know Casby? I was hired by him to carry out some work."

"What kind of work?"

He lowered his eyes. "Espionage."

"You're a spy?"

"Yes."

"And for which nation do you…do this kind of work?"

"Germany."

"Germany! The enemy? Good God, how…?"

"Yes."

"What on earth has possessed you to work for them?"

"I come from an extremely poor family in Scotland. Both my parents died when I turned twelve. We were sent to live with an uncle and aunt who we had never even met. They were poor, as well. I worked hard over many years to earn enough money to study medicine in Berlin, Germany. After I announced to my poor uncle and aunt I would be packing for Berlin within two months, they revealed I had a distant relative living there who might be willing to give me a room which I could rent. I wrote with much doubt that any good would come of my imploring for help from a relative whom I knew nothing about. To my surprise, a few weeks later, I received a letter from a Sir Arnold MacCrae, my uncle. He begged me to come to Berlin and offered me to be a guest in his home throughout my stay. When I arrived at my uncle's home three months later, I was shocked by his extravagance of living. He had a city home and a country home. He welcomed me with open arms, and I enjoyed the fine surplus of his living. He was a government official who had had close ties to the kaiser.

"At the time, we were not at war. I received my medical training there and set up a medical practice. I was horrified when my uncle informed me of the start of the war. What misconceptions and absurd notions everyone had! One day I was at a bar drinking some beer; for I had had a hard day at work. Casby sat next to me, wallowing in his own sorrows with his drink for a companion. What I considered some comfort were his chains. We started to talk about the war. He asked if I had family; I told him of my family's situation. He then promised me the pot of gold at the end of the rainbow if only I would do some espionage work for Germany. Of course, I immediately refused, not wanting to be entangled in these kinds of affairs; but I was hunted down several times and once barely escaped with my life. I decided I could do my family more good alive than dead."

"When was this? I mean when did you first meet Casby?"

"I believe it was November 1914."

"That must have been the time he asked for a month leave. He said his mother was dying, that she had asked him to be by her side. Yet the whole time…That bast…"

"Evelyn, please calm yourself. Do not resort to vulgarity. By that time I had set enough money aside to send to my older brother who wanted to learn a trade, the law; but I still had four other brothers and sisters who were suffering in their poverty not having any means to aspire to become something great or even to get a good education. I needed more money. He offered much, much more, enough to send all my siblings to school and more. The temptation was too great. I accepted. I have been stuck in this rat hole ever since."

"If you hate it so much, why do you do it?"

"I wanted to get out…once I started to have feelings for you. At the ball, Casby and I met. I told him I wanted no more part of it. He said I could not, that I was in too deep. I said I didn't care, that I would do anything to get out. Then he said that if I even tried, my uncle Sir Arnold MacCrae would finish me off. I was so…shocked to find out my uncle was behind all of it, that he had set up Casby to lure me into doing his own dirty work. 'One shot and you are done,' Casby said. The threat still rings in my ears. I do this for my family. This is the only way I can help them."

"There are always other ways."

"If there are, I don't know them."

Wait! If he knew Casby and they were working together, then all those months ago that cold night when she was home alone….

"Was that you who met with Casby the night two weeks before the explosion in my old home?"

"Yes."

"How could you?"

"When I realized who you were, I felt much remorse for my previous actions."

"The captain of the *HMCS Niobe* is he truly your friend?"

"I regret to say that that time when I found him in the street shot—I was in league with the shooter. I was ordered to befriend him and to steal naval secrets which he has in his possession. My whole friendship with him has been fabricated with lies and truth mixed together. I really do view him as a good friend; yet I betray him time and time again. It is a guilt I have had to carry."

"Therefore that time at the dinner party, the cigar was not the only thing you were after, was it?"

"I did steal some documents that night."

"I cannot believe it! All this time…what a fool I have been! And your love…is it real?"

"How can you say that!" He peeked a glance toward the hall where Clyde's bedroom was situated. He let out a gust of breath. "I just proposed an offer of marriage! I have no gain in marrying you for espionage purposes, save only in the purpose of having the honour of being your husband. To have you by my side helping me fulfill my ambitions, to love you and honour you is what I want. I want to grow old with you; I want you to bear my children. I even envisioned opening our own clinic for the poor and for those who have no money to afford the care for their health. Of course, we would not turn away those who could afford. I have callings and so do you; I want us to fulfill our callings side by side."

So much unsaid, so much hidden; but even through this confession, Evelyn's heart yearned to be his, to be his wife.

"I still have one more delivery to do before my contract ends."

"Do not do it, Gerald."

"I must."

"Please, don't. I will marry you. But please…do not bring yourself down."

"I will, Evelyn. I need to, for those I love."

"I will not follow you down this path."

"I am not asking you to. When all is said and done, I will come back for you and marry you. I promise you."

"I'm not sure that that is something you can promise."

"I trust you, Evelyn, to not reveal my secret to a single soul."

Could she betray her own country in his favour? She didn't know.

"Gerald, I…"

He cut off her words with a passionate kiss, like a momentous wave rolling over its prey. Her hands moved in his curls, feeling every fiber. His fingertips curved around her arms and down her back, sending shivers of extreme pleasure all over her body, shortening her breath. This physical love was too controlling. His fierce movements eventually calmed to soft caresses.

"I love you."

"Thank you…for telling me everything."

"Thank you for listening."

"I must go now. It's getting late."

"Yes, goodnight, my love."

"Goodnight." She fled from his infecting presence and cooled her body in the night's fresh air.

When the sun sets, shadows, that showed at noon
But small, appear most long and terrible.
Nathaniel Lee
Oedipus (1679), IV.i

Chapter 24

What had Evelyn done to deserve such a man who cared for his loved ones so much that he would lay his own dignity on the line? What had she done by telling him she would marry him! She had entangled herself in a real web of danger that she wasn't sure how she had fallen into.

She knew she shouldn't continue to walk in the deathly quiescent streets at this time of night, but she needed to walk off the thoughts of her perturbed mind. So she crossed the street and started to walk in the direction of the Commons. When she at last arrived, instead of sitting on the uncomfortable seating of the benches, she lowered herself onto the luscious grass. She fingered each strand and ripped some out to smell its earthy scent. She listened, listened to the thundering of her own heart and the clashing in her mind. Amidst all the internal cacophony, she did not hear the soft footfalls padding upon the grass behind her. A clammy wrinkled hand suddenly clamped down upon her mouth and partly upon her nose. Someone drew her up to a standing position and dragged her to a nearby tree in which the stranger pressed her against it, searing the uncomfortable landscape of the bark into her back. She tried to let out a scream, to bring to someone's attention of her assailant's attack. After one useless attempt, she knew it would be pointless to continue; for no soul was out roaming nearby. A breath reeking of alcohol wafted to one of her uncovered nostrils.

"Hello, my dear mistress. So sorry to terrify you at this time. I've been following you ever since you discovered my hideaway." He let go of his hold on her because she had stopped stirring.

"I am not surprised in the least, you cur."

"Good, I saw you slip into your new lover's apartment. Jumping into another man's arms after your husband's death—that was…quick. Perhaps you'll jump from him to me. I could do with a young pretty woman like you." His fingers started to slither down her blouse.

She stomped on his feet several times; he immediately stopped his untoward advances while grasping his foot in pain.

"On the other hand, you are…a bit too feisty for me. I like a woman who just falls into my lap."

"You mean one who falls into a trap."

"Tush, tush, harsh words are those."

"How did you ever conceal your ruse for two or more years? We thought of you as a faithful servant. What did we ever do to you?

"Oh, it has nothing to do with what you did. See, it's more about money, power, ambition. You and your husband were accidentally thrown into the mixture."

"Those can fade away just as quickly as you can gain them."

"I don't think so. Not the way I'm going about it anyway." He did a little hop. "I'm guessing your love told you his dark secret."

"What of it?"

"Well, I cannot have you running around with information that can ruin me, now can I?"

"I promise not to tell another living soul."

"What makes you think I should trust you?"

"Do you really think I would risk turning in the man I have come to love and have promised to marry?"

"Now that is a sad turn of events. In any case, that's good. Because if you do, I will come for you, and you'll be dead."

"I understand your terms."

"I know you'll keep them. Having lived with you and your husband for two years accounts for something; and if I kill you now, there will be a higher possibility that they'll link the murder to my hands. If I do come after you at a later date, it'll be planned. I will never be suspected. I will run away free. I have men watching you. See that you do not dishonour your word." He chuckled uncannily.

"May I go now?"

"Yes," He released her from his steely grasp. He walked away, and she watched him the whole time as his body slithered away into an alley.

Her body shook slightly as she digested the whole conversation with the slick Casby. Now she had no choice but to keep quiet or else her life would be in danger of ending. She could only hope that someone else would learn the truth and put a stop to this madness.

She entered...home. All the lights were out. She surmised Betsie had already returned from her date and gone to sleep. Just to make sure, she opened her friend's door a peak to see the bed occupied appropriately. She then lumbered to her own bed to surrender to a goodnight's rest.

***

The next morning she walked to the hospital with Gerald and Betsie. Once they arrived, Gerald and Evelyn left Betsie's side, sneaked in through a side door and stole a few kisses from each other. It was difficult to not share this good news with the whole world. The ring he had given her was being kept safe in its box in her dresser drawer. Her mind was filled with giddiness, but her conscience questioned her. What was she doing marrying a spy? Every time she asked, she kept that doubt at peace by saying he only had one more package to deliver, and then he would be free. He was doing this for his family's well being. Both worked long and hard. Whenever they had a few minutes to themselves, they met in his office and stole some more kisses from each other. All day she was sailing in the clouds despite the horrific evening yesterday.

***

That evening she went down to the docks to tell John what good news she did have. She knew he would not judge a dear friend such as she.

"John!"

"Hello. Come on over. My brother is around here somewhere. I asked him to go to the small grocery store at the corner to buy me a beer. I am so thirsty." No sooner had he said so that Mr. Cox came around the bend and returned with a beer in his hand for his brother.

"Here you go, John. Now do not go drinking too much of it."

"It's just a bottle."

The elder brother turned his attention to Evelyn. "Hello, Evelyn. It is so good to see you. What brings you to the shore?"

"Do I really need a reason to see my favourite set of brothers?"

"No, you don't. We are the reason ourselves," John said.

"That is true. But I do have something to tell the both of you."

"Oh, please do," said Mr. Cox.

"Well, gentlemen, I am going to be married."

Both men stopped smiling and became very serious.

"Really? But custom…oh, hogwash!" exclaimed John.

"How is this possible?" Mr. Cox asked.

"I have been courted by a local doctor for some months now. And he has asked me to marry him."

"How wonderful!" said John.

"Are you making this news public? Many will not appreciate the fact that a widow has accepted an offer as soon as this. We, however, are happy for you." Mr. Cox voiced with concern.

"Thank you. I appreciate the fact you are happy for me and you do not judge me according to…social custom. Please do not tell anyone else of this news. This is to be a secret between the three of us."

"We swear not to tell another soul," said John, putting his hand over his heart. "I know this is a sensitive topic, Evelyn, but how went your meeting with your mother?"

"I am glad to say that all misconceptions between us have been addressed and that…we are on good terms with one another. Even more than good terms. I feel as if I have a true mother, one to which I can turn when I have need of advice and companionship."

"God has blessed you greatly to have restored to you a broken relationship you thought you would never have the privilege of enjoying." Mr. Cox said.

"Yes…he has. John, how is your protege doing?"

"He is…better, if you can call it that. He has started to eat again and gone back to what he used to do."

"Good, I am very happy to hear he is mending." She uncovered a basket she had brought with her. "I baked some cookies for him. My fiance thinks they are divine. I thought your guest would like them, as well."

"Thank you. I'll be sure to give these to him."

"I was wondering if maybe sometime I could visit him. My husband, God rest his soul—when he returned from the war, he talked of the horrors he had seen. Perhaps what this man needs his someone to listen to him. I would be willing to come and do that."

"I think it an excellent idea. Perhaps a woman's touch is needed."

"May I come by this Sunday afternoon?"

"Of course, I'll be ready to take you to him."

After conversing a few minutes more, Evelyn hurried home, not wanting to be out after dark again. When she arrived, Betsie had already prepared supper. Evelyn helped her set the table for the two of them. Each woman took turns cooking supper each night. Tonight was cheese spinach souffle with some breaded chicken. Just as both women were picking up their food to eat, Evelyn asked, "May we say a quick prayer?"

Surprise registered on Betsie's face. "Of course."

"Umm…Thank you, Lord, for this food and for the glad tidings you bring our way. Amen."

"Amen." Betsie carefully picked up her chicken and eyed Evelyn with new interest.

"Betsie, I must tell you something."

"Yes?"

"Gerald has asked me to marry him."

"Well, well, I wondered when the time would finally arrive." Although she half-heartedly bantered, her eyes drooped, betraying a silent sadness.

"Are you not happy for me?"

"I am. Please forgive me if I am not my usual self. I'm quite tired today of all days."

"That's all right. I was thinking…I would be honoured if you would be my maid of honour."

"Oh, don't ask me. I am too old for such things."

"Nonsense, you are perfect for the position. You are one of my dearest friends. You and I have been through so much together, please."

"Then I will."

"Thank you."

The rest of the meal was eaten in plentiful silence.

When Evelyn retired to her bedchamber, she was a little concerned for Betsie. Something was not quite right. She was almost certain that Betsie would eventually tell her what was on her mind.

*It is one thing to show a man that he is in error; and
another to put him in possession of truth.*
John Locke
*An Essay concerning Human Understanding (1690) bk.iv, ch.7, sec.
11*

Chapter 25

Evelyn requested the following day off. She was told it was not possible because of the usual lower number of employees working on Sunday, but at the end of the day she had found someone who could take her place. Relief washed over her; for she was eager to be of some help to John's friend. Perhaps all he needed was someone to entice him into the light.

She flitted to Gerald's office and was met by one of his sweet kisses. "Gerald."

"Evelyn, I'm so glad you came. I've been thinking about you all day."

"I've been doing the same." She fondly nudged her nose against his.

He looked down at his shoes. "I'm sorry I have put you in a difficult position, in a quandary."

She thought back to two nights ago when she was accosted by her previous butler. "We'll manage. We will pull through this together. Our love is strong; and I pray nothing will tear it apart."

"Thank you for standing by my side, for understanding."

"It is my greatest pleasure. I wanted to let you know I won't be in tomorrow."

"Oh, and why is that?"

"Well, John has a man in his keep who will not talk to anyone nor show his face. I thought that if I went to visit him and tell him I am there to listen, perhaps it would do him some good."

"I think…that is very kind of you." He encircled his arms around her pressing her to himself and kissed the tip of her left ear.

"I'll bake some cookies for him, as well. Maybe whetting his appetite will incline him to come out of his shell."

"When have you ever baked cookies for me?" He murmured, his breath warming her cheek.

Evelyn laid a hand on his chest and pushed against it to create a small distance. Her breath hitched. "Don't you worry. I'll bring some over to you before I leave tomorrow."

"Where does John live?"

"Out of the city, in the country. It is really quite beautiful out there. Long lane ways, bushes of trees around farmhouses. The scenery is quite romantic."

"You will be back tomorrow night?"

"Yes."

"Well, then," he let her go. "I'll let you get on. I have a few medical papers to read."

"Goodbye."

That night once she arrived home, she whipped up a large batch of whipped creamery cookies to bring to Gerald and the man she was going to see the next day. She placed each cookie neatly on a plate, covered it with a kitchen towel, and went to her room to sleep.

***

The sound of robins singing serenaded Evelyn from her state of dreamy sleep to a state of pleasant awareness. It was now morning. She was strangely excited to see this stranger. Perhaps she could learn his identity, learn his history. She always had a fascination with meeting new faces. The whole circumstance was a delicious mystery!

She dressed in a lavender day dress with long ivory sleeves. She draped across her arm a white woollen shawl and linked the basket of cookies in the other. She had woken up mid-morning. Betsie had already gone out to work; so she locked the door behind her. She strolled over to Gerald's home. Although he was at work, he had left the door unlocked.

He was wanting my cookies badly.

She set his plate upon the kitchen table and left a note that said,

My dearest love,

Here are the cookies I promised to bring to you before I left. I only wish you were here to greet me, so that I could touch your handsome face. I love you. I will see you tonight. Think of me, my love, as I think of you in the deepest parts of my heart.

With a smile of satisfaction, she left her gift and headed out the door. The sun was shining bright. Months after the explosion, life had returned to its stream. Wounds had been healed and turned into visible scars, scars which would bring to remembrance the good that had come of a wrong.

I was wrong. Maybe God is not so distant after all. Perhaps He is closer than I realize, and has more of a hand in the affairs of men than I ever thought. I would like to hear what is said at Mr. Cox's church.

She walked toward the tar-paper church, a little self-conscious of who would see her walk into its walls. Opening the door, she was embarrassed to have most of the parishioner's eyes upon her now still form.

The preacher became cognizant of her abashment; therefore he spared her from further strange scrutiny by clearing his throat and declaring, "Hear ye what the Lord has to say concerning His command!"

All eyes left her to focus their attention on their preacher. She scanned the crowd for an empty seat in the back. Once she spotted one, she sat upon it and listened intently to what the man of God had to say. All of a sudden, she felt a hand upon her shoulder. She turned her head to the right to see a young woman about her age wearing a bonnet with a bow; one of its strands framed her heart-shaped face prettily.

"Good morning, my name is Rebecca. What is yours?" she whispered.

"Evelyn," her reply a whisper.

"I just wanted to welcome you to our service. Are you new in town?"

"No, I have lived here for many years."

"Well, I am glad you finally stopped by."

"Thank you."

Evelyn continued to listen to the sermon with much interest. The preacher spoke upon the power of prayer, how prayer was an essential part of worship, that it brought one closer to God. Yet, throughout the entire sermon, she was touched the most by Rebecca's kind and sincere gesture. The sermon ended and the preacher prayed to end the service.

God, I do not truly know who you are. I do not know if could ever fully know you, but I want to. I need someone to lean on other than myself. I fail so many times; I cannot pick myself up most of the time. Teach me to depend on you.

"Evelyn, would you like to come to my family's home for lunch? My parents always enjoy meeting new people who visit." Rebecca pointed down the row to her family who were rising from their seats to talk to the other churchgoers.

"I would love to, but I already have an important previous engagement. However, I would love to come back another time so that I could accept your offer."

"Wonderful, perhaps next week?"

"Next week, I must get going. Thank you."

She exited the quaint church with a little difficulty; for many of the attendees blocked her way as they were conversing with one another. Before she walked out, she looked once more at the scene. Surely there was a sense of unity and love amongst the people. This was a place where she could be, where she could give.

***

She hailed a cab and asked to be driven to the outskirts of town. She planned to walk the rest of the distance, which was forty-five minutes to John's home. Once she was dropped off, she hiked up her skirt a little bit to avoid brushing it against the spots of drying mud on the country road. As she walked, she bid good morning to a few other travellers who crossed her way. She soaked in the sun's rays and slowly breathed in the smells of farmland. At times, she pictured Carl and her walking hand in hand around a bend admiring the view of the sky; and at other times, she pictured Gerald and her whispering love sayings into each other's ears, heads bent down together. What a different life she would be leading if the explosion had never happened. Back and forth her mind swayed between two different ideas, not being able to make up her mind which she liked best.

She finally arrived at the seaman's home. She placed her hand above her eyes to shield them from the hot sun, trying to see if any person was on the property although she had no need to do such a gesture for her wide-brimmed straw sun hat provided enough shelter for her eyes already. There sitting upon a bench which was situated under a maple tree was a man. He was bent over, folded hands over his head. She strode toward him. Even though she neared him enough for him to be aware of her presence, he moved not but sat still as a carving. His eyes never gazed upward to see who was approaching. She sat upon the bench next to him, breathing in and out and wondering how to approach a man whose soul's life seemed to evade him. What would be the best thing to do? She picked up her basket and uncovered the plate of cookies she had brought.

"I brought you some cookies. Did you like the ones…" She was interrupted by a quick movement of his hand grasping hers in an iron grip. Was this man mad? He was strong to be sure, his grip almost too tight it could hurt.

"Speak." She heard him barely whisper the one word.

"What would you like me to say?"

For the first time, he brought himself up to a full sitting position. Something about this man was…familiar. She had no time to think what made him so; for his next word pinned her to her seat and knocked all breath out of her.

"Evelyn," He turned his face toward the sunlight.

"Carl?" She thought she would never see his face again. For so long she had searched for him and nothing had turned up. For so long she had thought of him waking, sleeping. Living? She could not believe it; yet there he was, his sunken eyes staring into hers. The planes of his face, although bristly with unkempt hair, were before her. She could not deny it. A hint of a smile played upon his lips. Oh, the anguish and joy of seeing him before her eyes.

"Carl," she said his name again thinking that saying his name over and over again would wake her from this dream. No, this was reality.

"Evelyn."

His speaking her name melted her heart. Her head fell into his lap and stayed in its resting place. He was here…with her. How could this be? All this time…he was right under her nose. How could she have not seen it?

He draped his arm over her limp form and slid his hand up and down her back in a rhythmic soothing manner. She did not want to leave this place. She had finally found…home.

"Carl?"

"Mmm."

"I have so many questions to ask you."

"Then ask them one by one."

Her flutterings ceased. He had calmed the storm inside her with only a few of his words. She realized he had no more crutches. "What happened to your leg?"

"After a month of living here with John, he paid the doctor to give me a prosthetic leg. I have no more need of crutches."

"Oh, that is wonderful. How long did it take you to walk with your new leg?"

"I would say I had to practice a week before I was fully accustomed to walking with it."

"I…I do not know what to say. Oh, forgive me for crying in front of…"

"I missed your tears."

She could not control the flow anymore. She let open the floodgates which had been kept shut for so long. Her body, racked with pain, ache, and macabre joy, moulded into his. "I tried to find you. For months I searched, and I could not find you. You were here all along. I thought I had lost you. Why had you never come to find me?"

"I am sorry, my love. I…There is so much to tell."

"Tell me."

"That morning when I went to work, I was thinking about you, about the love we had finally rekindled. My body was burning to be back home with you, but I had duties to perform at the job. So I went. I think I was…no, no, no that's not right. I believe I was putting a file into the cabinet. I looked up and saw…it. I never knew what consequences it would play in my future. Then I saw it happen, the explosion. I saw the factory's windows shatter in an instant before I ducked down to protect myself from the glass that I knew in less than a second would fly my way. I was too late. A few pieces of glass cut my right eye. My left eye was saved. The pain was excruciating. I could barely hold on to a thread of reason and logic. The pain screamed louder and louder in my ears. I held my hand to my eye; and when I pulled it away, I could see the blood seeping onto it, colouring it. My sudden instinct was to go to the hospital. No sooner had I escaped the wreckage of the office that I saw some people screaming and crying on the streets. The ringing grew louder in my ears. I tried to find my way to a hospital, but nothing looked the same. I thought I would never find my way through that hell, but by following a medical team, I finally reached the hospital. I sat on a chair and stared at the chaos before me."

The doctor had told the truth. He had seen Carl.

"I sat there in my own world, as if I were separated from this one on the other side of a sheet of glass. I looked around with the one good eye I had. I saw that there were so many more ahead of me who were in desperate need of medical attention. Guts were spilling out, others had serious burns—my injuries were nothing compared to the masses of others who were dying. My eyesight I knew had already…died. So I decided to leave to find you at our home."

That explains why he left.

"I stumbled through the streets, the images surrounding me being imprinted upon my mind. I found our home or what I think was our home…in shambles. No one was around; Death stung in the air. I fell to my knees, hardly being able to breathe; for I thought…I had lost you, that you had died in the rubble. I wanted to forget what I saw so I left Richmond in the distance, behind my back. I walked and walked; the pain in my eyes was almost nothing compared to the pain that throbbed in my soul. Your loss was all that was on my mind. The next days were…a blur. I do not remember much. All I remember is darkness, loneliness, silence. Even though the whole world around me teemed with activity, I heard nothing, saw nothing. John found me somehow. I cannot even remember how he found me, but he did. He asked the town doctor to patch my eye and overlook its healing. Thank God, I can still see with my left eye to see your beautiful face. Oh, that face that I have wanted to touch over and over again, to hold. These past few months, I have been in solitude, in slumber not wanting to be approached by another human being except John. My nightmares have become my companions. My mind has been continually plagued with scenes from the war, the explosion. They are my constant demons. It has almost become unbearable until now. Just now when I heard your voice, your intonation, I thought to myself how ludicrous it was, that my mind was playing tricks; but it wasn't. You are real, you are here. You have brought me into the light again. I am never letting you go."

All the wonderings, all the mysteries concerning Carl had come together, piecing themselves in Evelyn's mind. Everything made sense! How she had been foolish! He had been here all along. He was here now.

"Let me take a good look at you," he said, moving her face directly in front of his. He wiped away her tears with his smooth thumb, gently kissing her upon her forehead, nose, cheeks, and finally her mouth. "We have each other again."

"Yes, we do." The sense of joy that now welled up in her chest was overpowering, the sense of guilt overbearing. What was she to do? She was now married and betrothed to two very different men. She loved them both in unique ways. One moment her thoughts settled upon Carl and the next upon Gerald. She was torn. Carl knew nothing about Gerald. What was she to tell him? That she had given up trying to find him and found comfort in the arms of another man?! Not now, did she want to taint one of the happiest moments of her life with a scandal such as this. She would tell him…soon. It would be the hardest thing she would ever have to do, break his heart; but she needed to tell him the truth. He had to trust her. Her heart was his. He would trust or so she hoped.

"Carl?"

"Yes?"

"I…I am so happy to have you again in my arms after so long."

He smiled, its warmth as hot as the sun. "Do you think I may have a cookie? I loved the ones you baked before."

"Of course. Wait! John never mentioned who baked them."

"No, he only said it came from a good friend of his who had a heart of gold. He was right."

She reached into the basket and pulled out a cookie. She inched the cookie closer and closer to his lips until he could not stand the distance any longer. Piece by piece she fed him. Once he had chewed the last piece, he drew her head to his and swooped down to give a kiss which grew in intensity and passion. This kiss was not one she was afraid of. No, she was hungry for more. This kiss was the one in which she felt free. There were no boundaries to bar her from happiness.

"I love you, Evelyn."

"Yes, I know you do."

The old know what they want; the young are sad and bewildered.
Logan Pearsall Smith
Last Words (1933)

Chapter 26

She remained in Carl's company all afternoon. How could she not? There was so much to say without saying a word. They sat under the bench for hours reminiscing of the day they met, their journey of love together. They walked around the property and down the adjoining road. Daylight turned to twilight, the stars twinkled brighter until the whole sky was shrouded in melted silver night. Eventually, they spied someone coming down the lane. Of course, John! They drifted toward the front of the house arm in arm, her temple resting upon his arm.

"John," Evelyn called out.

"Evelyn? You're still here." He stopped short when he saw the both of them connected in such an...intimate way. "What is going on?"

She descended from the rickety porch and touched John's arm. "John...meet my husband Carl."

His jaw instantly dropped at the unexpected news.

"Shall we have some tea?" She tried to lead his stiff body up the stairs and into the house.

He nodded.

Once she had settled both men upon some comfortable seating, she relayed to John the whole story of the misunderstandings which had infiltrated their entire lives in the course of the past few months.

"I can hardly believe it!"

"That is what I said to myself when I first heard her delicate voice. Now she is here with me." Carl reached his hand out to Evelyn. She kneeled upon the floor in front of him and brushed her thumb against his gruff cheek. He really must not have had a full grasp of his senses to have let himself forsake his cleanly habits.

"I believe, gentlemen, that I really must leave to go to my home. It is getting late."

"Evelyn, where is your home? I mean…of course, you must have had some place in which to live. Must you really leave me tonight? I just found you."

"I regret that…I must. I live with a friend with whom I work. She'll be wondering where I am."

"You work? Where?"

"I will tell you another time."

She kissed the top of his hand as he in turn kissed her hands over and over again. She pulled them from his grasp with some difficulty and bid John goodnight.

"Here let me see you to the door." John opened the front door and stepped out with her onto the porch.

"John, I know this is a lot to take in. I have told you recently that I am engaged to…another man. I ask you do not tell Carl a thing about the situation."

"But…"

"Please, I will tell him myself; but I need to think…about this. Do you promise?"

"I promise."

"Good, please, take care of him, goodnight."

"Goodnight." John for the most part of the evening had become mute which was the strangest thing; for he was normally the one who could not keep quiet in company. She didn't blame him for having been made silent through the fantastic truths which had been told this night. On the way home, she could not utter a word herself.

What am I going to do? Carl doesn't know about Gerald. Now Gerald doesn't know about Carl. I am in such a mess. What way out is there?

Throughout the chaos, one thought stood out. She was Carl's wife. They had been apart for so long. She needed to tell Carl of her deeds and hope he would forgive her; and Gerald…she did not want to let him go. Her heart pulled in both directions threatening to rip her body, mind, and soul apart.

When she arrived home, all the lights were out. She struggled to make up her mind whether she should go to Gerald; for she had told him so in the note. He would have to do without her appearance. She needed to think, to mend. She settled into bed, trying to row away from the storm brewing in her mind.

***

Violent shaking awoke her from her few hours of slumber. For most of the night, her eyes had remained wide open and her mind more awake than ever.

"Evelyn! Where were you last night? I was starting to worry something had happened to you. I would have fetched the police if I did not see you in your bed this morning."

"Betsie, I'm all right."

"Come now to the kitchen table and tell me exactly what happened to have made you come so late last night."

"All right. I'm coming." She sat down upon her chair, feeling that she was now at a mock police station being inquired about her involvement in some crime.

"What happened?"

"Betsie, I found…him."

"What are you talking about? Found whom?"

"I found Carl."

Her mouth was open for a full minute before she could utter one word."What?"

"Yes."

"Where?"

"I found him at John's place."

"But I thought you were going to help some man who…Oh." Her eyes brightened at the enlightening facts; and her lips moved incessantly, but no words came out. "Really? All this time?"

Evelyn nodded.

"How could that be?"

"Before the explosion, when he returned home from the war, Carl was already suffering from…trauma. It must be that the explosion augmented the fragility of his mind to a higher degree. He thought he had lost me. He passed by our old home to see it in ruin. He believed that…there was no hope for him to live a life of happiness. So he stayed in his own shadow never venturing to turn his face toward the sun. He has suffered so much."

Betsie's hand covered Evelyn's. "What are you going to do? Your husband is still alive, but…you are to marry Gerald. Does Gerald know?"

"No, I was supposed to see him last night, but I arrived late. I could not bring myself to see him. I have to make a decision. I need time to think."

"Of course. I'll be at the hospital the whole day."

"All right."

Once Betsie had left, she meandered to her mirroir and stared at herself. Who was she, really, without either men? Yes, both of them had helped her to become better in different ways. Without them, she was a woman who had changed so much in the span of a few months. She had found good friends who would be her guides throughout her life. She had lost love and then had found it again. She had become more confident in more ways than she could have ever imagined. Hope had been restored. She was now a woman who had faith in something greater than herself. She was herself.

Carl had changed so much and…so little. He was still his gentle self and his strength seemed to have been sapped. His heart had changed. It had become more soft and caring.

Gerald—she had not known for very long but felt as if she had known him all her life. He was her leader, a man in every sense of the word. He stayed true to his convictions and word even during the hardest of times, but he was living a lie.

Both men had captured her heart and set their claims upon it. They both loved her. They both wanted her. Whom could she give the most of her love? Whom could she make the happiest? With whom did she want to spend the rest of her life? With whom could she open her heart to the fullest and let see the deepest part of her soul? Carl or Gerald—Carl would be by her side and revel in the delights she offered; and he in return would show true affection, affection in which she could rest assuredly. Gerald would lead her, comfort her and praise her for her accomplishments; and he would join her in every venture she would want to pursue.

*Let no guilty man escape, if it can be avoided...No
personal considerations should stand in the way of
performing a public duty.*
Ulysses S. Grant
Indorsement of a letter relating to the Whiskey Ring, 29 July 1875

Chapter 27

Evelyn journeyed to the country where her husband had lived all this time several days after his reappearance. She was ready to tell him the truth, tell him what she had done during the time they were without one another. She had demanded him to tell her where he had been. Now she knew it was her turn to show him the respect he was due. He was her husband and nothing could change that.

She found him upon the sofa reading poetry by Robert Burns. The smile on his face when she stepped into the room augmented the guilt preying upon her with a thirsty vengeance. It had been a long time since she saw him this happy; yet her news would shatter whatever happiness he had left.

"Come sit, please." He gestured to the space beside him. He put his arm around her and whispered into her ear. "Nothing in this world makes me happier than you do."

"How have you been?" She stroked some long stray hairs behind his ear.

"Sometimes I sit here, and I cannot help it. My mind—it wanders back, back to blood, death. I even hear the guns rocketing in my ears. I try to block out the sound, but it's no use. Only thoughts of you are what save me from insanity, knowing you are safe and alive; and seeing you drives the horrible memories away for a little while longer."

"I cannot imagine what you must be going through. I'm so sorry that you are the one to carry this burden."

"Please don't be. I have you." He gazed down at her lips and back up to her green eyes. He swept her lips with his and pressed on. His gentle touch activated all her nerves to tingle, and she melted. He brought his head closer to hers and drank in her smell as he released her. "I have missed you."

"Carl, do you not wonder what has happened to me over these past few months?"

"Yes, I do. I'm sorry I never asked. I believe I have become so caught up with the thought of having you again that I have forgotten all else. Please, tell me your story."

"Well," she folded her hands upon her lap. "I received a third-degree burn from the fire that overtook our home after the explosion. Someone pulled me out from the rubble. I don't know whom. I would have liked to thank the man or woman who did so." She lifted her sleeve for him to see the jagged scars. "I had to stay in the hospital for several weeks until I fully recovered.

"Once I did, I traveled to Dartmouth to visit my mother to see if she had been hurt. She was in full health so I returned to try to find you. I searched every medical centre on the Dartmouth side first and then the Richmond side afterward. During this search, I started to work at the hospital where I had received my operation. They were looking for volunteers. I thought that since I had received some medical training before I married you I could be of some help. That is where I became more acquainted with Betsie, another nurse on staff. We became very good friends to the point that we found an apartment and moved in together. Meanwhile, I searched everywhere for you. You were never listed as dead but missing. I could not find you. That hospital that you said you went to—well, I talked to one of the doctors. He said that he thought he had seen you, but he couldn't be too sure; so I wasn't sure that that was any evidence at all. I gave up searching for you in February."

Carl sat there stoically, the corners of his lips drooping. She wanted him to scream at her, say what a horrible wife she had been. Instead he looked upon her with compassion.

"I don't know what to say, Carl. I let you down. I gave up. Many times my conscience pounded me with ready guilt, but I ignored it. I thought I needed to move on with my life. Then Gerald...the doctor who had operated on my arm, Doctor MacCrae—he started to take a fancy to me. My heart aching for some sort of love became vulnerable to his advances. Mind you, he was never indecent, and he always treated me well. He asked to court me a few months ago. I consented, and a week ago...he asked to marry me."

"What did you say?" Hesitation to listen to her answer was written all over his face.

"I said yes."

He hung his head in defeat.

"Please say something."

"I...cannot."

"Carl, please."

"I suppose I cannot hold against you the fact that you gave up on me. Blast, I gave up on you immediately. I should have been the one searching for you, but I did not. I only assumed you were dead, and I wallowed in self-pity all these months. But...I would never have thought that you would take comfort in the arms of another man so soon."

"Carl, I..."

"What are you going to do now?"

"What do you mean?"

"I mean exactly what I asked you."

She thought he would be stomping all over the room, shaking his fist at her, but he didn't. She expected him to fight for her, but no, he gave her the freedom to choose. She did not want any of it. She had already made her choice.

She fell to her knees in front of him. She raised his chin with her fingers. "Please look at me."

His eyes darted left and right before they tentatively settled upon hers.

"Before you left me that fateful morning, December 6, do you remember the way you kissed me in our bed, the looks you bestowed my way? I would like to know what changed you? You had finally returned to the spirit of the man I once knew."

He answered, "When we would dine together, I would watch you when you didn't notice. I saw that you thought you were leading an utterly miserable life with me. I thought to myself that if I wanted to make you happy, if I wanted to spend the rest of my life with you in full assurance that you would not leave me, I had to try. That morning I not only tried but loved, truly loved."

She nodded. "I felt that love. I choose you. I love you. I am not going to leave you for someone else. You are my husband. You are all I will and ever want."

His eyes started to glisten with tears. He cradled the sides of her head in his hands. "Please don't leave me."

"I won't."

"What will you tell…what was the gentleman's name? Gerald?"

"Yes, Gerald is his name. To tell you the truth, I have no idea what I'm going to say to him, but I do owe him an explanation."

"Will you stay here for the night?"

He was her husband after all. There was nothing wrong with being with him in this intimate way. She was sure Betsie would conclude why she was missing that night.

"Yes, I will stay."

He led her to his room and started to unbutton her outer clothing. "I just want to hold you tonight," he whispered lightly in her ear, his breath sending slivers of shivers down her exposed neck.

She didn't care what happened. She was with him again. For a long time she had missed this kind of love he was giving her. He slipped into bed and bid her come by his side. She slid in and moulded into his hunched form. He put his arm over her and held her close. In each other's company, they both slept in peace that night. No nightmares invaded her mind, and she surmised that it was the same for him. He had fallen asleep a very short while after they had crawled into bed. His breathing moved in a rhythmic pattern. His heartbeat throbbed like a river. She was home in his arms; she was safe. How could she have ever let him go? How could she have ever lost hope that she would find him again?

***

The next morning, a myriad of country birds chanted their songs. Their symphony was so loud yet hauntingly soothing. A smile drew upon Evelyn's face; she felt Carl's arm around her warm body and hugged it tighter around her. She never wanted to be let go. She stayed under his umbrella for ten minutes before he was awakened by the same noise.

"Evelyn?"

"Yes."

"You're still here."

"I am still here."

They put on their clothing and went into the dining room to eat. However, no breakfast was ready to eat. So Evelyn rummaged through the kitchen and found oatmeal.

"I need to go back and…talk to Gerald, talk to Betsie."

"Yes, you must. I am not sure if you have thought of this or not, but well, I thought…let me say it this way. I found a quaint cottage for sale in this town yesterday, only five minutes walking distance from here. Perhaps we could see it together and figure whether we can afford it with the salary you have received these months."

"I would love to see it. Perhaps we could go see it tomorrow."

"Of course, until tomorrow then."

She left after they had breakfast and returned to her apartment. "Betsie."

"Yes?" She came out of the kitchen with a towel in her hands. "Well?"

"I need to speak to Gerald."

"What have you chosen to do, Evelyn?"

"I love Carl, and I am married to him. I would never leave him now, not even for Gerald."

"Good."

"I need to go."

"I know. Go. I believe Gerald is home. I didn't see him at the hospital this morning."

"All right. I'll be back." She sighed. "Please pray a little word for me."

"I will." Fear was in Betsie's eyes.

Evelyn left immediately, bringing the ring Gerald had given her.

After one knock, Gerald answered the door. He drew her in with his one arm and planted a passionate kiss upon her trembling lips. She tried to fight against him: but his touch was too strong, and she found herself succumbing. She finally stomped on his foot.

"Aaah!" He cried, twisting and stomping his foot upon the wooden floor to fight the pain. "Evelyn, have you gone mad?"

"No."

"Why the…?"

"Gerald, I found Carl."

His eyes grew wide, and his lips parted open. "What?"

"Is Clyde here?"

"No, he's out playing with some chaps."

"The man John has been taking care of all along—that was Carl the whole time. I found him. That means I'm still married to him." She procured the ring from her clasped fist. "I cannot be your wife."

He took the ring from her, devastation stamped upon his face. "Can you tell me by looking me in the eyes that he has not forced you to choose him?"

"Yes, I have chosen him."

"Why?"

"Gerald, he is my husband, and I love him. When I thought I had lost him…I thought my world had ended. Then you came along and brought me to the surface. I…I thank you for doing so."

"You played me? Was your love for me only one based upon gratitude?" He ran his fingers through his hair in frustration.

"How dare you say that? I did love you with all my heart. You were the key to my locket, the calm to my storm. I…I still love you. But…"

"How on earth can you love me…and him at the same time?"

"I do not know."

"Carl is just a ghost in the past. I am here, now. I want you for my own. Please, Evelyn, I am begging you to reconsider your choice."

She took a step near him and kissed him on the cheek. "I cannot." She looked up into his beautiful eyes and pleaded with him to understand her choice. This—a fight for her heart—is what she had wanted from Carl in the first place. Here Gerald was fulfilling that desire. Once done, once felt—it was extremely overbearing. Freedom or chains? Now she understood the immensity of Carl's love.

Suddenly, furious knocking banged upon Gerald's front door.

"Yes, I'm coming."

"Provincial Police, is there a Doctor Gerald MacCrae residing here?"

"Yes, I am he."

"You are under arrest for the betrayal of this country the Crown Dominion of Canada under His Majesty Henry V."

Gerald looked to Evelyn in defeat. The extreme pain clouding his eyes cut her to the heart. She moved not a step. He turned back his head to the authorities.

"Take me." He willingly offered his yet unbound hands.

"Uh-hum, well, carry on men."

"Wait!" Evelyn cried. "Don't take him. Please!"

They heeded not her pleading.

"Goodbye, Evelyn."

The authorities handcuffed him and shoved him out the door.

"I love you." She did not know if her words touched his ears. In a blink of an eye, he was gone.

She had never told a soul the secret he had entrusted to her keep. Someone else must have known for the authorities to find out. But whom?

Her heart ached as she had seen her love being dragged away to who knew what. She knew she would have no chance of procuring a visit with him. She hoped one day she could right the wrong she had done toward him. Yet in a way, she was relieved. She had no choice but to be with Carl. Gerald's presence was overwhelming for her supple heart. He was gone forever. She would never see his strong jawline or the hard flint of bronze metal in his eyes. Those lips that she had kissed so many times had now vanished. She would not be tempted to run back into his arms if anything were ever to go amiss with Carl and her.

All there was to do was to move on with her life with Carl next to her side. She promised never to forget the love she had for Gerald, the love that had saved her life when she thought it had ended.

Of all that is most beauteous—imaged there
In happier beauty; more pellucid streams,
An ampler ether, a diviner air,
And fields invested with puerperal gleams.
William Wordsworth
Lasodamia (1815), 1.103

Chapter 28

She awoke in the middle of the night to the piercing shouts of Gerald calling out to her. The toes of his shoes, scuffed as they scratched the wooden floors of his house, ripped up the floorboards leaving gaping holes over which Evelyn tried to pass but could not. Once they dragged him through the door, the door banged shut leaving her in the darkness alone. Or so she thought.

"Evelyn," Carl was calling out to her softly and then more and more strongly. "Evelyn."

She awoke from her nightmare. She turned over from her tummy to stare into her husband's eyes.

"Carl? What…How did you get here?"

He sat upon the edge of her bed and held her hand. "John brought me here to your apartment. I must say you have done a beautiful job of making it a home. It reminds me of our old house."

She yawned and raised her arms above her head, her features crinkling into a cute pout. "Betsie was kind enough to give me full leash on how to decorate our apartment. She says she has no decorative sense in the least."

"She was wise in letting you take charge. I was wondering how you would manage to have say over her if she did not agree with your ideas. She seems to be a very headstrong woman."

"Yes, she is. How did you know?"

"Observation, my dear," he tapped his finger upon his temple. The nerdy quirk made her chuckle. "I arrived and Betsie let me in. She was very happy to see me. She rushed me in and pointed to your bedroom door."

"I'm so happy to see you."

"You were tossing and turning as I entered your room. Are you all right? Are you ill?"

"Yes, I mean no. I mean I am all right, and I'm not ill."

He helped her up to a sitting position and fingered the neckline of her nightgown. "Would you like to see the house today?"

"Yes, I would like that very much."

***

They traveled down the country lane, glad the sun did not shine its full force upon them. The clouds had graciously protected them the whole journey to the country.

"What happened yesterday when you told Gerald about us?"

"He was…incredibly upset. He wanted to know if you had forced me to make the decision I had already made on my own. I insisted you had played the honourable part in giving me a choice. He tried fighting for me, pleaded with me to reconsider. I told him I would not, that I could not. The funny thing is is that when you asked me what I was going to do, you were giving me the freedom to make up my own mind. I must admit I was angry with you because I wanted you to fight for me; but when Gerald did what I had desired you to do, I was hurt. I realized that your love is irrefutable. Yes…"

"What? What is it?"

She wasn't sure if she should tell her husband who Gerald really was. What would he think of her, of him? Although Gerald was a spy, he was a good man who practiced many good virtues. She did not want to give Carl information of him that would make Carl gloat in his victory even more. No, Carl was nothing like that. He would take the news like a gentleman. He would pay his rival respect.

"The police came to take him away."

"Why on earth did they take him away?"

"He was a German spy."

"Good Lord, Evelyn, what did you get yourself mixed into?"

"He told me the night he asked to marry me. I begged him not to bring the last bit of information to his contact, but he said he must. You see, he was doing it for his family. He was trying to garner enough money for all of his siblings to be able to attain higher learning so that they would be able to rise from their poverty. They live in Scotland. Now, their brother…he cannot help them."

"The things people will do for those they love. I do feel sorry for his family."

"They'll probably remain in poverty unless some miracle happens."

"Yes, who was this…contact?"

"His contact was Casby."

"Casby?"

"Yes, do you remember that time before the explosion when I ran into your office asking you to return to the house because I had seen a strange man enter the house late at night?"

"Yes?"

"That was Gerald who had come to the house to see Casby. Back then they were already in league with one another."

"That explains everything."

There was no need to tell him that Casby had followed her one night and scared her silly out of her wits. She did not want him to be concerned about the matter more than he already was.

"I believe I shall never see him again."

"That makes you sad, I see. You still love him."

"Carl, I…it is in different ways that I love him. He has given so much to me. When I thought you were gone, he gave me hope for a still bright future. He was a friend to me who even encouraged me to find you. I am the one who gave up. I am the one who did you wrong."

"I understand."

"You don't hate me?"

"Evelyn, I could never hate you. Yes, you have hurt me through your actions, but your renewed love for me covers the wounds and heals them." He closed the gap between their lips. The softness of his lips wiped away all her tears. His hunger for her lips was more than she could take. She had expected him to be repulsed by her, but, no, he wanted her for himself.

They rounded a bend in the road to view a quaint cottage. It had a sturdy dark blue roof. The house's white paint needed retouching. The gardens had been abandoned for quite some time, but there was promise for a new life in this house. One of the neighbours came by and opened the door with a rusty key. The door swung open and closed sleekly. Although the house was covered in dust, Evelyn could visualize the cleanliness that could brighten this home a hundred times more. At the entrance of the home, there was a staircase in front of them to the left. It was embellished by a beautiful barricade which had been hand-carved. The room to the left was the living room, a smallish space, although there would be enough room for a sofa, a love seat, and a small coffee table. There was a large window overlooking the meadow in the yard. Adjoining the living room were the facilities, a tub to bathe in. They crossed back into the entrance and into the other side of the house. There was a good size dining room, big enough to have a dinner table that would seat eight people. Separating the dining area from the kitchen was one small step. The kitchen sported one large window. The cabinets were a rustic pine. They looked at all the other rooms, three bedrooms, a pantry, and a sitting room. The whole house oozed charm and simplicity.

"What do you think?" Carl asked.

"I adore it."

"You haven't said much the whole time."

"That is because I've been picturing in my mind what I would like to do with this place.There is so much potential here. Now it is time to think of the price."

"Let us go to the management office in town and ask how much they want for it."

They strolled into the village and asked a few people where the office was located. Once they entered the office, they approached the front desk.

"Excuse me, we would like to buy a house located on the outskirts of this village."

The clerk, a young man with a stubby nose upholding his drooping glasses quite adequately, reached underneath his desk to bring out a map. "Which house are you interested in?"

Carl studied the map for a moment. His finger hovered over the map until he found the exact spot. "Here it is!"

"Ah, yes, let me just take a look at the records."

He found the sheet and then rambled off the history of the house and anything of significance. He finally announced the price.

"I believe I have enough money saved up to put a down payment upon the house. I will have to recheck my funds, but I think it is possible," said Evelyn in earnest.

"Wonderful." Carl squeezed her hand.

After they had left the office, Evelyn commenced to tell Carl about Clyde whom she regretted forgetting for the past two days. For the past two days, Gerald was gone. How was Clyde faring? Where was he?

"Carl, throughout the time we were separated I met a boy who had been orphaned because of the explosion." She continued to tell him of all of Clyde's excellent qualities and how much she loved him. "I was planning to adopt him when…Gerald and I were to be married."

"Go on."

"Now I have you. I believe you would love him just as much as I do. Would you like to meet him?"

"Yes, I would."

***

They made their way to the hospital. She thought the hospital would be the most likely place to find him since Gerald had been taken away. Everyone greeted her when she arrived. She introduced Carl to several people. They all nodded their understanding of the situation. They were glad she had found him again. Many people knew of her loss, and now many would know of her gain. No one had known of her secret courtship with Gerald. Her reputation had remained intact.

She pointed to the popularly overlooked door. "He resides in there." She opened the door and entered the room. "Clyde."

"Evelyn!" He jumped up from his seat and hugged Evelyn fiercely. "It is so good to see you again." He then looked behind her to Carl. "Hello." He stood in front of Carl.

Carl bent down at Clyde's eye level. "Hello. I am Carl, Evelyn's husband. You must be Clyde. I have heard so much about you."

Chapter 29

"You found him!" Clyde said in amazement. "That is wonderful! It is so good to finally meet you, sir. I have heard many things about you in return."

"I hear you are good with numbers. Would you like to show me?" Carl asked.

Clyde scuttled over to his bed and waved Carl over. Carl sat beside him as he watched Clyde work at his arithmetic.

"Evelyn wasn't exaggerating at how good you really are!"

Carl and Clyde—they bantered back and forth, both so much at ease with each other. Clyde was fascinated with him.

"What do you do, sir?"

"Well, before the explosion, I was an editor for the *Halifax Gazette*. In trade, I'm a writer. One day, I plan to write a history of the recent events which have engulfed our city."

"Really? That would be jolly good. I would be the first one to read it, I promise."

"I'll remember that. I would very much appreciate another's opinion before I submit it to the hungry wolves."

"Do you mind my asking, sir, what the war was like when you were a part of it?"

A part of it, how true. The war would always be a part of him no matter how hard he tried to release it from his memory. He would have to embrace the trials he had gone through and not fight them. The way Clyde had asked with his blue eyes larger and deeper than the original well from which he drew his extreme sincerity caused Carl to relay the exact truth to his questioner and himself.

"No, I do not mind at all."

While Carl talked about the different tactics which he and his band of men had used to capture German trenches and about the victories that the Canadians had claimed, Clyde's face was fully enraptured with what he was listening to. "Is it hard for you to say these things, sir, to talk about your experiences?"

"Yes, it is, but life is hard. One cannot change this fact. One can work with it."

"I understand. Evelyn, I was wondering, what happened to Doctor MacCrae? I haven't seen him for two days."

"You weren't at his home two days ago when…he left?"

"No, what do you mean? I was out playing with some of the lads. When I was done, I returned to the house, but no one was there. I decided to come here and wait for him. I haven't seen him since."

Both Carl and Evelyn looked at each other, both knowing of Gerald's tragic fate.

Evelyn spoke, "Clyde, I am so sorry you have been given cause to worry about the well being of another and yourself. You should not have had to go through this hardship. Gerald has been taken away to prison. I am truly sorry I did not seek you out sooner than I did."

"Prison? What for? It's not because of me is it?"

"No, Clyde, it is not you. Doctor MacCrae was…a German spy. He only did this to help provide for his family in Scotland."

Clyde was stunned into silence. His good friend—he would never see him again. Clyde had heard rumours of German spies actively residing in Halifax, but he never believed it until now. "I cannot believe it."

"It is true. I was there myself when they took him away."

Clyde looked to Carl. "Evelyn and Doctor MacCrae were good friends."

"Yes, I know that."

"He was so good to me."

"He loved you, Clyde. Do not doubt it." Evelyn fervently whispered.

"I don't. Do you think I could have a few moments to myself to pray for Doctor MacCrae?"

"Of course," Evelyn replied. "We will return in about half an hour."

***

Evelyn led Carl to the Public Gardens. She refrained from bringing him to the bench near Egg Pond she had always shared with Gerald. Instead she steered clear of that very private area of her life and led him to the Upper Bridge.

"What are you thinking, Carl?"

"He is an extraordinary boy! He truly is! I see why you love him so much. I see why you want to adopt him."

She clutched his hands tightly, excitement building inside. She hoped he would say yes.

"What would you like?" Carl put his arms around her shoulders.

"I…would like to adopt him."

"Are you sure?"

"Yes."

"All right then. I believe we shall have a son."

"Ahh!" She screamed in delight, jumping to hold onto Carl. "Thank you, thank you, thank you. Oh, I love you."

"Now, I cannot promise you everything will go smoothly. We'll probably have to do some paperwork and deal with some authorities, but…I think we'll make it through."

"Oh, I am so happy. I can barely speak."

They held unto each other like so for the rest of the time. Evelyn could not wait any longer to tell Clyde what they wanted to do. She knew that Clyde would love to live with them He was a young boy who needed parents, who needed love. Both Carl and she were more than willing to give this.

So excited was she that she had to restrain herself not to run back into his room and shout out the news at the top of her lungs. She knocked on his door softly.

"Come in!"

"Hello, Clyde. Carl and I…we have something to tell you."

"What is it?"

"We want to adopt you. We would like you to be our son."

"You would be my father and mother?"

"Yes, if that is what you would like."

"Really? You would do that for me?"

"I would do anything for you."

He ran up to both of them and tried to wrap his small arms around them. "I would love to come live with you." All of a sudden a shyness stole over him. "Does that mean I may call you father and mother?"

"Yes," Evelyn said with tears streaming down her cheeks.

"You will come live with us in the countryside and go to school there. We will feed you and clothe you. We will care for you," Carl announced. "But we must first file you for adoption. Once we have done that and they have accepted, you will come with us."

"It's a dream come true," Clyde effused.

***

A few weeks later, all the paperwork and interviews with the board in charge of finding homes for orphaned children had been done, and Clyde had become their son. They had bought the quaint cottage in the country and were now doing minor repairs to the dilapidated house. Clyde enjoyed helping Carl with renovations while Evelyn painted the porch white in the hot afternoon sun. They had become a strong family. Loving each other was first and foremost in their minds. One day, as Evelyn stroked her paintbrush up and down one of the porch posts, she thought of her mother and how she had not seen her in a long while.

During supper, she asked Carl, "Do you think we could go visit my mother tomorrow? I have written to her of our house purchase, and she knows about Clyde. She would very much like to meet him. Do you think we could take a break from our house duties and make a special trip into Dartmouth?"

"I think we can do that. What do you say Clyde? Would you like to see your grandmother?"

"Yes, I would very much like to." Clyde stuffed a spoonful of peas in his mouth. "I never knew my original grandparents. I think this grandmother is very special."

All retired after supper to get a goodnight's sleep.

***

Early the next morning, everyone prepared themselves for a long journey. They dressed, brought some fare for transportation, doffed their hats, and strolled outside. As they rumbled in the coach from the countryside to the city, Clyde was having a hard time sitting silently in his seat. He looked out the window and pointed at all the wonders presenting themselves outside. He chattered on about how he was excited to go back to school and learn other subjects than the mathematics. He had already met some boys and girls his age in the town nearby.

Carl also relayed to Evelyn the requirements and duties of his job as a writer to the local town newspaper. On the side, he had started to write his nonfiction manuscript. She listened, enraptured by his passion for writing. Once they arrived in Richmond, they walked to the ferry. There they saw John, tying knots in his ropes.

"John!"

"Good morning, neighbours! Come on in. We'll be leaving in ten minutes. Tell me how it's going at Meadow Stream."

Meadow Stream was the name they had given their house. There was a large meadow situated in the front of the house with a stream snaking through it.

"We're off to see my grandmother!" shouted Clyde in excitement.

"Well, now. I hope you have a grand time."

The whole trip to Dartmouth was spent with the Richardson family conversing with John. John informed them his brother was doing well and he was going to visit him in two days.

"I insist you come, as well," John said.

"We will if only you'll let me help you cook," Evelyn replied.

"All right. You always know how to weaken my resolve."

"Of course."

Once they reached the other shore, they bid John farewell and walked to Mrs. Moore's home. They opened the gate. Clyde's mouth dropped open as he took in the breathtaking sight of the beautiful gardens blooming graciously under Mr. Thompson's hand. They knocked upon the door and waited for the maid to answer.

"Oh, hello, Mr. and Mrs. Richardson, Master Richardson, come in." She led them into the parlour where there sat Mrs. Moore.

She turned from her sunbath and gazed at the happy family standing before her. "Good morning, Evelyn, Carl," she hugged each one. "Clyde, my grandson, it is a pleasure to finally meet you."

"The pleasure is all mine, Grandmother."

"Oh, and he has such manners," remarked Mrs. Moore.

"We can thank his deceased parents for such good training," Evelyn responded.

"Come, shall we have some hot tea and hot cross buns?"

The whole visit was a splendid one. No ill words were said between mother and daughter, mother and son-in-law. Happiness reigned there that day.

***

On the way back, they passed by Evelyn's old apartment to check in on Betsie. However, she wasn't there. She was still working at the hospital.

"Carl, Clyde, go on back home without me. I would really like to see Betsie. I'll wait until she comes back. I'd like to visit with her for a little while. Once I'm done, I'll return home."

"Come on, Clyde. Shall we?" Carl nudged him toward the door.

"Goodbye, Mother, be careful when you come back."

"I will."

She placed a peck upon Clyde's head and kissed Carl fully on the lips. Evelyn made herself at home until Betsie arrived at five o'clock in the afternoon. She came into her apartment and skittered sideways when she saw Evelyn sitting on her sofa.

"Hello, Betsie." Evelyn rose from her seat and with arms wide open.

"Hello, Evelyn. It is good to see you. What…? I've been thinking about you these days. The apartment is a lot more empty with you gone, but now you have a family! Tell me about it."

So Evelyn indulged Betsie with tales of calm family life.

"I would love to have my own family one day."

"Do you not have Rupert?"

"Yes, I do, but he hasn't asked me anything yet. Maybe he never will."

"Do not be so quick to doom your future. He may ask at the most unexpected time."

"I'm sure you're right. Oh, I must tell you—how shall I say this? The hospital is auctioning off all of Gerald's things. His books, his microscope, desk, everything—it will all be auctioned off next Saturday. I thought you might want some of his things."

"Thank you for telling me. I don't believe I have room for…keepsakes."

More of Gerald's objects in her life? She wasn't so sure if she could handle the memories.

For all sad words of tongue or pen,
The saddest are these: "It might have been!"
John Greenleaf Whittier
Maud Mauller, 1.105

Chapter 30

Crowds pressing in and over each other like waves merging in current with one another threatened to suffocate the air she hastened to breathe. A large amount of the public had come to see the belongings of a spy who had been in their midst. A well-respected doctor who had brought healing to many through the skill of his hands and the knowledge of his mind—he was the talk of the day. Everywhere she turned she heard his name, Doctor MacCrae this...Doctor MacCrae that. So many untrue rumours were floating around about his being a lethal killer, his having been a high-ranking official in the German government. None of them were true, but they were in such manifold numbers that after a while it was hard not to believe these wild accusations were false. Evelyn steeled her mind against these accusations that the people delivered with death blows to her past love. She had come to see what they would auction off. She made her way through the mass until she found Betsie at the front near the table where all his belongings lay. The auctioneer made a signal to start the auction.

"All right, right here we have several medical books in pristine condition. Why don't we say fifty dollars? Fifty dollars?" He started to ramble off in the jargon which auctioneers employ so excellently. He started selling off the smaller items first, then the bookcase, the desk, and then…the microscope.

Her mind traveled to that time when he had first showed it to her, how he had let her peer through the wonderful machine, and how he had hovered over her. Even then his presence had sent shivers down her spine.

She battled for the microscope, the slides, and eyepieces that came with it against one of Gerald's coworkers. After it had gone on past her rival's patience, he threw his hands into the air. Automatically, Evelyn won the prize.

"Here's to the lucky lady, sold for one hundred dollars!"

The young man who held up the items as the auctioneer rattled off his words, wrapped it up in its packaging and gave it to her. She now held an exquisite black leather box. Other items went on sale until the last one finally made an appearance.

"Now ladies and gentlemen, here is a diamond ring surrounded by sapphires. A beauty isn't it? No one knows who this lady love was, but what a tragic ending there must have been to this unknown romance."

At the sight of it, her heart sank. She could not bear seeing it. She remembered the exact way he had put it upon her finger, and the way she had given it back to him. She picked up her only prize and left. She stepped out of the doors and didn't know where to go. She felt stranded. So instead she just sat upon an entrance bench and stared into the blue sky, trying to listen for a heartbeat. Listen. Listen for his heartbeat.

She couldn't tell how long she had been outside sitting, listening. Then Betsie strolled out.

"Evelyn?"

"Mmm."

"I need to talk to you." The stress in her voice bade Evelyn get up and follow her. Betsie led her to an eerily familiar spot.

"Do you remember this place?"

"Yes."

The grass upon which she had lowered herself, the bark of the tree that had ground her back—she didn't remember being here with Betsie before.

"Why do you ask? I have never come here with you before."

"No, we never have…with your knowing about it."

"Betsie, what are you saying?"

"I was there that night."

"What night?"

"The night you were here with a man named Casby. I heard everything he told you."

"What do you mean?"

"That night after I came back from my date with Rupert, I saw you come out of Gerald's home down the street. When Rupert and I approached the apartment, you weren't coming home. So I told him I had to follow you, and I did. Goodness, I was so afraid when I saw Casby grab you and pin you to the tree. I froze in place. Then I heard him talking to you about Gerald…the espionage work…everything."

"You knew, as well."

"Yes, I knew. Once he walked away, I ran back to our apartment before you arrived so that you wouldn't know I was there the whole time."

"Why are you telling me this now?"

"Evelyn, I'm the one who went to the police and reported Gerald and Casby. I said that if they could get Gerald, they would find the others who were involved."

"Why? Why did you do it?"

"Once you told me you had chosen Carl…I wanted to help you. So I told the police so that…you would never have to physically deal with Gerald again."

Evelyn felt the heat rising in her face. Betsie had no right to determine her future. However, her love for her friend cooled the rising fire, creating nothing but fading steam inside.

"Evelyn, please say something."

"Thank you for doing what you did. I know…you did what you thought was best for me. And yet…I don't know what…I cannot think."

"You asked me why I'm telling you this now."

"Yes?"

"I'm telling you this now because I received this in the mail."

She handed a dirty envelope to Evelyn. On it was marked *Evelyn Richardson* and the apartment's address. Her eyes caught the name of the sender,   Gerald.

"When did you receive this?"

"Yesterday, I had a feeling you would come to the auction today." She turned around and reached into her pocket. "I have something else for you." She pulled out the ring from the auction, Evelyn's engagement ring. "I bought it back for you. I thought you would want to have it."

Evelyn carefully grasped this treasure she had given up months ago. Now it had come back to her.

"Thank you."

"When they brought it out, I saw the expression on your face. I saw fear but I also saw want. That's why I got it back."

"Thank you. It must have cost you a lot." Tears welled in her eyes. "I must go back home."

***

Dusk was setting. She came home to laughter filling the yard. There was Carl teaching Clyde the techniques of baseball. Clyde was licking his lips and holding the baseball bat. His brows were furrowed, intent on concentrating at the task at hand. Carl was laughing his heart away. When he saw her elegant form approaching, he put down his gear, ran to her and picked her up in his arms and twirled her around.

This was all she needed. A family to love through the good and bad. They were here for her, and she was here for them.

"Carl, I'll be inside for a few moments, alone."

He quickly glanced at what she held in her hand, an envelope with Gerald's name upon it.

"Go on, in. We'll be out here for a little while yet, until the sun fully goes to sleep. Right Clyde?"

"Yes, father."

He looked at her with understanding. "Go."

She took her leave. She sat upon the sofa in the living room and moved her trembling fingers over the paper. She opened it with her letter opener. A yellowed paper rose from the depths of its covering. She took a deep breath and opened the letter to view its contents.

Dearest Evelyn,

How I long to see your face in this dank prison. These walls do not bind me from the freedom my love for you gives me. I know I was angry when you told me you wouldn't marry me because your husband had been found. Please know that it was wrong of me to be angry with you and with the circumstances Fate had dealt me.

I miss you, my love. The way your eyes sparkle and your smooth lips…Oh, these things haunt me throughout my days here. I love you. I always will, even in death. I am due for execution in a week. Just to read one written word from your hand would give me peace in my passing.

I know you are not the one who betrayed me. I have trusted you with my heart, with everything that was mine.

With all my love,
Gerald

He still viewed her honourably even though all the evidence pointed to her as the culprit. She took up a paper and pen and penned her own note to send to him immediately.

Dearest Gerald,

I received your letter. I thank you for the goodness with which you shower me. You still yet trust me with everything that is yours. They auctioned off all your belongings today. I bought back your microscope. Betsie—she bought back the ring you gave me.

I am truly sorry for everything wrong that has happened to you. I pray you would have a swift death, one of ease. I could not bear for you to hurt. I care for you even now. However, now that I have found Carl, I cannot love you in the way I had. It is not right for me to do so. I have pledged all I have to him, and that is the way it must remain. Thank you for the love you have shown me; I will never forget it. You are that hidden ray of sun that shines upon me each day.

> *Your dearest friend,*
> *Evelyn*

There it was. All the words she wanted to say to him, written on this piece of paper. She left immediately to post it, knowing it would bring him happiness during his last few moments on earth.

She returned home to watch Carl and Clyde play together, father and son. She was blessed by Providence. She had redeemed her past from the ashes.

After all, my erstwhile dear,
My no longer cherished,
Need we say it was not love,
Just because it perished?
Edna St. Vincent Millay
Passer Mortus Est.

EPILOGUE

"Mother!" A refined, older Clyde of twenty-two years waved to Evelyn just before he looked left and right down the street to cross it. His short blonde curls bounced lightly as he jogged toward her. "May we take a walk in the Commons before we leave town today? Father already said we could."

"Of course. It's been a long while since we have walked its peaceful paths."

He extended his crooked arm her way.

"And where is your father?"

"He should return shortly with little Clara, Robert, and Gerald. We were walking down the street past a candy shop. As soon as the children saw it, they begged Father to buy some candy. You know how Father is. He can hardly say no to them when they're all tugging on his trousers with little pouts on their sheepish faces."

"No, he can't. He has a good heart."

"He said we could go on before him. Shall we?"

"Yes."

She had not visited the Commons for many months. She always enjoyed the beauty blooming within its landscape whether it was the flowers unfurling their brilliant petals or the winter frost creating a brittle mosaic of crystals. One place to where she had not been for years was…that comely bench. Gerald—it had been ten years. Suddenly, memories of the past flooded her mind, and curiosity to see a past trysting place impelled her quickening feet to follow.

"Clyde, wait here, please. I'll return in ten minutes. There is something I must see."

"Are you all right, Mother?"

"Yes, yes, just…please."

"All right. I'll be right here. Do you mind if I take a few steps toward this handsome tree?"

"Clyde, how you drive me to desperation sometimes! Yes, plant your nose on it if you like."

"Really?"

"No! I'll be back."

The need to see the past ravaged her. Her brisk walk became a jog which then became a run. So crazed was she to see the bench. When she arrived, she was out of breath. She bent over slightly and stared at the grass beneath the toes of her boots. Hesitant to look, she squeezed her eyes shut then strained to tilt her chin up to face the reality, the curiosity. There it still was, the way she had always remembered it. Yet the smooth slats of wood were disrupted by a handful of greenery. She walked a few paces closer. Wax-flowers.

Strange, who left them there?

Only one person knew these were her favourite flowers. There they lay, waiting for her to find them, all bundled into a perfect bouquet tied with a red silk ribbon. Carl—she had never enlightened him of the small, seemingly insignificant fact that her preference for lilies had changed. The only one who had known died ten years ago. *He* had been executed. She grabbed them with trembling fingers and brought them to her nose to smell their tender fragrance. She looked around and saw no one. The brushing of leaves and the faint footsteps of strangers in the vicinity were her only companions.

Who put them here for me?

Acknowledgments

First of all, most important of all, I want to give all the praise and glory to my Lord and Saviour Jesus Christ who always holds me in the palm of his hands. There I am safe; and even though troubles come, He is the refuge I run to. You always hear me when I call; your ear is inclined toward me even when I am silent. You are faithful.

To my lover, my best friend, and husband—James, you have been by my side the whole time listening to my chattering about publishing, social media, books, and so much more. You've taken a whole-hearted sincere interest in this author's world I inhabit. You've given me encouragement when I needed it and great business ideas to incorporate in the marketing of this book. I do love you and will forevermore.

To Felicity—I love your infectious personality. Thank you for sharing your zest for life with me on my down days.

To Edward—your cuddles are always a comfort. I'm really enjoying watching you form more words with your mouth each day.

To Elena—keep smiling every second of every day. Your love for people is an inspiration.

To Dad and Mom—thank you for being the first ones to recognize my gift and passion for writing. You fostered and encouraged me to be the best that I could be. Thank you for paying for my correspondence course with the Institute for Children's Literature. Which leads me to…

I could not have attained the skills I know and employ today without the tutelage under Virginia Kroll, an instructor for the Institute for Children's Literature. Each lesson helped me better a different aspect of writing.

Phil, thank you, thank you, thank you for helping me self-publish my first book ever. Your enthusiasm in this project has been a huge source of support. Thank you for all your prayers.

Denise, thank you for taking the time to look over the first two chapters and pointing out where my writing could be stronger, and for all the constructive criticism you gave me. You are a great agent!

Alexis, Mckenna, Holly, and Lea—you all were AMAZING on the cover shoot.

Mckenna, Lea, and Saraih—thank you for helping me bring my vision for the book trailer to life.

Thank you to the Friends of the St. Raphael's Ruins, the Willow Inn, and Cooper's Marsh for providing me with the locations for the book trailer.

Alexis, the cover would not have been perfect without you. Thanks a million for your expertise.

Cathy, I could not have formatted this book without you. Your help was indispensable. Thank you for so generously giving your time.

To all my friends who showed sincere interest in my book, you helped me go through this journey. Just the fact that many of you want to buy this book blows me away.

Tommy, thank you for being a colourful inspiration for the little lad named Tommy at the beginning of my novel. I had a good laugh.

I also want to extend a warm thanks to the Friends of the Public Gardens and the Halifax Regional Municipality Archives for helping confirm or correct my research.

www.ingramcontent.com/pod-product-compliance
Lightning Source LLC
Chambersburg PA
CBHW021003120726
47905CB00009B/2823